ANGEL OF DOOM

Recent Titles by Christopher Nicole from Severn House

The Secret Service Series

ANGEL FROM HELL
ANGEL IN RED
ANGEL OF VENGEANCE
ANGEL IN JEOPARDY
ANGEL OF DOOM

The Jessica Jones series

THE FOLLOWERS
A FEARFUL THING

The Russian Sagas

THE SEEDS OF POWER
THE MASTERS
THE RED TIDE
THE RED GODS
THE SCARLET GENERATION
DEATH OF A TYRANT

The Arms of War Series

THE TRADE
SHADOWS IN THE SUN
GUNS IN THE DESERT
PRELUDE TO WAR

TO ALL ETERNITY
THE QUEST
BE NOT AFRAID
THE SEARCH
RANSOM ISLAND
POOR DARLING
THE PURSUIT
THE VOYAGE
DEMON
THE FALLS OF DEATH

ANGEL OF DOOM

Christopher Nicole

This first world edition published in Great Britain 2008 by
SEVERN HOUSE PUBLISHERS LTD of
9–15 High Street, Sutton, Surrey SM1 1DF.
This first world edition published in the USA 2008 by
SEVERN HOUSE PUBLISHERS INC of
595 Madison Avenue, New York, N.Y. 10022.

British Library Cataloguing in Publication Data

Nicole, Christopher
  Angel of doom
  1. Hitler, Adolf, 1889-1945 - Assassination attempts -
  Fiction 2. Fehrbach, Anna (Fictitious character) - Fiction
  3. World War, 1939-1945 - Secret service - Germany -
  Fiction 4. Women spies - Fiction 5. Suspense fiction
  I. Title
  823.9'14[F

  ISBN-13: 978-0-7278-6606-6 (cased)

All Severn House titles are printed on acid-free paper.

Typeset by Palimpsest Book Production Ltd.,
Grangemouth, Stirlingshire, Scotland.
Printed and bound in Great Britain by
MPG Books Ltd., Bodmin, Cornwall.

Prologue

W*e dined at one of the many bar-restaurants that line the front at Arenal, the resort village situated just south of the little port of Jávea, on Spain's Costa Blanca. Persuading Anna Fehrbach alias the Honourable Mrs Ballantine Bordman, alias the Countess von Widerstand, alias some other names she had not yet confided to me, to dine out was a triumph in itself: she normally preferred the privacy, and indeed, the safety, of her villa, perched in splendid isolation high on Montgo, the mountain that overlooks the entire surrounding countryside, as well as the beach and the sea.*

Sitting next to her in the summer twilight munching calamari and sipping Marquis de Caceres would, I imagine, make any man feel he was hovering on the edge of paradise. Although some might think it could be the other place.

She attracted attention. Even in her late eighties she was a beautiful woman, only an inch short of six feet tall, utterly elegant in every movement. I had never seen her legs, because nowadays she always wore pants, but it was easy to tell that they were very long, and slender, and as on a warm evening she was bare-footed, her ankles exposed and her splendid toes thrust into sandals, one could envisage the perfection that lay above, just as the loose shirt, occasionally drawing tight as she moved, could yet indicate the irresistible sexuality, that combined with her perfect features, her flawless bone structure, her soft blue eyes, and even her hair, no longer pale yellow but quite white, and cut short where once it had brushed her thighs, had lured so many men, and women, to destruction: twenty-nine at the last count, and I knew that she had not yet finished recalling the events of her remarkable life. The whole was set off by the quality of her jewellery, the gold bar earrings, the huge ruby solitaire on the first finger of her right hand, the gold chain that disappeared into her shirt front and from which I knew was suspended the gold crucifix that was the sole reminder of her Roman Catholic girlhood. Just as the man's gold Rolex on her wrist was indicative of the equality – indeed, the superiority – she had established in a man's world.

That she had agreed to recount her life to me, after more than fifty years of utter privacy, utter secrecy, remained the most remarkable aspect of our relationship. Most historians assumed that she was dead; quite a few refused to believe that she had ever existed. But I had come across her name while researching a book on the Nazi regime, and been struck by the excitingly evocative if indistinct reference to her as 'the most beautiful and dangerous woman of her time.'

Thus had begun a lifetime's search, whenever I had been able to spare the time from earning a living. The references I had gleaned from various news items, memoirs and autobiographies, always scant and often tantalizingly enigmatic, had given no indication that those who supposed her long dead, consumed in the holocaust of the collapsing Nazi regime of 1945, were wrong. Save for an instinct, or more properly, an urgent desire, to satisfy myself that such a figure could not possibly have dwindled into nothing. And here I was, seated beside her, now, I felt, her closest friend and confidant.

I knew I had been fortunate. I did not doubt that any phantom from her past would have been dealt with in the manner she had dealt with so many adversaries in that past, in a matter of seconds. But she had ascertained that I was what I claimed to be, a professional journalist and author who had not even been born when Hitler had tried to tear the world apart. She had been intrigued, and as Anna, whatever her skills and her profession, was all woman, flattered that I should have devoted so much of my life to finding her. And although she knew that her name had not been forgotten in certain areas – as for instance the many successors to the NKVD – and by people who would have given a great deal to be able to locate her, she was no longer concerned at anything they might do even if they did succeed in finding her.

Anna's life had conditioned her never to be handicapped by fear, but in any event she knew that that life was drawing to a close. She had wanted to leave something behind, and here was I, innocent of any connection with her past, clearly in love with her, for all that she was old enough to be my mother, and eager to take down the facts, however disturbing some of them might be.

She ate daintily, as she did everything with the utmost grace, smiled at the passers-by, who could not resist staring at her.

Yet for all her radiant good humour she was pensive. During our talks, in which she had, with amazing frankness, discussed her life, she had revealed a pragmatic acceptance, combined with, in certain instances, a good deal of girlish pleasure, of many of the things she had been forced to do, or indeed had been forced to suffer. Perhaps this was a result of the Irish ebullience she had inherited from her mother. Or perhaps it was simply that after all that had happened to her and around her there was simply nothing left for her to experience, except of course for that death which she had so many times so narrowly escaped.

Thus when she had told me how she, and her entire family, had been arrested by the Gestapo following the Anchluss in March 1938, because her Austrian father, a liberal journalist, had been writing anti-Nazi articles, her bitterness had been tempered by the fact that she had risen above the trauma of being a seventeen-year-old girl, aware of her beauty and equally of the fact that she was in the hands of utterly cold-blooded and obviously lustful men. And women.

She accepted that her survival had been because the senior SS officer to whom she had been presented as a prize had recognized that in her striking looks, her athletic ability, her IQ of 173, and above all, the speed and decisiveness of her reactions, he had uncovered a prize indeed. She could still be bitter at the stark choice with which she had been presented: work for the Reich, and your family will survive; refuse and they, and you, will go to a concentration camp. But she could also be proud of the way she had triumphed over the quite horrendous training she had been forced to undergo, to the extent that she had been taken into the most secret of German secret services, the SD the Sicherheitsdienst, the world within even the private world of the SS, becoming in the process the protégé of Reinhard Heydrich.

She could be amused as she recalled her, on the surface, disastrous marriage to the Honourable Ballantine Bordman, when she had spied for the Reich in the very heart of the British Establishment, just as her eyes could still soften as she remembered Clive Bartley, the MI6 agent who had 'turned' her and got her back to Germany as a double agent. Equally she could be amused at her affair with the American agent Joe Andrews, the man who had got her out of the Lubianka Prison in Moscow, where she had been awaiting trial for an attempt on the life of Joseph Stalin.

That had made her a triple agent, and vastly increased the dangers to which she had been exposed; for if the Americans and the British had soon afterwards found themselves fighting on the same side, they had had very different ideas on how their prime secret agent should be used. She had made it very clear that her real allegiance had always been to Clive Bartley, and it had been on his instructions that she had overseen the assassination of 'Hangman' Heydrich in Prague in 1942, a coup that still gave her immense satisfaction, even if she deeply regretted the repercussions the Czech people had been forced to suffer.

But then the Allies had determined that her talents should be used for the assassination of Hitler himself. And it had all gone disastrously wrong.

I knew she was still brooding on that, as we had reached this point in her life story when last we had talked. I touched her hand. 'It cannot possibly be considered your fault,' I argued. 'MI6, the OSS, whoever it was, gave you duff material to work with.'

'I accept that.' Her voice was low and enchantingly musical. 'But to plant it . . .'

'You had to sleep with Hitler. I understand how ghastly that must have been.'

She squeezed my fingers, an unforgettable gesture of intimacy. 'You do not understand at all.'

'Well . . . I suppose I wouldn't, really.'

She gave a delightful gurgle of amusement. 'Oh, having sex with him was a chore. That was because of all the pills that quack Morell pumped into him, so that he found erection difficult and at times impossible. But I made him ejaculate and be happy.' Even after all her experiences she could still take pride in her sexual skills. 'But I could not stop myself . . . feeling sympathy for him. I knew he was a monster on an unprecedented scale. I knew he was responsible for millions of deaths. I knew that if he were even to suspect that I was a British agent he would have me tortured to death, and probably watch it *happening. Yet I felt sorry for him. He was such a tortured little man in himself. He had created a horror world with himself as its centre, first in his mind and then, I'm not sure even he knew exactly how it had happened, in reality. He was terrified, because he was prematurely old and mentally exhausted, because he wanted to get out to fulfil his dream of rebuilding Vienna as the most beautiful city in the world, and there was no way he could. And of course –' she gave a quick smile – 'when I was with him I assumed that within a couple of hours he would be dead. All I had to do was place my bag containing the bomb beside his bed, set the timer, kiss him goodbye, and leave.'*

'And it didn't go off.'

'The bag was even returned to me, with the bomb still inside. I can tell you, that flight back to Berlin was the longest three hours of my life. I didn't know what had happened, or more correctly, what had not happened. All I knew was that I was sitting with enough explosive on my lap to blow the plane and everyone in it to Kingdom Come. At any moment.'

'But you sat it out. Did I ever tell you that you have got to have more guts than any woman who ever lived? Or any man, either.'

Another quick squeeze of the fingers. 'You say the sweetest things.'

'But the second bomb did go off. Only a couple of hours after you had left Rastenburg on that second visit. And still he wasn't killed. All because a staff officer had moved Stauffenberg's briefcase to the other side of an upright. Almost makes you believe in Fate.'

'Almost,' Anna said. 'Hitler certainly believed it was an Act of God. It never crossed his mind that perhaps neither God nor the Devil wanted the problem of dealing with him.'

'But it still had to count as a failure, to the Allies. What was London's reaction?'

'I imagine they were disappointed.'

'But they didn't blame you.'

'At the time, I didn't see how they could. As far as they were concerned, I had had nothing to do with it. After the first failure they pulled me out of any further attempts, but they still wanted me to control the assassination plot, from a safe distance. They didn't realize how deeply I was already involved. On Himmler's instructions I had "infiltrated" the conspiracy. When I did that,*

I realized how little secrecy was being maintained, how everyone seemed to know what was going on. I was aghast. And Himmler wanted names, more and more names. I stalled him as long as I could. But then Hitler became suspicious himself. I had to produce my list and my evidence. That would have condemned everyone to death. The only possible solution was for Hitler to die before he could read the list.'

'And as he didn't die . . .'

'Five thousand people, men, women, and children, were tortured to death.' She gave a little shudder. 'Do you suppose either God or the Devil will want to receive me?'

'You were doing a job. You hadn't asked for it. And you—'

'Oh, I was a heroine of the Third Reich, Hitler's favourite woman. After Eva Braun. He preferred Eva because of her essentially docile personality.'

'And so you survived, to the end. Was it very traumatic?'

She turned her head to look at me, and I felt a chill. Anna Fehrbach had looked at so many people like that, seconds before she had killed them. 'Traumatic,' she mused. 'I was the most wanted woman in the world. And only a few, a very few, actually wanted to rescue me.'

'But you stayed with Himmler to the end. Even if you hated him.'

'I hated him more than any other man I have ever known. But I had no choice He would not release my parents, even at the very end. I was fortunate that I had other friends in high places.'

'Were you with him, when he died?'

Anna Fehrbach smiled.

The Hunters

'Colonel Tserchenko is here, Comrade Commissar,' said the female secretary, smart in her green uniform.

'Then show him in.' Lavrenty Beria rose from behind his

desk, slowly. He did most things slowly, because of his bulk. He was both very tall and very heavy, his size accentuated by the great hairless head, the large, bland features on which the pince-nez seemed out of place. But as commander of the NKVD he was the second most powerful man in Russia, and the man entering his office did so apprehensively. No one willingly visited the Lubianka Prison, and to find himself actually in the office of the commissar was terrifying.

But Beria was smiling. 'Colonel Tserchenko,' he said, coming round the desk with outstretched hand. 'Nikolai! It is good of you to come.'

'I obey orders, Comrade Commissar.'

'Well, we all do that, do we not? Sit down.'

Tserchenko took off his cap and sank into the chair before the desk. It creaked. He also was a heavy man, although a head shorter than the policeman, with matching features and grey-streaked black hair, cut very short; he wore the uniform of a tank commander.

Beria returned behind his desk and also sat. 'Yours has been a hard war, Nikolai,' he remarked.

'As it has for all of us, Comrade Commissar.'

'Indeed. But some have suffered more than others. I am thinking of your poor dear sister.'

Tserchenko frowned: his sister Ludmilla had died three years ago.

'She was one of my closest and most trusted associates.' Beria looked ready to cry. 'A woman of immense talent. A woman with an unlimited future. To be cut off in the prime of life.'

'Accidents will happen, Comrade Commissar.' Tserchenko and his late sister had not been close.

'Accidents,' Beria remarked, perhaps to himself. He picked up the photograph lying on his desk and held it out. 'Have you ever seen this woman before?'

Tserchenko took it, cautiously, studied it. 'No, sir.'

'What do you think of her?'

'Well, sir . . . she is quite beautiful.'

'She is that. She is also the most vicious assassin who has ever walked the face of this earth.'

'Sir?'

'I am not certain of her real name, but she masquerades

under the title of Countess von Widerstand. I understand that she is half Austrian, half Irish, but she works for the Nazis. Four years ago, which is when that photograph was taken, they sent her here to use her beauty and her seductive skills to worm her way into our society, gain access to the Kremlin, and assassinate Premier Stalin.'

Tserchenko stared at him with his mouth open.

'She didn't succeed, obviously,' Beria said. 'We arrested her before she could complete her mission, and placed her here in the Lubianka to await trial. However, she managed to escape. She is the only person ever to have done so. This was the day after the Nazis invaded us. Everyone was very agitated. Even I, I admit it. I knew that we were in serious danger of being overrun, and thus I allowed myself to be duped by a smooth-talking American diplomat named Joseph Andrews, who told me that this woman was wanted in America for an attempt on the life of President Roosevelt, and that it would encourage the United States to grant us aid if we were seen to be prepared to cooperate with them, in this instance by handing this criminal over to them for trial, and, he assured me, certain execution. It seemed a small price to pay for the assistance we so desperately needed.'

He paused: the colonel was looking distracted. 'My sister died on 23 June 1941,' he said slowly. 'And she was—'

'Yes. At that time she was in command of the women's section of the prison, where this countess was being held.'

'But . . . I was told that she died of a broken neck after a fall down a flight of stairs.'

'That is what everyone was told, Colonel. It was not considered appropriate to reveal the truth at that time, and indeed what I am telling you now must remain confidential. Your sister's death was certainly the result of a broken neck, but not as the result of an accidental fall. Despite the written release I had mistakenly given this man Andrews, Ludmilla became suspicious and insisted upon confirmation, whereupon this countess attacked her and broke her neck, and then took her pistol and shot dead the commissar to whom your sister was appealing. This man. Ewfim Chalyapov, was a personal friend of Premier Stalin.'

'But if she was being returned to America to stand trial—'

'That was a fabrication on the part of Andrews, her lover. She had never been in the United States at that time, and had never made an attempt on the life of the president. Having extricated her from the Lubianka, Andrews then turned her loose to continue her blood-stained career. Later that same year she shot and killed six of our agents who attempted to arrest her and return her here for trial.'

Tserchenko looked at the photograph more closely. 'This young girl shot six of our people?'

'Yes, she did. You are entitled to ask if she is entirely human. Do you wish to avenge your sister, and bring this arch-criminal to justice?'

'Of course I would like to do that, sir. But—'

'That is also the wish of Premier Stalin.'

'Yes, sir. I can understand that. But—'

'I am relieving you of your duties in the field, Colonel, and appointing you to the NKVD.'

Tserchenko swallowed. 'You are sending me to America?'

'No, no, no. I have told you, Andrews turned her loose. She seems to have the power to bewitch men. So she returned to Germany and resumed working for the SS. Do you know that only two days ago there was an attempt on the life of Adolf Hitler? It failed, and we have not yet obtained any details, but Berlin Radio is saying that it failed principally because of the efforts of this Countess von Widerstand, who they describe as Herr Himmler's personal assistant. So we know she is in Berlin.'

'Berlin,' Tserchenko muttered.

Beria smiled. 'I am not asking you to commit either a miracle or suicide, Nikolai. Our armies are going to be in Berlin in the very near future. Within a week they will be across the Vistula, and one of the last natural barriers protecting Germany will have been overcome. I am thus transferring you to Marshall Rokossovsky's Front, as a political commissar. You will have carte blanche to requisition whoever and whatever you require to complete your mission, which will be to return the Countess von Widerstand to the Soviet Union, to me personally. We know that she is at this moment in Berlin. You will accompany our forces in the capture of that city. However, there is the obvious possibility that when she realizes that the end is nigh, she will leave the city and seek to escape. You will follow her wherever she goes to bring her to justice.'

'If she is a friend of the Americans—'

'That is not relevant. She is an enemy of the free world. Even Andrews will not be able to protect her when the facts of her life are made public, which we intend to do.'

'And when you say, return her—'

'Believe me, Nikolai, I understand the difficulties. This woman is as deadly as a cobra, a black mamba, and a boa constrictor all in one. And she is all of those things while hiding under that mask of innocent girlhood you have in your hand. I have never met her myself, but I will read you some of the things said of her.' He picked up a sheet of paper. 'Hair like fine spun gold. Soft blue eyes that would tempt the devil himself to her bed. A voice like the cooing of a dove. A face of which Helen of Troy could only dream. And a body to turn the Venus de Milo green. And while you are admiring all of those assets, you are already a dead man. Apparently her lethal skills, with or without a weapon, are outstanding, and the speed with which she can apply them is phenomenal. This is perhaps hearsay, as the only people who can truly know of them are dead. But I would recommend that you approach her with extreme caution. I would dearly like you to bring her to me, alive, but if it is necessary to do so, kill her first. However, if you need to do that, I shall require irrefutable proof that she is dead. I wish her head.'

'Sir?'

'It is old-fashioned, and perhaps barbaric. But it is also irrefutable. Cut off her head, Nikolai. Pretend you are Perseus. After all, this woman, apart from her good looks, is very close to being a Gorgon. If by any mischance she has died or been killed before you can find her, you will locate the grave, dig up the corpse, and again, cut off the head and bring it here. From this moment on, the Countess von Widerstand is your sole objective, your sole reason for living. Do you understand me?'

Tserchenko swallowed. 'I understand you, Comrade Commissar.'

'Mr Andrews is here, Mr Bartley,' Amy Barstow announced. Her tone was disapproving. Amy Barstow disapproved of

Americans in general, for no very good reason save perhaps that the only American women she had ever seen were film actresses on the screen, and they were always slim, svelte and immaculately dressed, whereas she was overweight and clad in the utility clothes that were all that were available in Great Britain after five years of war.

But she also disliked Joseph Andrews in person. Not because she knew the man – she had only met him on a few occasions – but because he shared with her boss what she considered to be an unhealthy relationship with the countess von Widerstand. She had never met the countess at all, but she was in charge of the file on her, and while she could not fault the facts, which indicated that she was every bit as compulsive and dynamic, not to mention beautiful and sexual, as her reputation suggested, it was impossible not to loathe a woman the very mention of whose name could have such a man as Clive Bartley behaving like a schoolboy.

And he was always pleased to see his old friend, rising to his feet with a smile. Clive Bartley was six feet two inches tall, built like a second row forward, and with features to match, with lank black hair just beginning to show grey at the temples, although he was only forty-two years old. As he also had a mostly even personality, and a good sense of humour, he was a delight to work for – but not when that beastly woman turned up or was even mentioned. Yet Amy knew that this morning he was not a happy man, although he called, 'Joe! Come on in. Nice to see you. That will be all, thank you, Amy.'

Amy sidled past the American in the doorway.

Joe Andrews was the same height as Clive, but very thin. He also had a matching face, very aquiline. He shook hands. 'You've heard the news?'

Clive gestured him to a chair, sat down himself. 'This one at least went off. But the bugger seems to have a charmed life.'

'And Anna?'

'She wasn't involved, thank God.'

'Not involved? You mean on our side. According to Berlin Radio, she virtually put an end to the attempted revolt, while the conspirators were still assuming that Hitler was dead and were ready to go ahead.'

'She was out on a limb, and had no choice. We knew she was part of the actual conspiracy. We told her to join it, remember? You did.'

'We never suggested that she should betray them.'

'Look, we planted her, told her to be a Nazi one hundred per cent. She has done this so successfully that she is now Himmler's PA. He trusts her more than anyone else in the world. It is her business to make sure he never loses that trust. So when he gives her an order, she carries it out without hesitation, utterly and completely. He obviously told her to investigate rumours of this conspiracy. This she did. And more. She actually had a go herself, back in December, at enormous personal risk. For God's sake, to place the bomb she had to sleep with Hitler.'

'How do you know that?'

'She told Baxter.'

'I'm not with you.'

'Himmler sent her to Stockholm in January, with a personal message for Folke Bernadotte.'

'The Red Cross guy?'

'That's right.'

'And what was this personal message?'

'She doesn't know. The envelope was sealed, and she didn't feel that she could take the risk of breaking the seal. But she has a pretty good idea that Himmler is seeking some kind of personal salvation when the Reich comes crashing down.'

Andrews blew a raspberry, which Clive ignored. 'The point is that she took the opportunity, while in Stockholm, to contact us. Unfortunately, I was out of the country on another assignment. So Billy answered the call.'

'Baxter went to Stockholm, in January, to meet with Anna? I thought he never left this office.'

Clive allowed himself a grin. 'Wouldn't you break the rule of a lifetime, for a get together with Anna? Seems to me you once broke quite a few rules, in Washington, for that purpose.'

'OK, OK, she's a turn on. And Baxter?'

Clive shrugged. 'I don't really know. I don't know if Billy can be turned on by anyone. All I know is what he brought back, which was the goods, as always. She warned him that the V-bomb was about ready to go into action. That was no lie. And she brought him up to date on the plot. He says she was madder than a wet hen, because that first bomb had failed to go off, after all her spadework. She wanted out, but he told her to get involved with the conspirators and make sure they tried again. And as always, she obeyed orders.'

'Has it occurred to you, old buddy, that this is pretty circumstantial stuff? Anna tells Baxter that the bomb we gave her didn't explode. Do we know that she ever even activated it?'

Clive's gaze was suddenly hostile.

'Then she happily agrees to go along with instructions to get involved in the general conspiracy. Great. But the moment this second attempt fails, she starts executing the conspirators left and right. For Christ's sake, according to Berlin, she shot two of them in her own office in Gestapo Headquarters.'

'We don't know the truth about that,' Clive said defensively. 'We do know that Anna is inclined to resort to executive action if she feels her life is in danger.'

'How many does that make?'

'God knows. More than twenty, certainly.'

'Holy shit! But you still trust her absolutely.'

'Don't you?'

Andrews decided it was time to inspect his fingernails. 'Wild Bill isn't happy.'

'I got the impression that Donovan went for her?'

'Sure he did. Don't most men go for Anna, when they meet her? And according to your figures, maybe twenty of them have regretted it, all the way to the morgue.'

'A few of them were women,' Clive said absently. 'Tell me what's bothering Donovan.'

'You mean, apart from this Hitler fiasco? Shit, Clive, don't you think it's time for you to take a long, hard look at the situation? So you meet an absolutely stunning eighteen-year-old at an SS ball back in '38. You told me yourself that you were suspicious of her from the start, and even more so when she marries Bordman and becomes a wow in London society. Then purely by chance, so you say, you bump into her again in Berlin, and bingo, you're in bed. You didn't find that suspicious?'

'It was entirely by chance,' Clive said, patiently. 'And if you will take the trouble to remember the facts, she had just been savagely punished by Heydrich for a breach of security. That made her realize just how much she hated him, and the whole regime.'

'And you just happened to pop up at that moment. So you had sex with her. I assume you took your clothes off, and hers?'

Clive stared at him.

'So you must have seen all the marks left by this "savage" punishment.'

'There were some marks on her arse, yes.'

'Oh, for God's sake. So they spanked her. That's a savage punishment?'

'They used electric shocks. Those inflict maximum pain but leave no marks.'

'She told you this.'

'Yes, she did.'

'And then she asked you if she could work for MI6.'

'You really are being absurd, Joe. Of course she didn't ask to work for us. I persuaded her.'

'In between thrusts, I suppose. And she said yes without hesitation, in between gasps.'

'You know, Joe,' Clive said equably, 'if you weren't one of my oldest friends, I would throw you through that door without opening it, and send you the bill for the damage. Anna has worked for us, faithfully and at great personal risk, for five years. Her sole ambition is to bring the Nazis down so that she can get her family out of hock. In my book, that makes her the ultimate heroine of this war. When you found out about her, you virtually blackmailed us into having her work for you as well. Now, if you want to end that arrangement, that is all right by me. But if you do, she reverts to being our property and no one else's.'

'Because you trust her, no matter what.'

'No matter what.'

Andrews stood up. 'I hope you're right. I mean that. But . . . there's a chance you may be subject to higher authority.'

'Just what do you mean by that?'

'Like I said, Wild Bill's a guy who doesn't like to be made a fool of, and he's beginning to wonder if Anna hasn't been making fools of us all, for all of those five years. And he has the ear of a lot of important people, including FDR.'

'Are you threatening me? And by implication, Anna?'

'I wish you'd get *your* facts straight. I'm on you side. And hers. The thought of anything happening to Anna can keep a man awake at night. So I'm warning you of what may lie ahead. Can't you pull her out?'

'You know I can't do that, Joe. She won't come out as long as Himmler holds her parents.'

'Well, then, you want to be goddamn sure that when that house of cards comes tumbling down, which is liable to happen within the next few months, your people are there to dig her out, before either the Soviets or, sadly, us. The Reds want her more than anyone. And while we may merely put her on trial as a Nazi mass-murderess, God alone knows what those bastards will do to her if they can lay hands on her.'

'As you say, sort of keeps a man awake at night. Thank you for that warning, Joe.'

Clive waited until he was sure that Andrews had left the building, then went upstairs. He had already discussed the bomb fiasco with his boss, and as he had told the American, he knew that their minds were one as regards Anna. But Billy Baxter did not look very pleased to see him again.

Short and thin, invariably untidy, his sweater, the refuge of innumerable strands of spilt tobacco, he always did regard the world from a jaundiced point of view. 'What now?' he barked. 'Don't tell me she's slipped up and is under arrest.'

'Anna does not slip up. Unfortunately . . .' Clive sat before the desk and outlined his conversation with the American.

'I said from the beginning,' Baxter commented, 'that letting the Yanks muscle in was a mistake. Those bastards have only one god: pragmatism. Results, results and then more results. No results, no dice.'

'And Anna hasn't come up with the right result. That is in the main because since Bartoli bit the dust we have had no ready means of contacting her, and the damnable thing is that she has no idea of her situation. Oh, I think she knows that she can't afford to fall into the hands of the Russians, but she regards the Americans, and above all, Joe Andrews and Wild Bill Donovan, as her friends. You may not believe this, Billy, but Anna, for all her apparent cold-blooded ruthlessness, is at heart still just an eager little girl. Or maybe you do know that.'

Baxter began to fill his pipe. 'Just what does that mean?'

'Well . . . you managed to get close to her in Stockholm. Didn't you?'

'In a manner of speaking.'

'Now I think I'm entitled to ask, just what do you mean by *that*?'

'What I said. She opened her door to me with a pistol in her hand, and although she didn't shoot me out of hand, she was furious because the bomb we gave her didn't go off, after she had had to spend the night with Hitler.'

'So you told me. But you managed to calm her down.'

Baxter stuffed tobacco into his bowl. 'I think so.'

'And you never laid a finger on her?'

'No, I did not.' He struck a match, puffed contentedly for a few moments, then added, 'She did invite me to stay the night.'

'I see.'

'Well, it was snowing. You ever been to Stockholm in January?'

'I did not have that privilege,' Clive said bitterly. 'And you didn't take her up.'

'I had a plane waiting.'

'My heart bleeds for you.'

'But she did kiss me goodbye,' Baxter said, reminiscing.

'Now she needs more than a kiss. She has to be warned, firstly that she must not be in Berlin when the Russians arrive, and secondly, she must not surrender to the Yanks.'

'How are we supposed to do that? We have no contact. Only that fellow Johannsson.'

'That's out,' Clive said. 'Johannsson works for Andrews.'

'Hm. Well, unless she is sent on another mission to a neutral country by Himmler . . .'

Clive snapped his fingers. 'Belinda.'

Baxter raised his eyebrows. 'You'd risk her again? You mean she is no longer your mistress?'

'Well . . . yes and no.'

'I'm sorry. You'll have to say that again.'

'Belinda is my mistress.' Clive spoke carefully. 'When she is in the mood. That is actually the way it always has been. But over the past year the mood has been increasingly absent.'

'You mean she's found someone else. I don't blame her. And so you're quite happy to put her head on the block. Didn't she have a horrendous time on her last visit to Germany?'

'That was due to her own carelessness. She talks too much. And she was extricated from real trouble by Anna.'

'And you think she'd be willing to chance her arm again?'

'She has said she would.'

'She has guts.'

'Yes,' Clive said dryly. 'I think we want to remember that that incident was ten months ago. That is just short of a year, right?'

He gazed at Baxter, and Baxter gazed back. 'You're not suggesting . . .'

'I'm not suggesting anything, Billy. I can only afford to deal in facts. Because of her Italian mother, we got Belinda into Germany, to contact Anna. She got herself picked up by the Gestapo, and as I said, was rescued by Anna in her capacity as a senior officer in the SD. Anna kept her in Berlin for a night before sending her home. Since then she has been . . . not really interested in sex. At least with me.'

'That could be a concomitant of being tortured by the Gestapo.'

'Belinda was not tortured by the Gestapo, Billy. Oh, they may have roughed her up a little, but the actual torturing was done by Anna.'

'What?'

'As I said, she was able to intervene as a senior officer in the SD, sent by Himmler personally to interrogate the suspect. But there was a security camera in the room, so it could not be faked. Fortunately, she was able to warn Belinda – I don't know the details as to how she managed it – to put up with it as it was her only hope of getting out.'

'As our American friends would say, holy shit! And then you say they spent a night together?'

'Yes.'

Baxter knocked out his pipe. 'I suppose you'd take deep offence if I said, you have to laugh.'

'Yes, I would. Take deep offence.'

'Then I won't say it. However, if I have ever known a man hoist by his own petard, you are that man. You mean you never suspected that Anna was a lesbian?'

'Anna is not a lesbian. God, or the Devil, endowed her with certain gifts mostly denied to mere mortals. The intelligence of a genius, the speed of thought and reaction of a wildcat, the guts and determination of a champion boxer, and the beauty and allure of a supreme courtesan. Our concept of morals does not exist in her world; it was knocked out of her at the SS training camp. To achieve her immediate objective, she will employ any or all of those strengths that she considers necessary.' He sighed. 'And being Anna, for the most part she enjoys what she is doing.'

Baxter pointed with his pipe. 'And you are in love with her.'

'Yes, Billy, I am in love with her. I think I fell in love with her the moment I laid eyes on her, so utterly beautiful and, as I supposed, so utterly innocent, at that SS ball in 1938. But more important, when I persuaded her to come over to us, I swore to her that I would get her out, the moment it was practical, and she was willing to come. That is, the moment we could ensure the safety of her parents.'

'Another of those impossible commitments you keep making. Well, of course she must be warned, and if Belinda is the only courier we have who can do it, then we must use her. If she's willing to risk it.' He gazed at his sidekick. 'And if you are willing to risk it.'

Clive blew a raspberry.

'Why, Clive,' Belinda Hoskin said. 'How nice to see you. Have you come for a drink, dinner or the night?'

'Can't it be for all three?' Clive scooped her from the floor to kiss her; she was several inches shorter than him.

Her diminutive size went with her personality, inherited more from her Italian forebears than copied from her English stepfather, whom her mother had married after their flight from Italy only a couple of steps ahead of the Fascist blackshirts who had murdered her real father. That had been more than twenty years ago, and since then, apart from adopting her stepfather's name, she had become so English as to be indistinguishable from the real thing, on the surface. Only Clive knew how deep there remained the memories of her girlhood and the hatred for the thugs who had turned her life upside down. A deep-seated phobia which he had used in the past, callously as many people would say, and which he had to admit had now turned out along the lines of a French farce. Clive Bartley did not like French farces.

They had now been partners for eight years. Very early in

their relationship he had asked her to marry him. But she had just been appointed editor of the fashion section of a prominent London glossy, and had been thinking of careers more than sock-washing. And then had come Anna, both to disrupt their relationship, and then, it seemed almost certain, to replace him entirely. So now he would use her again, callously, but with an even greater risk to his ego.

'I suppose you could do all three,' she agreed. 'I have nothing on this evening. Let's start at the beginning. You can pour us both a drink, and then you can sit down and tell me what's really on your mind. Apart from nookie.'

Clive released her and went to the sideboard to pour two scotches, while reflecting that her perception was sometimes too sharp for her own good. But having been given the opening, there was no point in hanging about. 'We were wondering,' he said over his shoulder, 'if you would like to see Anna again.' There was no reply, so he turned to face her, a glass in each hand. There were pink spots on her cheeks. 'I suppose you wouldn't.'

Belinda took the glass and drank. 'I am perfectly willing to see Anna again,' she said. 'If it will help the war effort. And if it can be done. I offered to go back several months ago, and you said it would be too dangerous.'

'Things have changed. Now we can easily get you into Switzerland, and from there you should have no problem crossing the border.'

She considered, looking into the glass. 'Would I use the same cover?'

'Not the same name. It's quite possible that Claudia Ratosi is in a file somewhere. You'd stay in clothes, obviously, as a moment's conversation would convince anyone that you're an expert in that field. But we'd give you an entirely new identity, as an Italian-Swiss.'

'And the Gestapo?'

'The only Gestapo you encountered were the people in Lubeck, that's at the other end of Germany.'

'His name was Werter.' Belinda spoke quietly, but her voice was consumed with venom. 'I hope he rots in hell.'

'I'm sure he will,' Clive agreed. He knew that before Anna had got to the scene Belinda had been subjected to a strip search with all the unpleasantness that entailed. 'He probably is already, rotting in hell. But whether he is or not, I would still say that the odds on your running into him again have to be several million to one. So . . . are you game?'

Belinda finished her drink and held out the glass. 'I'm game.'

'Then listen very carefully to what I am going to say.'

The Scheme

Heinrich Himmler marched into the office and stood there, hands on hips. In his superbly tailored black uniform, his black tie neatly knotted against the collar of his white shirt, his highly polished black belts, his high-peaked black cap which he was now taking off, he suggested a dominating figure, so that it was almost possible to overlook the pale complexion, the thinning, equally pale hair, the coldly blue eyes sheltering behind their rimless spectacles. 'Anna!' he announced.

Anna Fehrbach had risen from behind her desk at his entry. Like him, she was in uniform, but hers was far more prosaic. She wore a black skirt and tie, a white shirt, and black silk stockings, but this rather austere garb only served to illustrate the length of her legs, the slenderness of her waist, the thrust of her bodice; her long pale yellow hair was confined in a tight bun on the back of her head, and this again served to enhance the superb bone structure of her face, slightly aquiline but utterly flawless, the big, relaxed but always watchful, deep blue eyes. She stood to attention. 'Herr Reichsführer! Welcome back. Is . . . ah . . .?'

'Come here,' Himmler commanded.

Anna went round the desk, and advanced, cautiously. With this man she never knew what was going to happen next. She had worked for him for six years, the last two in conditions of considerable intimacy . . . at work. She knew she was his trusted aide, his partner in crime, as it were. But except for one or two almost accidental occasions, he had never touched her. As he was the only man she had ever encountered who had not immediately reacted to both her beauty and her sexuality, she found it impossible to understand his reserve. Of course she had the reputation in the SS of being a lesbian, but that had never put other men off, and this man had to know that she was his to command, utterly and without reservation. At the same time, knowing him as well as she did, she was certain that *he* was not homosexual. So she had been forced to conclude that he was totally *a*sexual.

Throughout their years together, whenever they had met, after even the briefest of separations, he had looked as if he was about to embrace her, and then apparently changed his mind at the last moment. She was therefore taken completely by surprise when he waited for her to come right up to him, then put both his arms round her and hugged her with surprising strength.

As she was some inches taller than him, her gasp went over his head, but she managed a strangled, 'Sir?'

He released her, looking somewhat embarrassed. 'The Führer is well,' he announced. 'Well, as well as can be expected after such an ordeal.' He peered at her. 'I had no idea you had spent the night with him.'

'He sent for me,' Anna explained.

'And you never told me?'

'I was instructed to tell nobody.'

'Instructed by whom?'

Anna drew a deep breath. 'Dr Goebbels.'

Himmler went to the chair in front of the desk and sat down. 'Goebbels set up this meeting?'

Anna sat behind the desk. 'Yes, sir.'

'And you never told me that either?'

'Dr Goebbels insisted that my meetings with the Führer had to be kept absolutely secret.'

'*Meetings?*'

'I had been to Rastenburg once before last Wednesday, sir.'

Himmler considered for a few moments. 'I had supposed we had no secrets from each other,' he said at last.

If only you knew, Anna thought. 'I do not like having secrets from you, Herr Reichsführer. You know that my life is devoted to you.' *Until I am in a position to destroy you.* 'But this was a directive from the Führer. I did not dare disobey.'

He continued to stare at her.

Anna drew another deep breath. 'Would you like to punish

me, sir?' With her perverse wish to *experience,* she was actually curious as to what he might wish, or do. When she remembered the horrendous pain Heydrich had inflicted on her naked body with his electric shocks . . . Himmler was reputed to be far more demonic than even his dead henchman.

'Punish you?' he muttered. 'The Führer has commanded me to tell you that you will be for ever in his heart and mind as the greatest of all German women.'

Except that I am not German.

'He says that your company during that night helped him overcome the traumatic effects of the explosion. He is also very pleased with the list of potential conspirators you provided, not to mention the way you handled the situation here.'

'What will happen to the people on the list?'

'You should not ask. He is very angry. I have never seen him so angry. He wants them hunted down, every one, and their wives and their children, and exterminated.'

Oh, my God! Anna thought. *I have committed mass murder without realizing it.* She had had no choice but to provide the list, because Hitler had demanded it. But she had warned the conspirators, and they, and herself, had felt it would not matter, because he would be dead before he could act on the information. Instead of which he was alive . . .

'And you have already started on that, from what I have heard,' Himmler went on. 'Is it true you shot both Steinberg and Essermann right here in this office?' He looked right and left as if expecting still to see blood on the floor. 'I don't understand about that. Were they not both your lovers?'

'I have no lovers, Herr Reichsführer,' Anna said bravely. 'Where the lives of the Führer, and you, and Germany, are concerned.'

'But what *happened*? Essermann was working with you on the investigation.'

And had suddenly stumbled on the truth. 'I do not know the truth of it, Herr Reichsführer. Frankly, I had no idea what was going on. As you now know, I had spent the night with the Führer. He dismissed me just before ten that morning, and I was flown back here. As you were not here – I did not know that you had gone to Rastenburg yourself that very morning – I came to the office. Then my door was suddenly thrown open, and Steinberg rushed in. He was distraught, and babbling about something having happened to the Führer . . .'

'But he was not on your list,' Himmler interjected.

Because I dared not put him on it: he was the originator of the entire conspiracy, and if arrested, the first person he would have incriminated would have been me. 'No, sir,' she agreed. 'As you know, I investigated him very thoroughly, and found nothing to connect him with any plot. In fact, I don't think he *was* involved. I believe that he had found out something important, and had come to tell me about it. But Essermann had followed him in, and he shot him before he could say anything more.'

'But that means . . .'

'Yes, sir. It means that Essermann *was* in the conspiracy, and was determined to stop Steinberg telling me his suspicions. I can only say that I am sorry. He had always appeared so loyal, to you, to me, to the Reich . . . it never occurred to me to investigate him.'

'It never occurred to me, either,' Himmler said. 'And so you shot him. That is a pity. He would have had much to tell us.'

'I shot him, sir, because having killed Steinberg, he turned his gun on me.'

'And you are the fastest shot alive, eh? Ha ha.'

'I have managed to survive, sir,' Anna said modestly.

'Yes. And we have more than enough to work on.' He mused for a few seconds. 'Anna . . . you have never mentioned anything to the Führer about our private business?'

'Of course not, sir.'

'Or to Dr Goebbels?'

'Certainly not.' I did not mention it, she recalled; he mentioned it to me. *Because, you silly little man, Goebbels knows everything about you. But then, he is also a silly little man. Because like you, he trusts me absolutely.*

'That is excellent judgement,' Himmler said. 'Our private arrangements are our private arrangements, eh. And in fact it is time for you to make another trip to Switzerland.'

Can it be true? Anna thought. Switzerland! Peace and tranquillity! Henri! The only man she had ever met who wanted nothing from her but her love! How desperately she craved both of those avenues of escape from this madhouse in which she now found herself. 'Of course, sir,' she said. 'When do I leave?'

'Tomorrow. Laurent will be waiting for you in Lucerne. I want you back here as quickly as possible.'

There was a note of suppressed excitement in his voice. 'Sir?' Anna asked.

Himmler got up and took a turn around the office. Anna watched him in amazement; she had never seen him so agitated. In fact he prided himself on his habitual calm. He halted in front of her desk. 'I,' he announced, 'have been appointed, by the Führer, Commander-in-Chief of the Home Army!'

Now Anna stared at him in consternation. She had long understood that Hitler's powers were fading, but this? Himmler already commanded the Abwehr, the Gestapo, the SS, the SD, and therefore, by extension, every local police force in the country. The only possible counterweight to such enormous power was the Wehrmacht. But if he was now also to command every soldier in Germany . . .

'You do not approve?'

Anna pulled herself together. 'Of course I approve, Herr Reichsführer. But . . . General Fromm . . .?'

'Fromm is under arrest.'

'His name was not on my list. I found nothing against him.'

'But the fact is, he is, or was, Stauffenberg's commanding officer. He sent Stauffenberg to Rastenburg last Thursday.'

But he didn't know that Count von Stauffenberg was carrying a bomb.

'It really is a pity that stupid fellow Stieff shot Stauffenberg so immediately,' Himmler grumbled. 'He could have given us an even greater list than yours. And of course it raises questions as to his own loyalty. I have ordered his arrest as well.'

Oh, my God! Anna thought; General Stieff, commander of the Berlin Garrison, *was* a member of the conspiracy, which was no doubt why he had executed Stauffenberg the moment he had learned that Hitler had survived the explosion.

'There is so much to be done,' Himmler went on, still standing in front of her desk as if he were addressing a meeting. 'Guderian is to be my chief of staff.'

A touch of sanity in the madhouse. Guderian, the man who had led the Panzer army to victory in France in 1940, was probably the most capable general in the German Army.

'And do you know what he tells me?' Himmler complained. 'That within a fortnight, perhaps even a week, the Russians will have crossed the Vistula.'

'Oh my God!' This time Anna spoke the words aloud. She had a sudden pain in her chest.

'Oh, don't worry. We are not going to let them into Germany. Certainly not.'

Anna was not interested in meaningless optimistic rhetoric. 'Sir!' she said urgently. 'If the Russians are going to get across the Vistula, my parents . . .'

He frowned at her. 'I had forgotten about your parents.'

Does this cretin seriously suppose that I would still be seated behind this desk if he didn't hold them hostage for my loyalty? She drew another deep breath. 'I would like permission to bring them out.'

'Of course you must do that. We cannot let them fall into the hands of the Russians, eh?'

Anna could not believe her ears. The moment she had waited for, for six years. 'Thank you, sir. I will leave immediately.'

'No, no. The delivery first.' He watched her expression change. 'You are panicking. You, Anna, of all people, are panicking. I have told you, the Russians cannot possibly get across the Vistula for another week, at the very earliest. You will leave tomorrow morning, make the delivery to Laurent in Lucerne as usual. But instead of returning directly here, I will arrange for you to be taken to Poland to fetch your parents. You will bring them to Berlin. Will that satisfy you?'

'Of course, Herr Reichsführer.' Her brain was spinning with ideas, possible plans . . . and actually, going to Switzerland first might help to carry those plans forward, if she dared risk it.

'Excellent. Now we must get on. You will . . .' He was turning away from her, and now for the first time noticed that the door to the inner office was slightly ajar. 'What is in there?'

Shit! Anna thought. 'The Record Section, sir.'

Before she could move, Himmler had crossed the floor and opened the door wide, gazing at the young woman seated at the desk beyond. 'Who are you?'

'Ah . . .' The girl hastily stood up. 'Katherine Fehrbach, Herr Reichsführer.'

'Katherine . . . my God!'

'My sister,' Anna said at his shoulder. 'My secretary. You appointed her, Herr Reichsführer. To assist me in my investigation of the conspiracy.'

'Of course. I had forgotten. You resemble your sister, Fraulein. And you have done a good job. I congratulate you. Now I must go.' He closed the door, and seized Anna's arm. 'Why did you not tell me she was there?'

'I did not think it mattered, sir.'

'What? Do you think she heard what we were saying?'

'I think it is likely, sir.'

'Good God! What are we going to do?'

'Sir?'

'If she heard what we were saying—'

'With respect, sir, we were discussing the conspiracy. She assisted me in my inquiries. She can have heard nothing she did not already know. Except for your appointment. But you are going to make that public anyway, aren't you?'

'And your trip to Switzerland? No one is supposed to know about that.'

You silly little man, Anna thought again; everyone knows about my mysterious trips, even if no one knows for certain what I do on them. 'Katherine is entirely loyal to me and to the Reich,' she asserted. 'You may trust her absolutely, Herr Reichsführer.'

'I hope you're right,' Himmler said. 'The goods will be ready for you to pick up tomorrow morning.'

Anna waited until he had closed the door, then went into the inner office. Katherine had sat down again, but was still looking startled. She did indeed resemble her older sister, without quite matching her beauty. She was tall, but was still two inches shorter than Anna. Her figure was excellent, and indeed, voluptuous, but it lacked Anna's sensuality. Her hair was just as yellow, but thick, where Anna's suggested golden silk. And her features, although splendidly carved, failed to equal Anna's perfection, and were even a trifle coarse, while her eyes, if a matching blue, had none of Anna's come hither quality. But she aped Anna in every direction, from the way she wore her hair to her choice of clothes, without ever revealing the required elegance. Yet the real difference between them, Anna knew, was in their brains. Although they had received identical training at the SS school, albeit several years apart, Katherine had never achieved her sister's speed of thought, her instant reactions, and, she supposed, her ruthlessness.

'He gives me the creeps. Did he really forget who I was?' Katherine asked.

'It's possible,' Anna conceded. 'He has a lot on his mind. Did you hear everything that was said?'

'Well, I couldn't help it. Are you really going to bring Mama and Papa to Berlin? Do you think they want to be taken anywhere, by you?'

Anna gazed at her. How she wanted to trust her, as she had claimed she did to Himmler. But there was another difference between them, the most vital of all. She had been dragged into the world of the SD by the threat that if she ever failed the Reich her mother and father, and her little sister, would die. Her skills, and her loyalty, had been purchased by that simple proposition. It had never occurred to her Nazi masters that all those qualities they so valued in her could ever be used against them, as she had now done for five years. But Katherine had actually volunteered to serve the Reich. Anna did not suppose she truly understood the Nazi philosophy – although like her she would have been given *Mein Kampf* and the works of Nietzsche and Houston Chamberlain to study. She knew that her sister's sole motivation had been to get out of her parents' prison and hopefully follow in Anna's apparently successful footsteps. In doing this, she had adopted that philosophy absolutely. Thus for her ever to learn the truth could be catastrophic.

'They think you are a German whore,' Katherine said. 'They hate you.'

'And do they not hate you?'

'Well . . . I suppose they do. So . . .'

'They are still our parents, and it is our business to protect them if we can. We certainly cannot abandon them to the Russians. You do not have to see them if you don't want to.' And if the plan that was forming in her mind could be made to work, she would never see them again, she thought. That would mean abandoning *her* to the looming disaster that was about to overtake Germany, but . . .

'Then I shall not,' Katherine declared. 'If you knew the things they said to me when I told them I was joining the Party.'

. . . she had chosen her path, and must go along it to the end. 'The decision is yours,' Anna agreed. 'Now, I have things to do.'

She turned to the door.

'Anna!'

Anna waited.

Katherine licked her lips. 'When you go away for the Reichsführer . . . do you kill people?'

Anna turned back. 'What are you talking about?'

'That's what you do, isn't? Kill people for the SD. When I think of the way you drew your pistol and shot Hellmuth . . . and he was already pointing his gun at you.'

Hellmuth, Anna thought. It had not occurred to her that Katherine and Essermann, working together for so many months, to track down the conspirators, would have become close. 'Hellmuth was a traitor to the Reich,' she said.

'But he was your lover.'

'He betrayed me as much as the Führer.'

'So you killed him. Just like that. Anna . . .'

'There are some things it is better for you not to know.' Anna closed the door.

Since the block in which her once luxurious flat had been situated had been hit by a British bomb, Himmler had moved Anna to one of the apartments situated in the bowels of this building. She had made it as comfortable as possible, but it could never be enjoyable. It was terribly small, and although efficiently air-conditioned there could be no substitute for fresh air. It also contained her maid, Birgit. Birgit had now been with her for four years, and a considerable intimacy had grown up between them; the woman was often a great comfort. But she, like everyone else, was in a tremendous twitter over the events of this past week. She would know that Himmler had returned from Rastenburg, would want to discuss it, hope to learn some truths as opposed to the wild rumours that were still sweeping the city. Anna was not in the mood for that.

She went down through the Gestapo Headquarters, greeted deferentially by the various secretaries and agents she encountered, and out on to the street. It was a brilliant late July afternoon, the glowing sun accentuating the calamity with which she was surrounded. To every side there were rubbled houses and cratered streets. The emergency services were hard at work clearing up some of the mess left by the previous night's raid, but the men all stopped to look at the strikingly beautiful young woman in the secretarial uniform walking past them. As did the various other passers-by. Anna smiled at them all. This might be the last time she would ever walk the streets of Berlin. If her plan worked.

It had to work. She had to make it work. But it would need very careful calculation, and the utmost determination. She was not really worried about either of those aspects. But it would also depend upon Henri Laurent. The Swiss banker to whom she delivered the funds that Himmler carefully accumulated from every source he could think of for depositing in a numbered account, had claimed to have fallen utterly in love with her. Well, she enjoyed him too. But he knew her only as a dedicated Nazi agent, and while he had indicated that he did not approve of the regime, he also worked for them in his role as a money launderer.

How would he respond to the knowledge that she sought only their destruction? And the problem was compounded by the fact that it would be very difficult to tell him part of the truth without revealing all of it. It would then become a business of which mattered more to him, her love or his professional integrity. But without his aid, she did not see how she could get her parents to safety.

The last week had been the most stressful of even her life. She needed to stretch her muscles, to relax . . . and to be adored. She went to the SS gymnasium, which, buried half underground, had so far escaped destruction.

The doorman blinked at her. 'Countess?' It was mid-afternoon, and Anna usually did her training first thing in the morning.

'Good afternoon, Bruno,' Anna said. 'Is Stefan available?'

'Well, yes, Countess. But—'

'I'll surprise him.'

Anna stepped past the desk and went along the corridor. There were several training rooms, some empty, some in use. She went to her usual room, opened the door, and gazed at the couple who appeared to be wrestling on the mat, but as they were both naked it was difficult to suppose that either judo or karate was involved. 'Good afternoon,' she said.

Stefan rolled off the woman – she was hardly more than a girl – while she uttered a terrified squawk, scrambled to her feet and ran for the showers.

'Hard at it, as always,' Anna remarked, closing the door.

'Countess!' Stefan stood up, panting, whether from his recent endeavours or an anticipated crisis Anna wasn't immediately sure.

'I know,' she said sympathetically. 'This is not my usual time. But I need a work out.'

'Of course. The young lady got carried away.' He reached for his singlet and shorts.

'I think you should leave those off,' Anna recommended. 'You are quite a good-looking fellow, you know, Stefan. Worth a second glance, anyway.'

Stefan gulped even as he flushed. But she had meant it. As a professional trainer he was in the pink of condition, hard-muscled with a splendid torso. He was not very tall, and his overly-rounded features were a long way from handsome, but he had wavy yellow hair, and was certainly well equipped where it mattered, even if at this moment somewhat diminished by the interruption.

She was giving way, she knew, to that wicked sense of humour that was essential to survival for anyone in her profession. Stefan had now been her trainer for three years, and like so many men, had fallen desperately in love – or more correctly, lust – with her the first time he had seen her without her clothes. He had even made advances, and been firmly snubbed, although she understood that such adoration, which had lasted for all of those unrequited training sessions, might one day come in handy in the increasingly uncertain world in which she was forced to exist.

But today, for all the cloud of guilt that hung above her like a thunderstorm – so many men, with their wives and children, condemned for attempting what she had attempted, and also failed – suddenly there was light at the end of the tunnel. If she could just get to it.

'You have not brought a change,' Stefan said, hesitant as he considered what might lie ahead.

'Then I shall do without,' Anna agreed. 'It was an impulse.'

He uttered a little sigh of anticipated pleasure, as she went to the changing room, which was adjacent to the showers.

The girl, just stepping from her stall, gasped and grabbed a towel to hold in front of her.

'This is the Countess von Widerstand,' Stefan announced, proudly.

The girl gave another gasp and dropped the towel, hastily retrieving it before it reached the floor.

'I am not going to bite you,' Anna said reassuringly. 'But Stefan and I require to be alone.'

Stefan scooped the girl's clothes from the bench and stuffed them into the arms clutching the towel. 'Dress outside.'

Another gasp, and she scuttled from the room.

'I hadn't meant you to be quite so hard on her,' Anna said. 'Or has she already experienced that?'

'No,' he said, watching her release her tie and unbutton her shirt.

'You mean I interrupted you?' Anna slid her skirt past her thighs. 'I am a wretch.'

Stefan was showing signs of recovery. 'I have been so worried. All these rumours . . .'

'Well, it is all over now. So you can stop worrying.' She slipped the straps for her camiknickers from her shoulders, and they followed the skirt past her thighs, before reaching up to release her bun and allow her hair to cascade on to her shoulders and down her back.

Stefan gazed at those flawless breasts; his greatest ambition was one day to be able to hold them, but he knew that to interfere with Anna, unless Anna wished to be interfered with, was the shortest possible route to a hospital . . . at the very best. 'You,' he said. 'I was worried about you. They said there was shooting at Gestapo Headquarters.'

Anna unclipped her suspender belt and sat down to roll down her stockings. 'Yes, there was. And in answer to you next question, yes, I did some of it. But as you see, I am still here.'

But what she might have had to do was no longer important; he was staring at the blue mark on her right rib cage, where she had once been shot. He did not know the details.

'And I feel like doing some shooting now,' she said. 'Load a pistol for me and prepare a target, will you?'

'Of course, Countess.'

He went into the gymnasium. Anna followed, lay on the

mat beneath the weights and exercised her arms for several minutes; she was as skilled at unarmed combat as she was with a weapon, and while she knew that the secret of that art was timing and delivery, the ability to get all of one's weight into the blow at the decisive moment, she also knew that muscles were very necessary. Stefan, watching her with glowing eyes, dropped one of the cartridges he was inserting into the Luger's magazine with a clatter.

Anna ignored him, and satisfied, got up and began to run, round and round the large room, hair flopping behind her, breasts rising and falling, muscles flexing in her thighs. Round and round she went while sweat dribbled down her face and from her armpits. 'Next time,' she panted as she passed him for the twentieth time.

Stefan pulled himself together, rested his hand on the lever. Anna rounded the room and approached the table. Stefan waited until she was almost up to him, then said, 'Now!'

As he spoke, he pulled the lever, and the full size cardboard image of a man began to cross the far end of the room, some twenty yards away, from left to right. Anna stopped running and in the same movement turned, grasped the pistol, levelled it, and emptied the magazine. The cardboard shook as each bullet struck home. Anna laid down the empty gun, now at last breathing deeply. Stefan went forward to peer at the target. 'Four in the head, five in the body. Where did you aim first?'

'You know that I always aim at the head,' Anna said. 'Because that makes any other shots unnecessary. Thank you, Stefan.'

She returned to the changing room and stepped into the shower, face turned up as she flooded her hair and herself. Stefan stood in the doorway to watch her; he thought that he could do this for the rest of his life. When she turned off the water to soap herself, he asked, 'Was there really an attempted revolution, Countess?'

'I'm afraid there was,' Anna said. 'Didn't you hear the Führer's speech?'

'Yes, I did. But . . .'

Anna shampooed her hair. 'You no longer believe everything he says.' She smiled through the soap at his expression. 'I don't think you are unique. But in this case everything he said was true.'

'He mentioned you by name. He said that without the support of his loyal aides, such as the Countess von Widerstand, he could not have triumphed.'

Anna finished showering and dried herself, then towelled her hair. 'And you did not believe him.'

'Oh, I believe that. Any man who could be certain of your support would be invulnerable.'

Anna dressed herself. 'You say the sweetest things.'

Stefan licked his lips. 'Countess . . . Anna . . .'

She opened her shoulder bag, found her brush, and stroked her still wet hair.

'Can we win this war?'

'If you believe what the Führer says, then we will win it.'

'But do not, well . . . we may all die.'

'We are all going to die, one day, Stefan.' She encased the long golden strands in a tortoiseshell clip.

Another lick of the lips. 'To die, without having held you in my arms . . .'

Anna rested her hand on the side of his face, and his fingers closed on hers. 'You shall have your wish, Stefan.'

'Anna . . .' The fingers tightened.

'Before you die. I give you my word.'

She freed herself and left the gymnasium. Promises cost nothing.

The evening was still bright, and she felt better for both the exercise and for using the gun. She supposed she occasionally suffered from hubris, but the feeling of superiority her skills engendered was irresistible. And in her tortured existence, without a degree of hubris she did not think she could survive.

She walked back to Gestapo Headquarters; it still wanted a few hours before the RAF would appear, as nowadays they did almost every night. She needed to work out what was coming next, what she intended to have happen next, to think, and felt that the gym session had freshened up her brain. On the surface of it, the question was a simple one. Thanks to Himmler's blind faith in her loyalty, she was being given the opportunity to get her parents out of Nazi control . . . if Laurent would go along with her. It would also mean that as she would have to go with them, she would be able to end this horrendous existence she had endured for six years. As to where she could possibly wind up, and with whom, she had really no idea; those were bridges she would cross when the initial step had been taken . . . although she knew where she *wanted* to wind up, and with whom. But to take that step meant abandoning Katherine. Well, there could not really be a choice, and as she had thought earlier, Katherine had made her own bed of her own free will. But still, to write off one's sister . . .

She realized that a car was nosing along the pavement beside her, sufficiently unusual in petrol-starved Berlin. Now it stopped, and a man got out. 'Oh, shit!' she remarked. She did not recognize the man, but both the lounge suit and the car indicated only two possible sources, and one of them, the Gestapo, was *not* possible; much as they might want to, no Gestapo agent would nowadays dare interfere with the Countess von Widerstand. That meant it had to be . . .

'Countess?' the man asked, anxiously, having overheard her comment on his appearance.

'It must be on my shoes,' Anna suggested. 'Don't tell me: it's a matter of life and death.'

'The doctor wishes to see you, now, yes.'

'I thought he was in Rastenburg.'

'He has returned. This very afternoon.'

The vultures, all coming home to roost, she thought. But she said, 'And he immediately wishes to see me? How sweet of him.'

She got into the car and sat down. *And immediately wishes to get his hands under my skirt*, she thought. *Bugger it!* Although he had never actually tried that.

The man sat beside her, and the car moved off. 'Your name is on everyone's lips, Countess.'

'Put there by your absurd propaganda,' she pointed out.

'Deservedly,' he argued.

Anna looked out of the window. There went any prospect of thinking for the next hour. The car stopped at the Ministry of Propaganda, and she was ushered upstairs to the office.

'Anna!' Josef Goebbels limped towards her and threw both arms round her. As he was several inches shorter than her, he was able to bury his face between her breasts while his hands immediately closed on her buttocks. Then he stepped back. 'Anna of the black silk stockings and the black silk underwear. You smell so sweet. As if you have come straight from your bath. And your hair is wet.'

'That is because I *have* come straight from my bath, Herr Doctor. Or at least, a shower. I have been at the gymnasium.'

'What a woman,' he said. 'If she is not working, she is training.' He gestured at the settee against the wall, and she seated herself, crossing her knees although she knew that even that small measure of protection was not going to do her much good.

Her relationship with this man was unlike any she had known, with anyone else. He was short, and she liked tall men. He was grotesquely ugly, where she liked her men to be, if not necessarily handsome, at least pleasant to look at. And he had a club foot, where she liked her men to be, if not her equal physically – she had never met one who was – at least fit and well formed.

He had taken her over without a by-your-leave, not as an employee, but simply because he believed it was his God-given right to appropriate any woman he chose. But it was not a God-given right, there was the rub. It was a Führer-given right, and in Nazi Germany that was far more important. The first time she had been summoned to his office, as always being plucked off the street by his henchmen, she had not known what to expect. But she had known that, however easily she could have disposed of him with a few – and probably only one – well-placed blows, such a reaction would mean her instant destruction. So she had allowed herself to be virtually raped, and been surprised. If he was a very rough lover, he also knew how to turn a woman on.

But the spin-off had been far more important. He had intimated that not only could he get her into the Führer's bed, but that he thought she might be good for the great man. That had opened a path that had seemed like a dream come true to her MI6 and OSS employers, and had led to this catastrophic situation. Now she assumed that he considered her even more his creature, a weapon to be used in whichever direction he chose. Well, all her employers, beginning with Heydrich, and then Himmler, and then Clive Bartley and Billy Baxter, and now Wild Bill Donovan and Joe Andrews, had so considered her. The difference was that all of those had directed her against the enemies of the regime that employed *them*;

this man would use her to destroy his apparent brothers in arms. If she was around to be used. As that was not going to happen, she could stand even his company. But she had to act her role to the end, and accept and if possible enjoy whatever was about to happen to her.

However, for the moment he remained standing in front of her, surveying her. 'I have just returned from Rastenburg,' he announced.

'So they told me. Did you come back with the Reichsführer?'

This was an intended rhetorical barb; Himmler and Goebbels loathed each other.

'We used the same plane, yes.'

'And the Reichsführer is now Commander of the Home Army.'

'Such as it is. The Führer has appointed *me* Reich Plenipotentiary for Total War Effort.' He paused to peer at her. 'You are not impressed.'

'I would be, sir, if I knew what the position entails.'

'The position,' Goebbels declared, and now *he* was making a speech, 'means that I am the supreme commander of every aspect of German life. That includes the Home Army.'

'Then it is important. May I ask, does the Reichsführer know this?'

'If he does not, he is very soon going to find out. I am empowered to do any and everything I consider necessary for the victorious survival of the Third Reich. As of this moment, this country is at *war.*'

'Forgive me, Herr Doctor,' she said. 'But have we not been at war for five years?'

'The Wehrmacht has been at war. And the Luftwaffe. And the Navy. And the industrialists. Some of them,' he added darkly. 'But the nation . . . do you realize, Anna, that the Soviet Union has whole battalions, regiments, of women serving in the front line? That half the women in England are working either in the fields to produce more food, or in the factories to produce more tanks and airplanes? That half the women in the United States are also in the factories? While our women sit at home and wail. Apart from a few dedicated ladies like yourself. I know this was a deliberate decision on the part of the Führer: it is men's task to fight, women's to keep the home fires burning for their men, and have as many children as possible . . .' he paused. 'Why have you never had children, Anna?'

'I am not married, Herr Doctor.'

'You were married once. Couldn't that Englander manage it?'

'Apparently not, sir.' Although, she remembered, it had not been for lack of trying. 'In any event, I did not wish to have children by Bordman. I do not wish to have children at all, until the War is over and I can marry again and settle down.'

'So you take precautions. Very wise. I would hate to see you with a bulging belly. But they are not infallible, you know. As for settling down . . . you? As what? As for *marriage* . . . would any man dare? That fellow Essermann was your lover, was he not?'

'For a while, Herr Doctor.'

'And you shot him dead, without compunction.'

'I shot Hellmuth Essermann, Herr Doctor, because you had just given me orders to execute everyone I discovered implicated in the plot against the Führer. Besides, he had drawn his pistol against me.'

'The ultimate crime, eh? The ultimate fatal crime. Ha ha.' Without warning he hurled himself at her. As usual, she had to exert an effort of will not to destroy him, but she felt entitled to put up her hands in an entirely feminine and protective gesture.

That did not do her a great deal of good. He parted the hands and had her stretched across the settee, nuzzling her neck and then her breasts while he pulled up her skirt to get at her crotch. This was so unlike the previous times he had raped her – he apparently knew no other way to approach a woman, sexually – that she didn't know how to respond. Normally he wanted her to undress, slowly and sensually, so that he could take in all of her beauty, stage by stage. So she did nothing, and after worrying her, like a dog, for a few seconds he suddenly pushed himself away, rolling across the settee to sit up.

Anna also sat up. Her tie was askew, her shirt was out of her waistband, and she had an idea that her stockings were laddered. But there were, or could be, more important matters. 'Herr Doctor?' she asked.

'Making love to you is like making love to an iceberg,' he grumbled.

That is because you have never made *love* to me, she thought. 'I am sorry, Herr Doctor. You took me by surprise.'

'When last did you have sex?'

'I had sex last Wednesday night, sir. In Rastenburg.'

'Of course. With the Führer. He said you were magnificent.'

'Thank you, sir.'

'In fact, he said that it was that night with you that carried him through the trauma of the next day.'

'I am flattered, sir. May I straighten my clothes?'

'Oh . . . go home. I have too much to do to have sex.'

You are overwhelmed by your new powers. Anna thought, and so you, of all people, cannot erect. She supposed it was a sad indictment of the state Germany was in, that of the three most powerful men in the country, one wouldn't do it at all, the other found great difficulty in doing it, and the third, who boasted of being the greatest lover in the country, seemed to have run out of steam . . . after attempting to savage the most beautiful woman in the country.

She straightened her clothes. 'I hope you soon feel better, Herr Doctor.'

'Of course I will soon feel better. Then I will send for you again.'

'I will look forward to that, Herr Doctor.'

Because by the time he did, she would be beyond his reach, for ever.

Birgit bustled, as always. She was a small, dark, pretty woman, who valued her position but was terrified of her employer. She did not know precisely what Anna did, but she knew she was a senior officer in the SD, which was sufficiently intimidating. And over the years they had been together she had noticed that from time to time various people had dropped dead in her mistress's close vicinity.

But for the past few days the news, not only that there had been an attempted coup d'état against the regime, but that it had apparently been largely foiled by her mistress, had her in even more of a twitter than usual.

'I have prepared dinner, Countess,' she said hesitantly. She could never be sure when Anna was going to be in or out.

'Thank you, Birgit,' Anna said. 'I will have a bath first. But open a bottle of champagne, will you? Now.'

'Of course, Countess.' She hurried off.

Anna surveyed the tiny lounge/diner. How are the mighty

fallen, she reflected, thinking of the luxury that the RAF had forced her to abandon. The strange thing was that at this moment she was more powerful than at any time in her life. She was the heroine of the hour, and her word at every level below the very top, was just about law. She wondered what Clive was thinking of it all.

She went into the equally small bedroom, took off her clothes. Although it was hardly an hour since she had showered at the gymnasium, even five minutes of being pawed by Goebbels left her feeling as if she had been rolled in cow dung.

She turned on the taps in the bathroom she now had to share with Birgit, waited with some trepidation: it was impossible to be certain, in Berlin in July 1944, which mains might have been severed by the last air raid. But the water gushed out, and it was hot; at least in Gestapo Headquarters the boilers were always lit.

Clive, she thought, as she watched the tub fill. Was it possible that she could be with him, perhaps permanently, within the next couple of weeks? Sooner than that, if everything went according to her plan; once he knew that she was in Switzerland and prepared to come out, she was sure he would act very quickly; he had begged her to come out so often in the past five years.

But where would that leave Henri? Her plan would not work without his complete support. She did not know if she would obtain that. She actually knew almost nothing about him, save that he laundered money for Himmler, and also had other contacts in Germany. He claimed to loathe the Nazis, had indeed criticized her for working for them . . . but he worked for them himself, and they were clearly very important for the business of himself and his partners. Now she was going to have to ask him to endanger that relationship. For her. He also claimed to love her more than life itself, and if that were true he might very well go along with her. But would he go along if he knew that her ultimate objective was another man?

So the answer was simple. Do not mention any objectives save getting her parents out of Nazi Germany, until it was done. Was she that ruthless? Her employers, all the world, perhaps Clive himself, had no doubt that she was. But she had never betrayed a man's love before. She needed love too desperately.

She tied her hair on the trop of her head and sank into the suds. Birgit appeared with a tray on which there was a bottle and a glass. 'Thank you, Birgit. Why do you not take one for yourself?'

'Countess?'

'I would like you to join me in a drink.'

'Oh, yes, Countess.' She scurried off and came back with another glass, poured.

'Have you enjoyed working for me, Birgit?'

'Oh, yes, Countess.'

'Despite . . . well, some of the things that have happened?'

'I know that whatever you have done has been for the Reich.'

'That must be a very comforting thought.' Anna raised her glass. 'Well, then, to us. Our years together.'

'Oh, yes, Countess.' But the maid was frowning.

'I am going away tomorrow morning.' *And you will never see me again.*

'Am I to come with you?' Birgit asked.

'No. It is one of my trips for the Reichsführer.'

'I understand. But you almost sound as if you will not be coming back.'

How perceptive you are, Anna thought. But, however often she had to do it to stay alive, she hated telling lies. So she said, 'Have I not always come back in the past?'

Unusually, Anna slept badly. She was too excited, and next morning decided to skip a visit to the gym and go straight up to her office. She packed her valise with two changes of clothing – the rest of her wardrobe, including sadly, her sable, would have to be written off – but also with her best jewellery, apart from what she was wearing; made sure her shoulder bag contained her Luger and two spare magazines – she had no idea how much opposition she might encounter in Poland – kissed Birgit, much to the maid's surprise; and climbed the stairs to the ground floor, where the day staff were just coming in, smiled at them as she invariably did, and went to the next flight of stairs, to stare at the man who was coming down.

He was staring at her in turn, and whereas she was registering a mixture of surprise and irritation, his expression was one of apprehension, which did not go well with his rather harsh features, his heavy shoulders. 'Countess!'

He made to step past her, and she checked him. 'Herr Werter! What are you doing here?'

He was very close to the top of her hate list, as he undoubtedly knew. She had last seen him in January, when she had stepped off the Malmo ferry at Lubeck, after her trip to Stockholm for Himmler, and having been forced to kill three Gestapo agents who had unwisely attempted to arrest her. Before they had realized that they were going to die, they had told her they had been alerted to the fact that she might be fleeing Germany by this man. More importantly, she knew that in his capacity as commander of the Gestapo Lubeck office, he had been the man who had arrested Belinda Hoskin, and submitted her to the humiliation of a strip search. He had been planning to do a lot more than that when she had turned up, armed with an order from Himmler that the prisoner was to be released into her care. She fully intended to take care of him, when the opportunity arose. But she had never expected to see him here.

'I have been seconded,' he said proudly.

'You are joining the SS?'

'I have been recommended for membership of the SD.' His tone was prouder yet. 'Perhaps we will be working together.'

'I regard the possibility of us ever working together as remote. And I doubt that you would enjoy it, if it happened.'

Anna went upstairs, now feeling thoroughly out of sorts, but before she reached her office was accosted by one of Himmler's secretaries. 'The Reichsführer is waiting for you.'

He must still be agitated, she thought, to have come in so early. She went through to his office. 'Heil Hitler! Good morning, Herr Reichsführer.'

'Good morning, Anna. One attaché case.' He held it up. 'Here is the key.'

It was attached to a long loop of string. Anna knew what he required, dropped the loop over her head, fluffing out her hair over it, and settled the key inside her décolletage, beside her gold crucifix.

'Fortunate key,' Himmler remarked, as he always did. 'You look as if you are going to a party.'

I am, Anna thought. 'I find travelling easier when the men I meet are anxious to help me,' she explained.

This morning she was wearing a pale blue suit with a calf length skirt, a white shirt, flesh-coloured stockings, and a broad-brimmed straw hat with a pale blue ribbon. Her earrings were tiny gold bars dropping from gold clips – she had never had her ears pierced – and she wore an enormous ruby solitaire on the forefinger of the right hand, although this was concealed by her white gloves. The watch on her left wrist was a gold Junghans: she was travelling with all her most precious possessions.

'As long as you don't let any of these admirers get too close, eh? Ha ha.'

'Ha ha,' Anna agreed. 'I met Agent Werter on the stairs just now.'

'Ah. Yes. You know him, don't you?'

'Yes, sir. I know him.'

Himmler snapped his fingers. 'Of course. I remember. He was unhappy when you removed that woman . . . what was her name?'

'Her name was Claudia Ratosi, sir.'

'And you took quite a liking to her, as I recall.'

'I merely ascertained that she was innocent of the charges Werter wished to bring against her.'

'And he did not like that.'

'No, sir, he did not. May I ask what he is doing here?'

'Well, you know, he has spent two years in Lubeck. He was very efficient there. So when he applied to join the SD I thought it might be an idea to give him a chance. You don't have to see him if you don't want to. Now, tell me what you think of Laurent.'

Anna frowned; he had never before raised the question of their possible relationship. 'Sir?'

'I have never met him, you know.'

'Yet you trust him with all this money?'

'He was highly recommended. And he has proved trustworthy. Has he not?'

'As far as I am aware, sir.'

'So what sort of man is he? How old is he?'

And they have never met, Anna thought, and surrendered to her Irish sense of humour. 'I don't really know, sir. I suppose he's about sixty.'

'Hm. Has he ever made an advance?'

'Good heavens no, sir. Our relationship is strictly professional.' *At least, out of bed.*

'But he knows who you are.'

'He knows I am the Countess von Widerstand,' Anna said cautiously.

'And because of that business in Geneva last year he knows that you are a killer.'

'He knows that I am a member of the SD, sir,' Anna corrected primly. 'And therefore, trained to protect myself.'

'Just as he knows where this money –' he tapped the briefcase – 'comes from. Would you not say that he knows too much about us? Both of us?'

'Sir?' Alarm bells sounded in her brain.

'This transfer will bring my total deposit with his bank . . . our total deposit, Anna . . . to over three million US dollars. I think that is probably enough for us to go on with. In any event, the way things are going here, that is as much as we can hope to accumulate. I think the time is coming for us to terminate our business arrangement with Herr Laurent.'

Anna gazed at him. You unutterable scum, she thought. But hadn't she always known that?

'How many of his staff know of these transactions?'

'One or two, sir. But they only place the money on deposit in your . . . *our* numbered account. They do not know to whom the account belongs.'

'And we are the only ones who can access it. Apart from Laurent, of course.'

'*You* are the only one, sir,' Anna corrected.

'I shall give you the number when you return from this trip.'

'Thank you, sir.' But I am not going to return, she thought.

'But Laurent also knows the number. I will leave this in your hands, Anna.'

How casually he condemned people to death. And she knew, that on the rare occasions he had been present at an execution, he had been physically sick. 'Yes, sir. But you do realize that when I hand over the money, it takes at least twenty-four hours for it to reach the account?'

He nodded. 'Thus you will remain with him for those twenty-four hours. Or longer if you feel it necessary. Make his last hours happy, eh? You are accomplished at that.'

If ever she had felt physically sick, as now, it was in the company of this man. 'You flatter me, sir.'

'No man can do that, Anna. Now, your parents. You have not forgotten about them, eh? Ha ha.'

'I have not forgotten about them, sir.'

'I did not think so. When you are finished with Laurent, take the train to Berne. It is only eighty kilometres. I assume you will as always cover your tracks to give you time to get out ahead of the Swiss police. At Berne you will go to one of my agents, who will be waiting for you.' He pushed a piece of paper across the desk. 'Memorize that address and then destroy it. This agent will accompany you in the aeroplane. He will be your bodyguard, eh?'

'Did you say, aeroplane, sir?'

'You have flown before, have you not?'

'Yes, sir.' But it had only been four times, and each time she had been on her way to, or from, Hitler. Each occasion had been nightmarish . . . for different reasons.

'Then you will not be afraid. In any event, there is no alternative. It is eleven hundred kilometres from Lucerne to Posen. To make that journey, either by road or rail, in the present conditions, would take you several days, and God knows what you might encounter. By aeroplane it will take you only a few hours, all in perfect safety.'

With Russian fighters roaming at will? she wondered.

'At Posen, you will be met and driven to the internment camp.' This time he gave her a sheet of stiff, headed notepaper. 'Here is the order for the release of your parents, into your custody as the Countess von Widerstand. You don't want to burn that, eh? And here are your passes and your carte blanche as my agent. Then you, and they, will be driven back to Posen, where the aircraft will be waiting to bring you to Berlin. Is that satisfactory?'

'Very, sir.' But although she knew, in view of her plans, that it was a hypothetical question, she could not resist asking, 'And what will happen to them then, sir?'

'Why, we shall find them a new home, eh? Safe from the Russians.'

'Thank you, sir.' She stood up. 'The car will be waiting. So, *auf wiedersehen.*'

To her surprise, he also stood up, came round the desk, and

held her shoulders. 'I am placing my absolute trust in your fidelity, Anna.'

He'd have her weeping in a moment. But they would be tears of joy. 'I understand that, sir.'

'Well, then . . .' To her utter consternation, he kissed her on the forehead.

Anna carried the attaché case and her valise into her office then placed the various passes and tickets in her shoulder bag, beside her Luger.

Katherine stood in the doorway of the inner office. 'When will you be back?'

'In a couple of days. Why, will you miss me?'

'With Essermann gone, and now you – well – it will be lonely. And now our investigation is over, I have nothing to do.'

'I will find you lots to do when I come back. Until then, rest up and read a good book. Come here.'

Katherine advanced, cautiously. Anna took her into her arms and hugged her tightly. Katherine gasped. 'You *are* coming back?'

Anna kissed her. 'Don't I always?'

The Best Laid Plans

This was Anna's third trip to Lucerne, and if it felt odd not to be escorted to the station by Essermann, as always in the past – this was an SS officer she had never met before, who was tongue-tied throughout the short car ride – the journey as before went off smoothly and peacefully, in such strong contrast to her first delivery to Switzerland, when she had been sent to Geneva. And wound up having to kill two other interfering Gestapo agents.

But she needed the peace, and having made it clear to the two businessmen sharing her first-class compartment, and who could not believe their luck at being cooped up for several hours with a beautiful woman, that she was interested in neither chitchat nor a flirtation, she was left alone with her thoughts.

For the first time in a long time she was at once impatient and apprehensive of the future, and this disturbed her. Her success had been built upon her patience, and her refusal to consider more than one step at a time, confident that, within the parameters of the overall plan she was required to carry out, she would be able to deal with each problem as it arose. But she had never before undertaken a project quite as large as this, and this time she was not acting on orders, confident of support if she really needed it. Now she was on her own. Certainly if she could not obtain the support of Laurent.

The staff at the Lakeview Hotel welcomed her as a favourite customer. Eyebrows were no longer raised at her peculiar habit of retiring to her room and remaining there, at least until she was visited by her gentleman friend; it had never occurred to any of them that she might be unable to abandon her luggage for a moment, and to go down to the bar or dinner lugging an obviously heavy attaché case would have made her too conspicuous.

So as always she had a room service supper and went to bed, remaining there until ten the next morning, when she had a bath and dressed. The temptation to use the phone to call Clive and tell him what she was planning had to be resisted; securing the active support of Laurent came first, otherwise she could be endangering Clive needlessly.

He always came at eleven, and punctually on the hour there was a tap on her door. Although she had no doubt who it was, Anna was so conditioned to caution, at least when not actually in Gestapo Headquarters, that as always she stood to one side of the door, her pistol, the silencer already screwed into place, resting against her shoulder. 'Come.'

She had unlocked the door, and a moment later was in his arms, the silencer resting on the nape of his neck. He took his mouth away from hers. 'Do you ever make mistakes?'

'I'm alive.'

'I meant, as regards the other chap.'

Anna released him, rested the gun on the table, while she remembered that unforgettable day in Prague when she had gunned down two obvious assassins, unaware that they were

British agents sent to dispose of the chief secretary to the German Protector. 'I have made mistakes,' she confessed.

'Then *I* should say, I'm alive.' He held her arms, and brought her back for another kiss. 'Seeing you is like watching the sun rise over the lake.'

'I like looking at you, too.'

This was no lie. Henri Laurent was by far the most handsome of all the many men with whom she had shared a bed, willingly or unwillingly. He was astonishingly young for a financial tycoon, still in his early thirties, and roughly her own height, which was always a bonus. His features were splendidly carved, only slightly aquiline, his black hair brushed straight back from his forehead, his eyes lively, and she knew that his body, presently encased in a flawless three-piece suit, was hard-muscled and filled with vigour.

They had known each other for just a year, since that first delivery, and he claimed to have fallen in love with her at first sight, even if the discovery of those two bodies in her hotel room immediately after she had left, had left him uncertain as to just what he had become involved with. Now he did not seem to care who or what she actually was, as long as from time to time she was his. But the operative word, this far, was 'seem'.

'So what does it feel like to be a heroine of the Third Reich?'

Anna made a face. 'If you start believing Goebbels' propaganda you're in deep trouble.'

He kissed her again, then released her and went to the attaché case, which waited on the settee. 'You'll need this,' she suggested, drawing the key from inside her shirt.

He took it. 'How warm it is. One day, when this is all over, I am going to set this key in stone, for all time.'

A cue? Anna took a deep breath. 'There is no time like the present.'

Henri had already inserted the key. Now he raised his head, slowly. 'Would you say that again?'

'If you will help me, I would like to come out.'

'Help you? My dearest girl. But I thought . . . you mean Himmler is letting you go? Because of what you did? Or is it this Russian breakthrough?'

'What Russian breakthrough?' Anna's voice was suddenly sharp.

'They crossed the Vistula last night. Didn't you know?'

'No,' Anna said, 'I did not know.' Because Himmler had not told her. That was the reason for his agitation, his suggestion that it might be too dangerous for her to travel by train or car. Yet he was letting her go to Posen, which might already be in Russian hands. Was he trying to get rid of her?

Then the penny dropped. She was to remain here until the money was safely deposited, then she was to kill Henri. And flee . . . into the arms of the Russians. But only Himmler would know that. To the Nazi hierarchy, and most importantly, to Hitler, he was bending over backwards to help her, allowing her to go to Poland to reclaim her parents. He would be heart-broken when news arrived that she had been overtaken by her most bitter enemies.

'The crossing was made well south of Warsaw,' Henri said. 'And your people are throwing everything they have into a counter-attack to drive them back. But frankly, they don't seem to have all that much to throw. And according to the latest bulletin, the Russians are holding. Anyway, that's not relevant if you're getting out. From what you have told me, I really never thought he'd let you go. Didn't you say he had some kind of hold on you?'

'Yes,' Anna said. 'I did.' Because, whatever Himmler had planned, or might be hoping would happen, she had to go through with it. She had spent six years protecting her mother and father; to abandon them now would make a nonsense of her life, and make her everything most people considered her.

Henri frowned. 'But he doesn't any more? I'm sorry. I don't understand.'

Anna sat beside him on the settee. 'Do you love me?'

'Love you, Anna? I adore you. To be able to . . . well . . .'

'I am about to place my life in your hands.'

He frowned. 'I had always supposed, that if push came to shove, my life would be in *your* hands.'

'That is quite true. I have been sent here to kill you.'

He stared at her, then looked at the pistol, which remained on the table.

'Do you suppose that I need a weapon to kill?' she asked. 'Or that I would tell you about it, if I intended to carry out my orders?'

'You have been ordered to kill me? By Himmler?'

'This is to be our last transfer. I suppose there is no one left to rob. I am to wait here with you until the money is deposited, and then I am to get rid of you. You are the only person who can identify the source of the money, you see.'

'And you are disobeying him? Because . . .?' He held her hands.

'Because I need your help.'

The grasp on her fingers only slightly relaxed. 'I have said that I will help you, in any possible way. So you would like the money, transferred to an account for your use?'

'Now, Henri, you know that is not possible. That money does not belong to me, any more than to Himmler.'

They had had this conversation before, to his incomprehension. 'I know, you want to give it all back. And as you can't possibly do that, as at least half the people from whom it was taken are dead, you want to give it all to charity. Three million dollars! I give up. So what are you planning to do?'

'I am going to leave here tomorrow, and hopefully return the same day, with two people. These people will have no identification, no papers at all, and they may be in a confused state. I need you to take care of them, and me, until I can make the necessary arrangements to get them to safety. Again, if you are prepared to help me, I can make those arrangements now, but it may take a day or two for them to be implemented.'

The frown was back. 'These people . . .'

'Are my parents.'

He stared at her for several seconds. 'Your parents. And they are . . .?'

'They are in a camp in Poland. Because of the Russian advance, Himmler has given me permission to remove them from the camp and take them to Germany.'

'My God! And they are . . .?'

'Yes. They are the reason that I have worked for him, and for the regime, for the past six years.'

The fingers had tightened again. 'Oh, my dear girl. My dear, dear girl. I knew you could never be a Nazi. Of course I will help you. But . . . he is letting you take the count and countess . . .' He frowned at her expression. 'Of course, they cannot be the count and countess, if you are a countess. Anna, what is your real name?' He had only ever known her as the Countess von Widerstand, or the name she had used, Anna O'Brien, on the occasion of their first meeting, and he now knew that had been an alias.

Anna hesitated. But again her years of having to protect herself were telling her, much as she wanted to, not to trust even this man absolutely . . . until he had proved worthy of that trust, absolutely. 'I can't tell you that, Henri.'

He gazed at her. 'But you want me to help you.'

'If you love me. Or have you changed your mind about that?'

'Of course I have not,' he protested, and took another tack. 'But the danger—'

'Is all on the other side. You must trust me.'

'I trust your skill. But what of the Russians? Suppose you fell into their hands? They may know you are an SD officer.'

They know a lot more than that, Anna thought. 'I think I have time, if they are still south of Warsaw. In any event, it is something I must do. I have spent the last six years carrying out the most dreadful crimes for the SD, simply to protect my parents. I am not going to abandon them now.'

'Of course. But your courage, your determination . . . is there nothing I can do to help? I can come with you . . .'

'Have you ever fired a gun, Henri?'

'Of course. I am a Swiss. I have done my national service.'

'Let me put that another way: have you ever killed man?'

'Well . . . no. But—'

'It is not something most people find easy to do.'

'And you find it easy to do.'

Anna made a moue. 'I have been trained for it.'

'Are you saying that those two men in Geneva were not the only men you have killed?'

Anna sighed. But he had to take her warts and all. 'I have killed twenty-nine people, Henri.'

His hands fell away.

'But some of them were women.'

'You have carried out twenty-nine assassinations for Himmler?'

The crunch moment had arrived. 'No. Less than a quarter were for the Reich. I have another, and superior employer.' Which was unfair on MI6; most of the remainder had been in her own self-defence. But that confession would have to come later, if at all.

Almost insensibly he had moved away from her, as if expecting her to claim to be an emissary of the Devil. Well, she thought, he would not be so very far wrong.

'My other employer,' she said, 'is my ultimate salvation. And more important, he is the salvation of my parents, to whom I wish you to deliver them.' And me, of course, she thought. But it would be unwise to say that at this moment.

'Anna . . . I am totally bewildered. This employer . . .?'

'I am going to telephone him now, and I would like you to speak to him.' She got up and picked up the phone. Like most continental phones, it had a duplicate earpiece, and this she handed to him. Then she gave the number to the switch-board operator.

'That is an English number,' Henri said.

'Yes, it is.'

'The lines are busy, Countess,' the switchboard said. 'If you will remain in your room, I will call you back the moment I have a connection.'

'Thank you.' Anna hung up.

Laurent was still gazing at her as if he had never seen her before. 'I do not understand,' he said again. 'You work for the Nazis, and yet you have a superior in England . . .'

'I told you that I was placing my life in your hands.'

'You mean . . .?'

'I have been an English agent since before the war started.'

He took his handkerchief from his breast pocket to wipe his forehead. 'Do they know what you do . . . what you have done, for Himmler?'

'Not everything. They are satisfied with the job I am doing for them.' At least, she thought, I hope they are.

'But . . . Berlin is telling the world how you saved the regime, saved Hitler . . .'

'It is a complicated business, which I will explain to you when we have the time. What I need to know is whether you will back me, despite what I have just told you.'

He licked his lips, and glanced at the pistol, which still lay on the table, beside the telephone and therefore close to her hand. He might never have seen her in action, but he could have no doubt of the consequences should he reject her.

'I had thought you loved me,' she said, quietly.

'I do,' he insisted. 'But you must understand . . . It will mean the end of my business.'

'Only as regards Herr Himmler. And as I have just explained, that business is terminated with this transfer.'

'But . . . will he not send another assassin when he discovers that I am not dead?'

'The way things are shaping up, by the time he discovers that, the war will be over, and he will be behind bars awaiting trial as a war criminal.' Unless he happens to be in his grave, she thought; that was the end she had in mind.

The telephone rang. 'I have your call, Countess.'

'Thank you.' Anna indicated the extension, and Henri put it to his ear.

'Countess?'

'Good morning, Miss Barstow.' Anna spoke in English. 'Is Mr Bartley available?'

'Yes, he is. But—'

'Just put me through.'

A moment later Clive was on the line. 'Anna! My God, but it is good to hear from you. Where are you?'

'Lucerne.'

'Lucerne? That's in Switzerland.'

'Yes, it is.' She frowned. 'Is that important?'

'My darling girl . . . can you stay there for a day or two?'

'Ah . . .' but she intended to return the following night. 'I will be here, yes.'

'That's splendid. Listen, Belinda is on her way to see you. We were going to get her into Switzerland, and she was going to cross the border as an Italo–Swiss national, and contact you. But if she can see you there . . .'

'It will be safer for everyone. Is there a problem?'

'There could be a problem, yes. She'll explain it when she sees you.'

'Then I'll be patient. Has she left yet?'

'We're still setting things up.'

'Well, it would be best if she could arrive tomorrow, or at worst the day after, and there are some things she must bring with her. Specifically, whatever documentation is necessary to get my parents and me into England, as well as blank passports and things like that.'

There was a moment's silence. 'Would you repeat that?'

'I think you heard me the first time,' Anna said. 'I have been given the opportunity to get my parents out of prison and myself out of Germany, and I am taking it.'

'That is the best news I've ever had. Of course she'll bring the documentation. Anything you could possibly need. Although the passports will have to wait until you are actually here. Tell you what: I'll come with her, just to make sure nothing goes wrong. This will absolutely make Billy's day.'

'You reckon?'

'He loves you too. Where can we contact you?'

'I can't tell you precisely where I'll be.' It might not be safe to return to this hotel, which was known to Himmler. 'But I have a contact here in Switzerland who will tell you where I am.'

Another brief silence. 'A contact.'

'He is absolutely trustworthy.' She smiled at Henri. 'He loves me too.'

'Anna . . . this contact . . . he's not OSS, is he?'

'I wish you could stop fighting over me,' Anna said. 'No, he is not OSS. He's here. Speak to him.' She handed the phone to Henri, who was looking more uncertain than ever. 'Mr Bartley is my MI6 controller,' she explained, reverting to German. 'He is fluent in German. Give him a contact number.'

Henri regarded the phone as if it might be about to explode, then took it. 'Henri Laurent, at you service, monsieur.'

'You're French.'

'No, monsieur, I am Swiss.'

'And you're prepared to help the countess get out?'

'Of course. I will give you a telephone number where I can be reached when you and your people are in the country. When you contact me we will set up a meeting. Will you write this down?' He gave the number, then handed the phone back to Anna, who was frowning; she had not realized that Henri was fluent in English, but he had to be if he had understood what they had said. 'He wishes another word.'

'Anna . . .'

'I know,' she said, continuing in German. 'I am breaking every rule in the book. But this is my first chance, and it may be my last. I cannot pass it up, Clive.'

'I understand that, and I, all of us, are on your side. I just hope to God this character doesn't let you down.'

'He's on the extension.'

'Ah! Well, then, Herr Laurent, I'll repeat that. If you let the lady down you'll have the entire staff of MI6 on your back. *Auf wiedersehen.*'

Henri replaced the receiver. 'Is that man your lover?'

'What makes you say that?'

'The way he spoke.'

'We have loved, yes,' Anna said carefully. 'I suppose it goes with the job. More importantly, he is my boss.'

'And what is this OSS he seems to be worried about?'

'Some American organization. He doesn't want them to know about me.'

'And this documentation he is bringing . . . it is to be for you too.'

She had already decided how this should be handled. 'Yes. There are two reasons. I need to have the same nationality as my parents, and whatever course you and I may choose to follow, it has to be safer for me to have a British passport than any other: I have been working for them for the past five years, and only they know that.'

He was still looking doubtful. It was time to move on.

'Listen . . .' She held his hand and led him to the settee. 'You understand that I cannot return to this hotel.'

He nodded. 'How are you getting to Poland?'

'By plane.'

'From where?'

'Berne.'

'And how are you coming back?'

'By the same plane.'

'But . . .?'

'I told you, I can take care of it.'

He considered for a few moments then said, 'When?'

'I am leaving tomorrow morning, and it is my intention to return tomorrow night. It may be quite late.'

'And this plane . . .?'

'Will be German. But I will be in control.'

He looked at the pistol on the table. Then he nodded. 'I will meet the plane, in Berne, tomorrow night.'

'Oh, my darling!' She kissed him. 'And now, we have had

nothing but business all morning. And I have to be off again at the crack of dawn. Let us have a room service lunch with a bottle of champagne, and then go to bed for the afternoon. And the night.'

He kissed her in turn. She knew there were huge problems ahead, but she felt that for the time being, at least, she had things here under control as well.

'Shall I come with you now?' Laurent asked, lying in bed and watching Anna emerge from the bathroom, towelling her hair. 'To Berne?'

'I don't think that would be a good idea.' She draped the towel across a chair and dressed, quickly and precisely as always. 'I am meeting a German agent there, and you are supposed to be dead, remember?'

'How could I forget?'

'But in any event, I shall be back tonight.'

'With your parents.'

'Indeed.' She added her jewellery, checked the contents of her shoulder bag, and smiled at him. 'Don't worry, they're not going to share our bed. But if I may, I will leave these two bags with you.'

'I know what is in the attaché case. Will you tell me what is in the other?'

'Of course. My clothes. Now I must hurry: the train leaves in half an hour.'

He caught her hand. 'And when you come back, we will be together, for always.'

'If that is what you would like.' She kissed him again, freed her hand, and went to the door. '*Ciao!*'

He watched the door close, remained lying still, staring at it. He thought, I have spent the night in the arms of a mass murderess! In Anna's presence, surrounded by the feel of her, the touch of her, that realization had only lurked at the edge of his consciousness. It was too bizarre to be taken seriously. But, thinking about her, thinking about what he *knew* of her, he knew it was true.

Could such a woman, such a creature, ever love, without reservation? Could she *be* loved, without reservation, with the knowledge that if they ever quarrelled she could, and very probably would, kill him without compunction? When one has killed twenty-nine times, does number thirty really matter? So perhaps he could make sure that she never had access to a weapon, but she had indicated that she did not need a weapon, to kill. And he believed that too.

She had promised to be his . . . what? He had actually considered marriage. But that was before she had revealed so much of herself. Without actually revealing anything! She would not even tell him her real name! And quite apart from her homicidal background, there was her emotional background to be considered. Could any woman who had worked hand in glove with the Nazis, and killed for them, be entirely normal? She had said it was all to protect her parents. If that were true, she could claim to be a heroine. But at the same time, did that not mean that she valued them above everything else in life . . . including every man? He had no desire to marry a family, only a woman.

She had also refused to consider using any, or all, of the $3 million. Was that another aspect of her essentially heroic character? Or just a sop to her conscience? A $100,000 a killing!

So she also claimed to be working, and have done most of her killing, for the British Secret Service, and like everything else she had said, that also appeared to be true. But if so, even if the war ended, as now appeared certain, in Nazi defeat, could she ever turn her back on such a commitment? And this man Clive . . . there had been more than merely servile admiration for her boss in her voice when she had spoken to him. So where did *he* fit into the emotional picture?

He swung his legs out of bed and sat up. It all came down to one simple question: with all her beauty, all of the desire she could generate . . . was she worth an open-ended involvement?

Anna was in Berne by ten, and took a taxi from the station to the address she had been given. As she hoped to be back in Lucerne in a few hours at the outside, she was carrying only her shoulder bag with her Luger, its spare magazines, and, of course, her precious passes and carte blanche.

For the moment, she felt totally relaxed, not only because she always did relax when actually started on an assignment, but because of what she had left behind . . . and would be returning to. Henri was a delightful lover, at once positive and yet gentle, more eager to please her than himself. She felt enormously guilty at her intention to abandon him the moment Clive appeared, but then she reflected that over the past year she had given him several hours of sexual bliss, and a relationship he could dine out on for the rest of his life. So, concentrate.

The door was opened for her by a young woman. 'Yes?'

'I am the Countess von Widerstand,' Anna said. 'I am to meet someone at this address.'

'Oh! Ah . . .' She turned. 'Herr Udermann. The lady is here.'

Shit, Anna thought. Udermann? Another unwanted relic from her past.

Udermann hurried into the hall to greet her; if she was irritated at having to come into contact with him again, he was obviously no less apprehensive than Werter had been. 'Countess!' he gushed. 'It is such a pleasure to be working with you again.' He was a stocky man with blunt features and a close-cropped head, on whom such hypocrisy did not sit well. 'Or perhaps you have forgotten me?'

Anna entered the hall. 'I remember you very well, Captain Udermann. You were with Colonel Essermann in Lisbon when I was last there. Three years ago.'

'I do assure you, Countess, that when I was appointed to Colonel Essermann's staff, I had no idea that he was contemplating treachery against the Reich.'

'I know that, Captain.' Because Essermann had had no idea either, she thought. 'Or you would not be here now.'

He ushered her into a small sitting room and produced a bottle of schnapps. 'I am a major, now.'

He was in civilian clothes. 'Then I congratulate you.' She raised her glass.

'And how is that charming maid of yours?'

'She is very well. I will mention you to her.' She recalled that on their return from Washington, to be unexpectedly met by their 'escort' from Portugal to Berlin, while she had had Essermann round her neck, Birgit had been both embarrassed and alarmed at the attentions of this man.

'I would like you to give her my regards. Perhaps I could see her when we return to Berlin.'

'I am sure she will be delighted.' He was, of course, going to have to die, but she did not think that would upset Birgit. 'Is everything ready?'

'I imagine so.'

'You imagine so?'

'Well, we did not expect you before tomorrow at the earliest.'

'I completed my business sooner than *I* expected. Did you know that the Russians are across the Vistula?'

'I did hear a rumour. But they will not stay there long. We will soon throw them back.'

'I am sure of it. But I still do not intend to take any risks. I wish to be in and out of Poland today.'

'I'm not sure that will be possible, Countess.'

'Is there not a plane waiting for me?'

'Well, yes but—'

'I understand it is a three-hour flight to Posen. We can be there by two this afternoon. From Posen it is an hour's drive to my destination, and an hour back. I do not intend to spend more than a few minutes there. We should certainly be able to take off again by six. As it should be only two hours from Posen to Berlin, we will be in Germany by eight o'clock tonight.'

'I suppose that it could be done . . .'

'Then it must be done. The plane is ready?'

'I will have to telephone. Like me, the pilot is not expecting you so soon.'

'Then telephone, Major Udermann.'

He gulped, and left the room.

It seemed to take him a long time to get through. Anna poured herself another glass of schnapps while she waited, forcing herself to sit still and keep calm. Her feeling of relaxed anticipation was beginning to dissipate.

The young woman appeared. 'Will you have lunch, Countess?'

'Thank you, no.'

She would not be able to eat a thing. Suddenly she was actually more apprehensive than on any lethal assignment for the SD, and it had nothing to do with any possible dangers. She had not seen her parents for four years, when, after her dramatic return from England, with, so far as anyone in Germany knew, every security service in Great Britain out for her blood, Heydrich had allowed her to visit them in their internment camp. Actually, as her father had

refused to see her at all, she had not laid eyes on *him* for
more than six years, ever since that dreadful day in March
1938 when the whole family had been arrested by the
Gestapo. Jane Haggerty Fehrbach had received her errant
daughter, but her anger and contempt at what she conceived
as Anna's betrayal had been unbearable; she had, of course,
no inkling of the truth, assumed that Anna, with her glowing
health, her expensive clothes and jewellery, had become at
best the mistress of some high-ranking party official at worst
an SS whore. Aware as she had been that the room in which
they met was bugged, there had been no way Anna could
give her mother even an inkling of the truth. And the attitudes of both her mother and her father would only have
hardened during their years of captivity. And now they had
lost Katherine as well.

And still there was no way she could tell them the truth,
until they were on their way to freedom, and by then they
would have had to watch her at work.

'There,' Udermann said. 'It is all arranged. Now all we have
to do is have lunch . . .'

'No lunch, Herr Udermann,' Anna said. 'I have told you
that I am in a hurry.'

'But—'

'No lunch.' She stood up. 'I am waiting.'

Half an hour later they were at the little airfield, and Anna
was gazing at the aircraft that was to be her ride to freedom.
'What is that?' she asked.

'It is a Storch, Countess,' the pilot said.

'It's very small.'

'It is a six-seater, Countess. I was told there will only be
four of you for the flight to Germany.'

'But it only has one engine.'

'As long as the engine works, Countess, you have nothing
to worry about. Will you board?'

Anna glared at him and then climbed through the small door.
She was again wearing her blue suit, and was forced to reveal
a lot of leg while stepping up. She slid across the seat and
Udermann sat beside her. 'You *have* flown before, Countess?'
he asked, solicitously, as she fumbled with her belt.

'Several times,' she snapped. She still hated the knowledge

that for all her skill and experience, her life was entirely in the hands of the pilot, and the weather.

They were airborne, but flying it seemed only a few hundred feet above the ground. 'Shouldn't we be higher up?' she asked Udermann.

'It is safer here, Countess. We are less likely to be seen by Russian aircraft.'

Shit, she thought, looking out of the window. But the sky appeared to be clear, although far to the east she could see dense clouds of smoke.

'That is our counter-attack,' Udermann said, proudly.

After what seemed an eternity they landed at Posen. The last time she had come here she had flown to Warsaw, further east.

'It is safer here,' Udermann explained. 'The Russians are approaching Praga. That is the suburb on the east bank of the river, you know. And there is some trouble in the city itself.'

'You mean Warsaw may fall?' So quickly, she thought.

'It is very strongly defended,' he pointed out.

The trouble with landing at Posen was that to get to the internment camp they had to go east, over a succession of bumpy roads, all clogged with troop movements. But they were flying an SS flag, and the driver was wearing the dreaded black uniform; once he hooted his horn, space was always made for them, while the exhausted men all gazed hungrily at the woman in the back of the command car, much to Udermann's obvious pleasure; he was seated beside her and able to give a convincing impression of being in charge of her.

Then they turned off along a deserted track, and the pine forest loomed in front of them.

'You have been here before?' Udermann asked.

'Yes.'

'Ah.'

The wire fence and the high gates were as she remembered. The driver hooted, and a sergeant emerged from the little guard house, beaming as he recognized the flag.

Udermann stepped down. 'I am Major Udermann,' he announced.

The sergeant stood to attention. 'Herr Major! You have brought the orders?'

Udermann approached the gate. 'What orders?'

'Why, Herr Major, to get out of here. The Ivans get closer every day.'

'The Ivans are still a long way away,' Udermann pointed out. 'Now open the gate. I have orders for the removal of two of your prisoners.'

'Two!' The sergeant looked past the officer at Anna. She was wearing her hat but had left her hair loose, and although she was travelling in an SS car it was obvious that she was not a prisoner. 'Lucky for some,' he remarked, and opened the gate.

Udermann returned to the car and they drove through, watched now by the other three members of the guard.

'I will telephone to let them know you are coming, Herr Major,' the sergeant said. 'Then they will keep the dogs under control.'

'Thank you.'

They followed a winding track through the trees, which clustered so thickly that even the July afternoon sunlight was diluted. 'A gloomy place,' he remarked.

'Yes,' Anna agreed. And Mama and Papa have been here for six years, she thought.

'You are not afraid of the dogs?'

'No. I have met them before.'

'Supposing these are the same dogs, eh?'

They swept round a last bend and came in sight of what might have been a holiday camp, a collection of neat little logwood cabins surrounding a larger building. But the relaxed image was dispelled by the two armed guards lounging outside the headquarters, and the two large Alsatians chained to a post.

As the car stopped, an officer, wearing the insignia of a major, emerged from the doorway. Anna opened her door and stepped down, and the officer came forward. 'Fraulein? You have business here?'

'I have come for Herr and Frau Fehrbach.'

The major looked at Udermann.

'We have the release papers,' he announced importantly.

Anna opened her shoulder bag and took out the required document.

The major scanned it, and raised his head; his complexion had paled. 'You are the Countess von Widerstand?'

'Who else should I be?'

He licked his lips. 'And you have come to . . .?' His gaze moved up and down, looking for the weapon she would use to carry out her assignment.

'Remove two of your prisoners, Herr Major. I am also in a hurry. I wish to be in Berlin by tonight.'

He gulped. 'Of course, Countess. If you will come inside. Please do not get too close to the dogs.'

Anna approached the two animals, who growled and bared their teeth. She stroked their heads and they began to pant contentedly. The two officers, and the guards, stared at her in consternation. 'Those dogs are trained to kill,' the major said.

'Thus we are in the same line of business,' Anna pointed out, and went inside. The officers trailed behind her like delinquent schoolboys. An orderly rose from behind his desk like a startled pheasant. 'What I would like you to do, Herr Major, is inform the Fehrbachs . . . I trust they are well?'

'Oh, yes. Yes, yes. They are well.' Her tone had contained a considerable degree of menace.

'Excellent. Now, you will inform them that they are to leave this place, and therefore that they must pack their belongings as quickly as possible. As soon as that is done, have them brought here.' She needed to act her role of SD officer and possibly executioner, to the very end.

'Of course. You heard the countess, Luther. Jump to it.'

The orderly hurried from the room.

'Would you like a glass of schnapps while you wait, Countess? Herr Major?'

'Thank you.' Anna sat in the chair before the desk.

He poured. 'I am Hans Neudorf.'

'I am pleased to make your acquaintance. This is Major Udermann. I'm afraid I have forgotten your first name, Udermann.'

Udermann took the proffered glass. 'It is Pieter. Countess. Prost.'

Anna drained the glass and placed it on the desk.

'Another?' Neudorf asked.

'Thank you, no.'

'Well, then . . .'

'Ignore me,' she said. 'Go on with your work.'

This he clearly found difficult to do, so she ignored *him*.

She was trying to conceal her nerves. She told herself that it had to be the height of absurdity for a woman who had experienced so much, who had been in imminent danger of her life so often, who had carried out so many fearful coups, both for the Allies and the Reich, to be nervous at the thought of meeting her parents after so long. But she was terrified. And as she had realized earlier, if she was to get them to the safety of Switzerland, they would have to see her at her blazing best . . . or would they regard it as her demonic worst?

The minutes ticked past, and Udermann pointedly started looking at his watch. But at last the orderly reappeared. 'I have the Fehrbachs outside, Herr Major.'

'Excellent,' Neudorf said, and stood up. 'Countess?'

Anna drew a deep breath, and also stood. The orderly held the door for her, and she went outside. Johann and Jane Fehrbach stood together, and Anna took another sharp breath. She knew that neither of them was yet fifty years old, but they looked well past that figure. Her father, never a big man, seemed to have shrunk – he had certainly lost weight – and his hair was white. Her mother – after whom she took – was still a tall woman although she also was thinner than Anna remembered. Her once golden hair was also streaked with grey, and if the superb features that Anna had inherited remained untarnished, the weight loss had them too outlined, and her blue eyes were dull where once they had bubbled with Irish vitality. Above all, the pair were shabby. That was understandable, as they were wearing the same clothes as six years ago, darned and patched, and because of their weight loss the garments hung on them. But even their two suitcases looked shabby.

Both seemed unable to believe their eyes as they gazed at their daughter. 'Anna?' Jane asked. 'What . . .?'

'I am to take you to Germany,' Anna said, resisting the overwhelming temptation to take her in her arms.

'Are we at last to be executed?' Johann asked.

'I am to take you to a place of safety.' Anna gestured at the car.

'Do you know these people?' Neudorf asked.

'They are my parents,' Anna told him.

They left him in a totally confused state, obviously realizing, in view of the complete absence of any fondness in her demeanour, that she was even more of a monster than her reputation indicated.

Udermann sat in front beside the driver, Anna in the back, her mother in the middle, her father on the other side. No one spoke until they were past the gate and well on to the lonely road leading to the highway. Anna was totally concentrated upon what had to be done. She hated carrying out cold-blooded executions, but she had waited six years for this moment, and Udermann was SD, while the driver was SS; if she were to make a move and hesitate for a moment, give them the slightest opportunity, she, and her parents, would be done. When she was satisfied that there was no one in sight in any direction, she asked, 'Did you not use to have a car, in Vienna, Papa?'

'Is that of interest now?'

'It is to me. Can you still drive a car?'

'Of course I can,' he snapped.

'That is very good. I have never learned how to drive.' She opened her shoulder bag. 'Stop the car, Udermann.'

'What?' He turned round and found himself looking down the barrel of Anna's Luger. 'Are you mad?'

Jane gave a little shriek and clutched her husband's arm.

'Stop the car,' Anna said again. 'Or I shall shoot you. And you,' she told the driver.

He braked.

'Switch off the ignition.'

He obeyed.

'Now get out, and you, Udermann.'

'You . . .' His hand hovered above his belt; there was obviously a holster concealed by his jacket.

'Touch that, and you are a dead man. Get out of the car and put your hands on your head.'

He gulped, but obeyed. 'Herr Himmler—'

'Is a very long way away. Turn round. You,' she told the driver. 'Stand beside him.'

He obeyed.

'You cannot just leave us here,' Udermann protested.

'You have nowhere to go,' Anna pointed out, also getting out. 'And the world has no more use for you.'

She shot him through the back of the head. The driver started to turn, and she shot him through the temple. Both men fell without a sound.

'My God!' Jane gasped. 'You shot them. Two men. Just like that.'

Thirty-one, Anna thought. 'They were SS, Mama, who would have shot you, without compunction, if commanded to do so.'

Her father was staring at her with his mouth open. 'Believe me,' she said, 'I know. I belong to the same organization.'

She dropped the pistol on the ground beside Udermann's body. When they were found, the bullets would be identified, but as both she and the dead man were wearing gloves, there was no way of telling who had used the gun. Of course, if her plans went as they should, it would not matter if she could be identified as the killer, but her years of training, of learning to cover every possible angle, made her act instinctively. She stooped beside Udermann, drew the pistol from his holster. It was, as she had expected, exactly the same make as her own and would use the same cartridges, even if the barrel would leave a different imprint. She dropped the pistol into her shoulder bag and returned to the car.

'Anna!' Jane said. 'Please tell us what is going on? We don't understand.'

'There is no time to explain: we must be far away from here before anyone comes along. Just remember three things. One is that I am your daughter, and that I love you more than life itself. Two is that I am trying to save your lives and get you away from Nazi Germany. Three, and this is the most important, until I give you the word, you are, and you act, my prisoners being removed to Berlin. Just act that part and leave any talking to me. Do you understand?'

'Yes,' Jane said. 'Yes, we understand. But those men . . . should we not . . .?'

'Now is not the time. Papa, will you drive? I will sit beside you.'

He got behind the wheel; his hands were trembling. 'That gun . . . you had it all the time? You have used it before?'

'Yes, Papa. It is my profession.'

'Using guns?'

'Killing people.'

Both of their brains were clearly teeming with questions, but fortunately only a few minutes later they had reached the highway and were back in the middle of the unceasing traffic flow. As it was six years since Johann had last driven, he needed all his concentration, and even so they several times scraped or banged against another vehicle. This brought curses but little else, as they were still flying the SS flag, until they had a heavier than usual prang, and were waved to a halt by an irate colonel, who had been a passenger in the vehicle they had just struck. 'Who are you?' he shouted, coming up to them. 'Where did you get that car? Where are you going?'

'We are going to Posen, Herr Colonel,' Anna explained, politely.

'In an SS car?' He advanced to stand beside it. 'You are under arrest.'

'And you are very tiresome,' Anna said. 'I am in a hurry. These people must be in Berlin tonight.'

'What? What?'

Anna opened her shoulder bag and took out her carte blanche. 'Perhaps you would like to look at this.'

He frowned as he glanced at it. 'This is signed by the Reichsführer.'

'I congratulate you on your eyesight. You are therefore capable of reading the rest of it.'

His frown deepened as he read. Then his jaw dropped as he raised his head. 'You are the Countess von Widerstand?'

'Yes. I am.'

He stared at her as if seeing her for the first time, then handed the paper back. 'My apologies, Countess.' He turned. 'Get out of the way,' he shouted. 'Clear a passage for this car.'

'I think we can move on now, Papa,' Anna said softly.

The car jerked forward, and then Johann got it under control.

'You, are the Countess von Widerstand?' Jane asked.

'Don't tell me you've heard of me?'

'The guards spoke of you. They said you are the most deadly woman in the world.'

'People do tend to say nice things about me,' Anna agreed.

Half an hour later they were in Posen. There was a check point as they approached the airfield, but the lieutenant was immediately obsequious as Anna showed her pass. 'Countess!' He saluted. 'Your escort is waiting.'

A sudden lump of lead formed in Anna's stomach. 'Escort?'

'Of course. The Reichsführer does not wish any risk to be taken with your safety.'

Anna looked past him at the four Messerschmitt 109 fighters drawn up immediately in front of the Storch.

A Matter of Morale

S hit! Anna thought. Shit, shit and shit. Perhaps Himmler had not, after all, intended her to be captured or killed by the Russians. Perhaps the appearance of these planes, which could surely have been put to better use elsewhere, meant that he really valued her. Or that he did not really trust her?

But whatever the reason for his solicitude, her plan was ruined. She might still be able to take over the Storch, but there was no way her escort was going to allow her to fly anywhere than to Berlin.

So . . . practice that determined patience that had kept her alive for six years. 'Thank you, Herr Lieutenant,' she said. 'You may drive on,' she told her father. 'But slowly,' she added in a low voice.

Johann obeyed.

'Something has happened,' Jane said.

'Yes,' Anna agreed. 'I did not expect these planes. This makes it impossible for us to fly to Berne as I had intended. We will have to accompany them to Berlin.'

'Then we are not going to escape,' her father said.

'At this time, no. I am more sorry than I can say. But you must not give up. Please listen very carefully. You know my secret now. I have preserved it for six years, have done everything I have had to do, to reach the day I could get you out. Please remember that one careless word from you will condemn us all to death. Your freedom has only been postponed. I will get you out, I swear it. Wherever you are sent, just wait for me to come for you. Will you do that?'

She was staring straight ahead as they slowly approached the waiting pilots. Now Jane touched her on the shoulder. 'Of course we will do that. And Anna, my dearest Anna, may we beg your forgiveness for everything we have thought of you over those six years?'

At least, Anna thought, there is so much happening that they have not asked about Katherine. She smiled at the pilots as the car stopped.

'Countess?' the Storch pilot inquired as they boarded. 'Is Major Udermann not with you?'

'That is obvious,' Anna pointed out.

'There has been no trouble?'

She had already determined how this had to be handled. 'Yes, the : has been trouble. We encountered a Russian patrol. Shots were fired. Major Udermann and our driver got out to engage the enemy, and told us to drive on as fast as I could. This I did.'

'But you do not know what happened to them?'

'No,' Anna said sadly. 'They were brave men.'

'Brave men,' the pilot agreed.

It was just dusk when they landed at Rangsdorf Military Airport, without having seen any sight of Russian aircraft. Two cars were waiting, and a bevy of black-uniformed SS men. 'Welcome, Countess,' the major in command said. 'We have been worried about you. Are these your prisoners?'

'They are not to be harmed.'

'Those are my orders, certainly.'

'So where are we going?'

'You are to return to Berlin, immediately.'

Alarm bells again jangled in Anna's brain, but she asked, 'And the prisoners?'

'Are to go to Potsdam tonight. They will be moved to their destination tomorrow.'

'Where is that?'

'I do not know, Countess.'

Almost she stamped her foot in irritation. Instead she turned to her parents. 'It seems that I must say goodbye, for the time being. Remember everything I told you, and you will prosper.' She took her mother in her arms and hugged her tightly. 'Trust me.'

'I do,' Jane whispered.

Anna turned to her father, hesitantly. But he opened his arms as well. 'I am so sorry,' she said as they embraced.

'And I am so happy,' Johann said. 'To have found you again. We will wait for you.'

They were escorted to one of the cars, and driven off. The major had been waiting patiently. He sat beside her in the back of the second car. 'Is there a crisis?' she asked.

'Is there not always a crisis, nowadays, Countess? You do not remember me.'

She turned to look at him, but in the gloom his face was indistinct. 'You will have to forgive me, Herr Major.'

'I do not blame you; we last met more than four years ago. I escorted you to the SS training camp at Görzke. You were not very sociable.'

'Gunther Gutemann,' Anna said.

'You do remember!' He was pleased.

'I remember the names.'

'Ah, yes. You suggested that they did not go together.'

'You must forgive me. I was very tense that morning.'

'I remember. You quarrelled with Dr Cleiner, and had to leave in disgrace.'

'But as you see, I am still here. Is he still there?'

'I do not know. But I should think it is probable.'

Cleiner, Anna thought. The bastard who had almost made her ashamed of her body, almost, and who had commanded her to shoot an innocent man – her first ever victim – just to prove to him that she could kill. He was not important enough in the Nazi hierarchy to hate, but she knew if she ever encountered him again she would destroy him. While this man . . . he had indeed escorted her to the camp, but he had also remained there throughout her week's training, watching her in every state of undress and in some very stressful situations. No wonder he was pleased to see her again.

'You have not yet told me what this crisis is,' she remarked.

'As I said, there are so many it seems that you can take your pick. But I know that Herr Himmler commanded that you should be taken directly to him on landing.'

Shit, she thought. On the other hand, there was no need to be agitated; he always wanted to see her immediately she returned from a mission to Switzerland. In any event, he could not possibly know of Udermann as yet, so she would be able to get in first on that subject.

'I was wondering,' Gutemann ventured, 'have you eaten?'

'No,' Anna said. My God, she thought, she had not had lunch either. Now she thought of it, she realized that she was starving.

'Well, then, after you have reported to the Reichsführer . . .'

Why not? she wondered. He was obviously very keen, no doubt activated by his memory, and the alternative was her underground apartment, and Birgit, and the tumult that was raging in her brain, the failed escape attempt, her inability to contact Laurent and tell him what had happened, the fact that Clive, and Belinda, would be in Switzerland, probably tomorrow, to collect her, the thought that this time tomorrow, or indeed, right now, she should be safe, and this ongoing torment be for ever behind her.

'Or does the Reichsführer require you to stay with him for a while?' Gutemann asked.

'No,' Anna said. 'He does not require me to stay with him. If you are prepared to wait a few minutes, Major Gutemann, I would be delighted to dine with you.'

'Countess!' Albrecht, Himmler's burly servant-cum-bodyguard, as always seemed delighted to see her. But this was mainly because of the perks that were involved. Anna gave him her shoulder bag, watched him empty the contents. As usual he inspected the pistol with great care, opened the chamber, and sniffed it and the barrel. 'This gun has not been fired.'

'Should it have?'

'Well, it makes a change. You have had a quiet trip.'

'Actually, no,' Anna said. 'But I was given no opportunity to use my weapon.'

He raised his eyebrows at her peculiar choice of words, but was also puzzled by something else. 'Where is your travelling bag, and the attaché case?'

'My valise, and the case, ' Anna said, with complete honesty, 'are in Lucerne. I had to leave there in rather a hurry.' Which was again the absolute truth, save for the inclusion of the word 'had'. 'I am sure, if you were to ask him, that the Reichsführer will explain it to you.'

He was more interested in completing his search. 'Then, if you would be so kind.'

Anna knew the drill, stood facing the wall, resting her hands on the wood, felt his hands moving over her body. They unbuttoned her jacket and quested inside, taking the opportunity to caress her breasts, before moving down her hips to raise her skirt and go between, sliding his hands up the insides of her thighs to touch the hem of her camiknickers. As with Stefan, she knew how he longed to do more, but dared not, less because he feared her skills – he had never seen her at work, even in training – than because he knew that she belonged to his boss.

'Don't you get tired of this?' she asked, as he stepped away and she was able to smooth her skirt and button her jacket.

'One could never get tired of you, Countess.'

'You say the sweetest things.' She opened the door and went into the apartment.

'Anna!' As it was still fairly early in the evening, Himmler was fully dressed, although in a dinner jacket rather than uniform; at least she was spared the sight of him in his usual striped pyjamas. 'I have been so worried.'

'About me, Herr Reichsführer?' She used her most dulcet tone.

'Well . . . do you know that those Red bastards have managed to cross the Vistula?'

'I did know that, sir.' Now was the time to fire the first shot. 'In fact, I encountered them.'

'What? But . . . they crossed south of Warsaw. That is a long way from Posen.'

'That may be, sir. But we ran into a patrol on our way back from the internment camp. That I am here at all is only thanks to the gallantry of Major Udermann.'

'My God!' Himmler went to the sideboard, poured two balloons of brandy and gave her one. 'What happened?'

'As I said, it appeared to be a patrol, perhaps half a dozen men. But they had motorbikes, and clearly intended to overtake us.'

'There was no help around?'

Anna sat on the settee and sipped her drink. 'No, sir. The road was deserted. So Udermann stopped the car, and he and the driver got out. They were both armed. He then told me to drive on and reach Posen, no matter what. I felt I should stay and help him, but—'

'Thank God you did not. You could have been killed. What happened to them? Udermann and the driver?'

'I do not know, sir. I heard shots behind me as I drove away. But I fear the worst.'

'Damnation! As you say, he was a very gallant officer. But at least you got away. You reached Posen without trouble?'

'There were delays, but nothing important. I can tell you, I was so happy to find those Messerschmitts waiting for me. Although I have no idea how they got there.'

'I sent them,' Himmler said proudly, and sat beside her. 'We had received so many reports of Russian air activity, I could not risk your being shot down.'

'May I ask how you knew I would be in Posen on that day?'

'Ah! Udermann telephoned from Berne to tell me that you were a day early. At least a day early.' He peered at her. 'Why were you a day early?'

'I had completed my business in Lucerne, sir. Our business. And I was in a hurry to get out of Switzerland and my parents out of Poland.'

'And they are all right?'

'They were a little shaken by our unexpected adventure. I don't think they had ever been under fire before. But they are all right, yes. May I ask where they are being taken?'

'To a safe place. You say our business in Switzerland has been completed?'

Anna wanted to scream at him, but she said, 'Yes, sir.' *Her* business, at any rate, even if she could not be there. 'Here is the receipt.'

He studied it, then nodded. 'Excellent. You are an absolute treasure. Now, I am sure that you must be very tired after such an ordeal. Go home and have a good night's rest. The Führer wishes to see you as soon as he has returned to Berlin. That will be in a few days' time.'

Anna gulped. 'Sir?'

'It is to be an official meeting of the General Staff. Or does that disappoint you? Perhaps you are expecting another summons to his bed?'

God forbid! she thought. But . . . what had she to do with OKW?

'Although,' Himmler went on, 'he may well wish the use of your peculiar services. He really is very fond of you, and, well, since the explosion he is not functioning properly.'

He has not functioned properly for a very long time, Anna thought.

'His left arm appears to be paralysed and he suffers from a twitch. But there is nothing the matter with his brain.'

If there was, you would not recognize it, Anna thought: there is too much wrong with your own brain.

'He remains extremely angry,' Himmler went on. 'I have never known him so angry. The first of the important conspirators are to be hanged next week. He wishes them strung up on piano wire, so that they strangle slowly. And do you know, he has commanded that they should not be allowed belts for their pants, so that as they writhe these will slowly slip down. Have you ever seen a man hanged, Anna?'

'No, sir.' Anna drained her brandy glass to avoid being sick.

'It affects the, well, the physical functions. You know what I mean?'

'A man being hanged slowly, erects, momentarily, when the pressure is applied to his spinal column,' Anna said.

'Ah . . . yes.' He finished his own goblet, took both glasses to the bar to refill them. 'Would you like to attend the executions?'

'Thank you, sir. But no.'

He gave her the glass. 'Because you have seen too many men erect, eh? Ha ha.'

'Ha ha,' Anna agreed.

'But in any event, the Führer has commanded that the executions should be filmed, so that he can study them at his leisure. I am sure he will let you look at the film.'

And I have had sex with *that*, Anna thought. Her shudder was entirely genuine.

'You are tired,' Himmler said again, sympathetically. 'Well, as I said, you rest up and await the summons. There are great things afoot.'

'Yes, sir.' Anna put down the still full glass and stood up. 'My parents—'

'I have said, they will be placed in absolute safety.'

'May I not see them?'

'You have just seen them, Anna. You know they are well. And you have my word that they will remain well.'

'Yes, sir.' Anna accepted defeat, for the moment. 'Thank you, sir. Good night.'

'Well, that did not take too long.' Gutemann was waiting for her in the downstairs lobby. 'Now, for dinner, I know the very place.'

'Ah . . .' Anna rested her hand on his arm. 'I really do not feel like eating right now.' As for sex, she thought, I would vomit all over you.

'But . . .' He was looking both shattered and bewildered.

'I must be more tired than I had thought.' She squeezed his arm. 'Listen. Ask me again in a couple of days, and I would love to dine with you. And . . . get to know you better.'

'You will?' Now he was delighted. 'But now . . .?'

'I would like you to take me to Gestapo Headquarters, so that I can go to bed.'

And weep, she thought.

'Herr Laurent?' Clive Bartley stood before the desk in the Geneva office. 'Clive Bartley.'

'Of course. And this is . . .?'

'Belinda Hoskin. My aide.'

Laurent shook hands with each of them, while they surveyed him, taken aback by his youth, as he also seemed surprised that Clive should be accompanied by a woman; they had just flown in, from France and Belinda was not looking at her best. Even if she had been assured – and she had observed for herself – that the Luftwaffe no longer had the aircraft to disrupt the Allies' activities in Normandy much less operate further south, she disliked flying as much as Anna. 'Do sit down.'

Clive placed two chairs before the desk, and he and Belinda sat together. 'So, where do you have Anna hidden? And her parents, I presume.'

'Sadly,' Laurent said, 'I do not have her hidden anywhere. Or her parents.'

Suddenly there was an atmosphere of hostility from the two Britons. 'Would you explain that?' Clive asked. 'We understood that you were assisting her.'

'I was,' Laurent agreed. 'And I would hope to do so again. But at this moment I do not know where she is.'

'On the telephone, she said she would be here, with you. And you confirmed that.'

'Yes, I did. But all I know is what she told me. Two days ago she flew to Poland to remove her parents from their internment camp. She was to return here that same night. But she never came.'

'Oh, my God!' Belinda said.

'I do not think there is any reason to assume that something has happened to her,' Laurent said. 'I understand that you are her controller at MI6, Mr Bartley?'

'Yes, I am.'

'Would I, therefore, be correct in assuming that you have worked with her for several years?'

'You would be correct.'

'Therefore you must know that Anna can take care of herself. Have you ever seen her at work?'

'Have you?'

'Not in so many words. I have seen, or know of, the evidence of her work, when she regards it as necessary.'

'You are thinking of here in Geneva last year.'

'That is correct. She sat exactly where you are sitting now, as cool as a cucumber, the epitome of innocent beauty, and she had just killed two men.'

'She had killed them the previous night,' Clive said, absently.

Laurent raised his eyebrows. 'You knew of this?'

'I had spent the night with her.'

Belinda blew a very loud raspberry.

Laurent looked from one to the other. 'You mean, *you* killed those men?'

'No, I did not. Anna had killed them before I arrived.'

'But . . . the bodies were found in the apartment the next morning.'

'Well, she couldn't get rid of them, you see.'

'And you mean, you—'

'What we did, or did not do, Herr Laurent, is none of your business. What I am trying to tell you is that I am fully aware that Anna can take care of herself in virtually any situation.' He recalled the six NKVD agents in Washington, who had surely supposed that they held all the high cards, with a naked Anna their prisoner. 'But I am also aware that when she says she is going to do something, she does it. Therefore, if she told you she was returning to Switzerland two nights ago, and she did not, something fairly catastrophic must have happened.'

'To Anna? My God! But I have heard nothing.'

'Would you have heard anything?'

'Well . . . no.'

'Right. So let's consider the alternatives.'

'If something has happened to Anna . . . I could not bear the thought of that.' It was, actually, an upsetting thought. Although, of course, it might also solve a great many problems.

'At least we seem to be on the same wavelength in one direction, at any rate,' Clive said. 'So let's consider. She went to Poland. I assume by a German aircraft?'

'She was to pick it up in Berne.'

'Berne is not a very big airport. Can you check and make sure that a German plane left there two days ago?'

'I have already done that. I went to Berne myself to meet her return flight.'

'Which never arrived. Right. She was going to Poland? Where in Poland?'

'Posen. My God! The Russians are across the Vistula.'

'Three days ago, yes. According to their last communiqué the crossing was made well south of Warsaw. Posen is well to the west. They cannot possibly have got up there in the next twenty-four hours.'

'But they have air superiority.'

Clive sighed. 'Yes. That is a possibility. All we can do is wait, and hope. How does she get in touch with you?'

'She doesn't.'

'What? But . . .'

Laurent had to choose his words carefully; he had no desire for his arrangement with Himmler to be known to the British Secret Service. 'For the past year I have been handling certain business matters for Herr Himmler. You know of him?'

'Of course I know of him,' Clive snapped.

'Then you will know that he is the second most powerful man in Germany. As you are Anna's controller, you will also know that she is his personal assistant. In that capacity she brings me certain . . . items, that need to be dealt with.'

'What items?'

'I am sorry, Mr Bartley, those are confidential.'

'Between you and Himmler. You are admitting that you are a Nazi sympathizer.'

'I suppose, when one is at war, it is an asset to be simplistic about these matters. I am a businessman, Mr Bartley. I perform certain functions for my clients. It is not my business to enquire into either their politics or their religion. I am sure that, shall we say, if you were to go to a bank in England to open an account, you would not be asked if you were a Protestant or a Roman Catholic, and be refused if your religious principles did not agree with those of the manager.'

'We are talking about the Nazis, not religion.'

'And they are objectionable to you because Great Britain and Nazi Germany are at war. Switzerland is not at war with anyone.'

Clive glared at him in frustrated anger, and Belinda decided it was time to abandon ethics in favour of practicality. 'So Anna comes to you with various messages or whatever from Himmler. But you must know she is coming?'

'I am informed, by the Reichsführer's office,' Laurent agreed. 'Never by Anna personally. For her to attempt a personal message would be far too risky.'

'But she comes regularly.'

'No. She comes whenever Himmler requires her to. We have only met four times in the past year.'

'But on those brief occasions you appear to have struck up a considerable rapport,' Clive said, acidly.

'She has learned to trust me, yes,' Laurent agreed, proudly.

'As she is now trusting you with her life.'

'I shall not fail her.'

'But you can't help her, either.'

'Oh, behave, Clive,' Belinda said. 'No one can help Anna unless she wants to be helped. It's time to decide what we're going to do. Which means getting to grips with certain facts.'

Clive glared at her, but she merely smiled at him. 'One: it is possible that Anna did run into the Russians, or a Russian aircraft, in which case she is either dead or in their hands. In which case there is not a lot we can do about it.'

'Do you know what they would do to her, if they captured her?' Clive asked.

'You can tell me about it, some time. That does not alter the fact that if that has happened, there is still nothing we can do save weep. However, possibility number two is surely equally likely, that for some reason her plans had to change, and instead of coming back here she had to return to Germany.'

'You mean she might have betrayed herself?' Laurent asked.

'Anna does not betray herself,' Clive snapped.

'Well, then, that someone else betrayed her. Although,' he added thoughtfully, 'as far as I am aware, she had confided her plan to no one.'

'Except you,' Clive pointed out.

There was another exchange of glares.

'I do think,' Belinda remarked, 'that we would make more progress if we concentrated on the business in hand.' She might have been addressing a board meeting at her magazine office. 'So, if we exclude point one from our calculations, and assume that Anna is back in Berlin, surely the first thing we need to do is contact her and find out the situation.'

'And how are we supposed to do that?' Clive enquired.

'For God's sake! Before this thing came up, weren't you sending me to Germany to see her. So, back to square one.'

'You can do this?' Laurent asked.

'I have done it before.'

'But how do you reach her?'

'I know where she lives.' She could not suppress a flush. 'I have stayed there.'

Laurent looked at Clive. Who was also looking slightly embarrassed. 'Well,' he said. 'I suppose in the circumstances . . .'

'Anna!' Adolf Hitler said, advancing towards her. 'My dear Anna!'

Always in their past meetings he had seized both her hands to squeeze them. Today he used his right hand only; as Himmler had warned, his left arm hung immobile at his side, its fingers from time to time twitching uncontrollably. But that was symptomatic of the whole. She had last seen him only a fortnight before, when she had shared his bed . . . the night before he had been blown up. She had never known a fully fit Führer; by the time she had been forced to enter his intimate circle he had already been existing on pills, and giving every evidence of the premature ageing brought on by his lifestyle, the amount of responsibility he had taken upon himself, and the quack medicines to which he subjected his body. But there had never been anything identifiably wrong with him.

Now she looked at a wreck. Apart from his left arm, his left leg trailed as he walked, his entire body seemed to have shrunk – he was, in any event, several inches shorter than her – and constantly trembled, and his face, still pitted and cut from bomb fragments, also twitched spasmodically while both his hair and his moustache were singed. Only the eyes, at once mesmerizing and demonic, gleamed with their old fervour. 'My Führer,' she said. 'I have been so worried.'

He squeezed her fingers. 'Am I not indestructible? This event has proved that to the world. Just as it has proved to the world that here in Germany we have a woman who can take her place on the same stage as well as any man. You know these gentlemen?'

Still holding her hand he turned to face the room. Anna's brain had already been tumbling as she had indeed met several of the men present. Keitel, the epitome of a Prussian junker with his close-cropped hair, his moustache, his military expression. Jodl, narrow-faced and anxious. Goering, red-faced and overweight, his uniform a mass of ribbons and stars. Guderian, very much a soldier's soldier. Several other staff officers she could not immediately name. But neither Himmler nor Goebbels, to her relief, were present.

But Hitler apart, her acquaintance with these men had always been at an entirely social level, nor had she ever been inside the huge conference room at the Chancellery, with its map-covered tables. And she had been given no indication as to the reason for her presence.

She could only be patient. 'I think I do, my Führer.'

'Well, they all know you, at least by repute. Gentlemen, I give you the Countess von Widerstand, our latest secret weapon.'

Anna gave him a startled glance, then had to submit to having her hands clasped by each man in turn, following which they formed a circle round her; she found herself thinking of Daniel. But most of the expressions were simply mystification. They had no more idea of what their leader intended than did she. Or what he had meant.

Hitler continued to stand beside her. 'As you know, Countess,' he now explained, 'our soldiers in the field have been having a difficult time. They are being forced to retreat, in the east, in the south, and now in the west. This is of course a temporary situation. Our new secret weapons, our V-2 rockets, which are twice as fast and have twice the range of the V-1, and will deliver twice the payload on English cities, are ready to be deployed. Our latest invention, the snorkel, will enable our submarines to remain underwater for as long as they wish, as their air will be constantly renewed. Our new King Tiger tanks are coming off the production line in ever increasing numbers. While our Messerschmitt 262 will soon be ready for combat. It is jet propelled, and is twice as fast as anything the Allies possess. It will revolutionize air warfare and regain for us total command of the skies. So you see, it is only a matter of months before we turn the tide of the war.'

He paused to beam at them all. Anna could not resist a quick glance at the various faces; none was looking entirely convinced.

'However,' Hitler went on, 'while eventual victory is assured, it is not always obvious to the man in the field, and as I have said, I am aware that morale is suffering due to our soldiers being repeatedly forced to retreat. Thus the countess.' He raised her arm. 'Due to her exploits in combating the subversive elements who have recently attempted to overthrow the Reich, the countess has become a household name. But very few of our troops have ever seen a picture of her, much less her in the flesh. I am thus appointing her to a position I have just created. The countess is now our Minister of Morale.'

He paused to stare at them; they were looking even less convinced. He turned back to her. 'Your duties, Countess, will consist of touring our military units. You will appear in person before our troops.' He allowed himself a smile. 'I am not suggesting that you get *too* close to any of them, no matter how much they might wish it. But you will let as many as possible see you in the flesh. Speak with as many as you can. You are the epitome of glorious German womanhood, of everything that our soldiers are fighting for, of everything they will one day return to.' Another brief smile. 'Not everyone they return to will be as beautiful as you, but every man carries a dream in his mind and in his heart. You are that dream.'

For a moment no one spoke, then Guderian ventured, 'Is there not a chance that some of our people may know that the countess is not a German, my Führer?'

'The countess was born in Vienna, General. I also was born in Austria. Are you suggesting that I am not a German?'

Guderian gulped, and the rest of the officers clapped.

'Thank you, gentlemen. This meeting is now ended. Anna, you will come to my office.'

Anna felt as if she were in a dream as she followed him along the gallery, past the saluting SS guards. There was no one else in the office, and he sat behind his desk, gesturing her to a chair. 'You do not look happy with your appointment,' he remarked.

Happy, she thought. She had had only two priorities, one to find out where her parents were now being held, the other to find some means of contacting Laurent and putting him, and thus Clive, in the picture. If she could not do that, they might well suppose her dead or captured by the Russians. Either way, they would have to write her off. Would Clive ever do that? She did not believe that he would, in his heart and mind. But if she disappeared beyond his reach, there could be no doubt that Baxter would close her file. And Donovan. She couldn't be sure about Joe Andrews.

But suddenly she realized that if she was going to be given maximum publicity, it would be sure to get back to London, as well as Geneva, and they would at least know that she was alive, even if at the moment beyond contact. But ... if she was being sent to 'entertain' the front line troops in France, was there not also the possibility of her being taken prisoner by the Allies? But that was not a practical solution, as it would mean abandoning her parents.

Hitler was waiting for a reply. 'I am overwhelmed, my Führer,' she said.

'You have merely to be yourself to succeed. A look at your face will inspire most men. Now. You will need a staff.'

'Yes, sir. May I ask, does the Reichsführer know of my appointment?'

'I have not told him yet. I will do so this morning. Does this concern you?'

Concern me? she thought. He will not be a happy man, as he will see me slipping further away from his control. 'No, sir. It is simply that at least one of the people I would like to take with me works in his office.'

'Indeed? Who is this?'

'My sister Katherine.'

'You never told me you had a sister.'

'I am sorry, sir. It did not occur to me that it might be important.'

'Is she anything like you?'

'She is very like me, my Führer, save that she is two years younger.' And the resemblance is only physical, she thought, not where it matters.

'And you say she is working in the Reichsführer's office? As what?'

'As my assistant, sir. She is SD.'

'How extraordinary.'

'She played an important role in the detection of the conspiracy.'

'Did she, indeed? I must meet this young lady. However, I quite understand that you would like to have her with you, and so you shall.'

'Thank you, sir. There is also my maid, Birgit.'

'Your maid. Yes, of course, a lady must have her maid. But I was thinking more of a personal escort. A bodyguard. I am sending Martin with you, in any event.'

'Sir?' Anna was aghast. She had never met Martin Bormann, but on her first visit to Rastenburg, she had been warned by one of the secretaries that the one mistake she could make would be to get on the wrong side of the shadowy figure of whom so little was known. What *was* known was that Bormann was a man with no military or political rank, who appeared to have no special talents, but who was close to the Führer, although invariably lurking in the background, and whose advice Hitler apparently always accepted. 'Is that necessary, sir? I mean, I know how important he is to you, to the military situation . . .'

'Yes, he is important. Which is a reflection of the importance I attach to your mission. And he can only be with you for a couple of weeks, just to make sure everything goes well. After that, you will be on your own, although the various commanding officers will be informed of your schedule and of your duties and will be required to offer you every facility. However, what I also wish you to have is a personal bodyguard, someone to be with you at all times to make sure of your immediate safety and also to handle any difficulties that may crop up. You say your sister is SD? That should mean that she is proficient in weapons.'

'She was certainly trained to use them, sir. But I do not believe she has ever fired a shot in anger.' One could hardly count the execution she had been required to carry out to prove her proficiency. And after she had qualified, having failed in her first assignment of seducing a Turkish diplomat – when he had tried to sodomize her she had run screaming from the room – she had been saved from the disgrace of being sent to an SS brothel simply because she was the sister of the famous Anna. But her duties had from then been strictly secretarial. She had never had the 'benefit' of working for someone like Heydrich.

'Hm,' Hitler commented. 'Pity. Obviously, the man who is appointed must be someone you find congenial.'

Anna appeared to consider, but she had already made her choice. 'May I suggest Major Gutemann?'

Hitler frowned. 'Do I know this man?'

'I should not think so. But I have known him for four years.' Which was stretching a point, as she had not met him between the summer of 1940 and his sudden reappearance a couple of weeks ago.

'I see. Is he your lover?'

She did not suppose he was jealous, simply curious. 'Certainly not, sir.' At least yet. While she had fulfilled her promise to have dinner with him, she had refused to allow him to come down to her apartment, and as the apartment was situated in the Gestapo Headquarters he had been unable to press the point. But she had no doubt that he was desperate to get together with her, and there could be no brighter prospect of intimacy than undertaking a tour together . . . certainly after they had unloaded Bormann.

'I will have him seconded,' Hitler said. 'Now, it will take a couple of weeks to set things up for you. So you can have a rest, eh?' He turned as the door opened. 'Martin! The very man! You have not met the Countess von Widerstand.'

'Countess!' Bormann bent over her hand. He was shorter than she, as were so many men, and was entirely unremarkable in either feature or body, with lank, thinning dark hair, a bland face, and a solid figure. He wore a black uniform, but without insignia, and even that failed to lend any personality to his appearance. Nor did he appear to find anything compelling in her, which was very *un*like most men. Now, after his perfunctory greeting, he straightened and turned to Hitler. 'There is important news from Warsaw.'

'Don't tell me it is under attack?'

'Ah . . .' Bormann glanced at Anna.

'I have no secrets from Anna,' Hitler said.

Bormann did not look pleased. 'There has been an uprising.'

'What? You mean the Jews are at it again? I thought we had got rid of all the Warsaw Jews.'

'This is not the Jews, my Führer. It is the Poles. The report says that the entire population of the city has risen, that they are well armed, and control large areas. This has happened, because they have learned that the Russians are very close.'

Anna watched Hitler's face slowly become crimson with white blotches. Oh, my God, she thought. She had been present when he had had one of his fits before, and although it had not been directed against her, it had still been terrifying to experience.

'The situation could be serious,' Bormann went on, seeming to ignore the suggestion of an incipient explosion. 'Because the Russians *are* close; they are just across the river in Praga.'

'Swine!' Hitler shouted. 'Bastards from the pit of hell,' he shrieked. 'Seeking to stab us in the back.'

To Anna's consternation he fell forward on to his knees and then on to his face. She immediately dropped to her own knees to see if she could help him, but felt Bormann's hand on her shoulder. She looked up, and he shook his head, then jerked it to indicate that she should rise.

He had apparently experienced these outbursts sufficient times before to know that they were not as serious as they looked, and indeed, after rolling about for a few moments, screaming unintelligibly and tearing at the carpet with his fingers, the Führer suddenly sat up, and then rose, straightening his tunic. Then he sat behind his desk and wiped foam from his lips. 'I wish them destroyed,' he said in a quiet voice, apparently unembarrassed by what had happened. 'Every last Pole in Warsaw. Men, women and children. I wish the city razed to the ground. Tell Guderian to detail two Waffen SS Panzer divisions to the task.'

'With respect, my Führer, the Waffen SS are heavily engaged with the Soviets across the river south of the city.'

'They can be replaced on a temporary basis for this purpose.

An example must be made of Warsaw, so that no other city thinks of revolting against our rule. What of Paris, eh? What of Stülpnagel?'

'General von Stülpnagel has committed suicide, sir.'

'What did you say?'

Bormann glanced at Anna. 'Evidence was supplied that he was one of the conspirators, but he killed himself before he could be arrested. He has been replaced by General Choltitz.'

'Choltitz?'

'He is absolutely reliable, sir.'

Hitler's cheeks were becoming inflamed again, and Anna feared another outburst. But Bormann remained calm. 'This tour that the countess and I are to undertake . . .'

'Ah, yes. You must undertake the tour, Anna. I wish you to begin in the East, but do not go near Warsaw until this business is sorted out. I do not wish you to be in any danger from some Polish madman.'

'Yes, my Führer.'

'But you will have to do without Martin. I need you here.' He addressed Bormann. 'Get Guderian in here. And Himmler.'

Bormann hurried from the room.

'Meanwhile,' Hitler said, 'you can assemble your staff. Your sister and this fellow . . . what did you say his name was?'

'Gutemann, sir. I will need authority.'

'You have it. Refer anyone who questions your requirements to me.'

Anna closed the door of her office behind her and went through to Records. 'We are going on a trip,' she announced.

Katherine looked up in alarm. 'Going where?'

'Various places. I will tell you when the time comes. I just wanted you to know. We need to travel light, but we are also required to look glamorous. Select what clothes you think you will require and I'll have a look at them. I had better inspect your entire wardrobe.'

Katherine licked her lips. 'This trip . . . for how long will we be away?'

'I have no idea. It may be a couple of months.'

'Months? But we are coming back?'

'Of course we are coming back.' Anna frowned. 'Don't tell me you have a boyfriend?'

'Well . . .' Katherine flushed. 'Should I not have a boyfriend?'

'Indeed you should. Every girl should have a boyfriend.'

'Except you. Now.' She was clearly thinking of Essermann.

'You could say I am resting. Tell me the name of this friend.'

Katherine's flush deepened. 'Joachim Rudent.'

'And he is . . .?'

'A captain in the Luftwaffe. He flies fighters.'

'Hm. Do you sleep with him?'

'Well . . .'

'I am not criticizing. But you need always to remember that you must never reveal anything about your work here, even when in the throes of an orgasm.'

Katherine blinked at her.

'Don't tell me you've never had an orgasm? Ah, well, I suppose there's time. And I am sure he can spare you for a few weeks. We are travelling on business for the Reich.'

'Oooh!' Katherine exclaimed.

'I will come to your quarters this evening to go through your things.' She returned to her own office, called the switchboard. 'I wish to see Major Gunther Gutemann,' she said. 'Will you please locate him, immediately, and send him to me?'

'I will do so, Countess,' the woman said.

Anna replaced the phone. She was quite excited herself, both at the idea of travelling and even more, of getting out of Berlin for a spell, escaping the cloying company of Himmler. Who at that moment opened the door and stalked into the office. 'I am informed that I am to lose you.'

'Regrettably, Herr Reichsführer.'

'But only for a few weeks, eh? Now, Anna, I wish you to be careful. Stay away from any actual fighting. It can be very fast-moving. As for example, our troops in Normandy, while they are resisting gloriously, are being pinched out. As a result, a withdrawal to the line of the Seine has been ordered.'

Anna frowned. 'But if our forces are withdrawing to the line of the Seine, does that not expose Paris?'

'Oh, they are not going to get Paris,' he assured her. 'It will be defended to the last man, and if it does look likely to fall, Choltitz has orders to destroy the entire city. All they will capture is a pile of dust.'

My God! she thought. Paris? 'Can he do that, sir?'

'Of course he can. It is simply a matter of placing sufficient explosives in the right places.'

'I meant, the responsibility . . .'

'It is a directive from the Führer, and he will obey it. Choltitz
is a good officer. Thank God we discovered the truth about
that traitorous lout Stülpnagel in time. But the point I am
trying to make is that after the withdrawal the Americans and
the British will be able to range across all of France. And, of
course, there are their aircraft. They have absolute air superiority. Their fighter-bombers fly low and shoot up everything
they can see. Everything that moves.'

'But what of our new jet fighters? The 262?'

'Do you seriously suppose they can make a difference? We
have perhaps fifty available. The RAF and the Americans have
ten thousand fighter-bombers.'

Anna regarded him. 'Herr Reichsführer, you are talking as
if you think we have lost the war.'

He took off his glasses and polished them. 'I am very much
afraid that we may have lost the war in France. But we still
hold the line of the Rhine. And in the East we will not give
up the line of the Oder.'

'But you think the Russians may get that far?'

'Yes, I do. I am unhappy with the quality of the men we
have there . . . Do you know that they have found the bodies
of Udermann and his driver?'

A crisis? 'The bodies, sir? You mean they were both killed
so that we could get away?'

'They are both dead,' Himmler said. 'But the circumstances
are very strange, and very disturbing. There was no sign of
any Russians in the vicinity, and when the bodies were examined it turned out that Udermann had shot the driver and then
apparently shot himself. Both the bullets came from the gun
lying beside his body, and they were the only two shots fired.
Can you believe it?'

'No, sir. Although . . . he was acting strangely throughout
our journey. He seemed to have something on his mind.'

'The only thing he should have had on his mind was you.
He didn't make an advance, did he?'

'No, sir.'

'Well, I don't suppose we will ever know what was going
through his head. But it is very disturbing to think that an

officer in the SD can be in such a state. Which is why I want
you to take great care on this tour. I would hate to lose you.'

'Thank you, sir,' Anna said. 'I would hate that too.'

Belinda Hoskin stood on the pavement and gazed at the pile of
rubble. My God! she thought. There were sufficient piles
of rubble in London, but never had she seen quite so much
concentrated destruction. And this building . . .

Workmen were picking at the stones. Belinda crossed the
road. 'Excuse me,' she said to one of them. 'This building . . .
when was it demolished?'

He scratched his head, and another man, somewhat better
dressed and clearly a foreman, joined them, looking her up
and down. She wore a quiet dark blue suit under a belted rain-
coat, a large floppy hat, and her only jewellery was a signet
ring, but that was invisible beneath her glove. She carried a
single suitcase. 'It was hit in a raid, oh, last December, Fraulein.
It was not demolished, but was so badly damaged it was
decided to knock it down.'

'What about the people who lived in it? Were they killed?'

But of course they couldn't have been, she realized. Anna
certainly, if Laurent had seen her a month ago.

'One or two may have been hurt,' the foreman said. 'I don't
think anyone was killed.'

'Do you know where they are now?'

'Oh, they will have been re-housed. Government employees,'
he said darkly. 'They were all government employees. The
whole building belonged to the government. Police. Oh, they
will have been looked after.' He frowned at her. 'Did you know
someone from here, Fraulein?' He could tell from her accent
that she was not a Berliner.

'Yes, I did. The Countess von Widerstand.'

'You are acquainted with the countess?'

'We have known each other for years,' Belinda said, with
absolute truthfulness.

His eyes shone. 'Our national heroine.'

'Oh, of course. I had forgotten.'

'You had forgotten? Where are you from?'

'I am Swiss.'

'Ah.' That clearly explained everything, including the accent.

'I would so like to see her again.'

'To do that, you will have to go to Gestapo Headquarters.'

'What?'

'That is where she now lives, Fraulein. Since this building was hit.'

'Oh. Right. Is it far?'

'About a mile. It is on the Prinz Albrechtstrasse. You intend to visit Gestapo Headquarters?'

'Should I not?'

He scratched his head, but made no further comment. Belinda picked up her suitcase and set off.

Was she being foolish? That oaf had certainly seemed to think so. But if she had nothing but unpleasant memories of the secret police, she had supreme confidence in Anna's position and power. Once she made contact with her, she would be utterly safe. And once she made contact with her . . .!

Throughout the very long time it had taken her to get here, her excitement had grown. The delays had been caused firstly by the fact that, because she and Clive had left for Switzerland in such a hurry, to pick Anna up, as they had supposed, there had been no time to complete her cover papers. It had in any event seemed irrelevant to do so, if she would no longer need to enter Germany. Thus, after Anna had failed to show, they had had to return to England to start the whole process over again.

Then it had been back to Switzerland. That charming man Laurent had taken her out to dinner. He had asked her a lot of questions about Anna, which she had been unable to answer, but she couldn't help wondering if he and Anna had something going. She supposed that was extremely likely, knowing Anna, and from Clive's mood since that first visit she suspected that he also held that opinion. But of the pair of them, *she* was the one who was first going to reach the goal.

Anna! She wondered if things would be the same between them after a year? If indeed Anna had ever felt anything for her, and had not been merely amusing herself. That also was in keeping with what she knew of Anna's character. But she didn't care. Throughout the horrendous journey across Germany, where it seemed that just about every railway line had been knocked out, very often half demolished by the Allied bombers, where delays had to be counted not in hours but days, often with only the most primitive accommodation available and the autumnal rains setting in, she had kept herself going with the thought of Anna at the end of it, an Anna who, whatever her real feelings, would have to be grateful for the warning she was conveying, of her danger, and not only from the Russians.

But now she was here. She gazed at the building, which at first sight did not appear the least forbidding. There was a Swastika flag on the roof – in which there were several holes just as most of the windows had been knocked out and were boarded up – and an armed sentry on the door, but he made no effort to stop her as she went up the steps. The door was actually open, and she drew a deep breath and stepped into a gloomy hallway. There was a desk to one side, and the man seated behind it regarded her with neither hostility nor curiosity. 'You have business?'

'Yes. I would like a word with the Countess von Widerstand.'

Now she had caught his interest. 'You wish to see the Countess von Widerstand?'

'That is what I have just said.'

'What do you wish to see her about?'

'We are old friends, and as I happen to be in Berlin . . .'

'You are an old friend of the countess?'

Belinda, who genetically operated on a very short fuse, began to feel irritated. 'There is really no need to repeat everything I say. Yes, we are old friends.'

'Where are you from?'

'Geneva. That is in Switzerland.'

The somewhat sleepy eyes became hostile; he knew she was deliberately putting him down. 'You have papers?'

'Of course.'

Belinda opened her bag and took out her passport, held it out. He opened it, looked from the photograph to her. 'Valentina Sabatini.' He closed the passport and handed it back. 'You cannot see the countess.'

'Look, if you will inform her that her old friend from Switzerland is here . . .'

'You cannot see the countess, because she is not here.'

'Oh. Could you not have said so at the beginning of this ridiculous conversation? When do you expect her back?'

'I cannot say. A month, two months, who knows.'

Belinda glared at him. 'You mean she is not in Berlin? Where has she gone?'

He shrugged. 'Here, there, everywhere. It is no business of yours.'

Damnation, Belinda thought. All this trouble for nothing. 'Well,' she said. 'As I am in Berlin, will you recommend a hotel for me?'

'A hotel? In Berlin? There are no hotels in Berlin any more.'

'Are you telling me that I am supposed to sleep in the street until I can get a train back to Switzerland?' And again face that terrible journey.

The man shrugged.

'Well,' Belinda said. 'I won't say thanks for you help, because you haven't given me any.' She returned to the front door, stood there for a moment. What the hell was she to do? She had anticipated spending the night in Anna's apartment, and even, perhaps, in her arms. Now . . .

A car stopped at the foot of the steps, and a man got out. Lucky for some, Belinda thought, and started down. The man came up, glanced at her as he passed her. Oh, shit! she thought. She had been assured that this could not happen. She pulled her hat over her eyes and hurried down the last few steps, but as she reached the pavement, the man said, 'Stop right there, Fraulein.'

Belinda stopped, drew a deep breath, and turned. Werter smiled at her. 'How nice to meet you again, Signorina Ratosi.'

'Now, really, Werter, what is this all about?' Himmler had been continually irritable since Anna's departure. 'You have obviously made another of your mistakes.'

'With respect, Herr Reichsführer, it is the woman Ratosi. Although I think even that may be a false name.'

'What are you talking about?'

Werter placed Belinda's signet ring on the desk. 'If you would care to look at that, sir.'

Himmler did so. 'Hm. Nine-carat gold. Not very valuable. I am an expert in these things, you know.'

'If you would look inside, sir.'

Himmler squinted. 'BH. Is that important?'

'I took that ring from the finger of this so-called Claudia Ratosi. Should it not be CR?'

Himmler picked up the passport and studied it. 'It says here that her name is Valentina Sabatini. Odd. I am sure that I have heard that name before.'

Werter sighed. 'It is also a false name, Herr Reichsführer, and I think is probably copied from the name of a writer of historical fiction who is very popular in England.'

'Extraordinary. But then, shouldn't it read VS? Anyway, the inscription must be that of a boyfriend, or favourite aunt, or something.'

'She claims it is that of a boyfriend, sir.'

'Then what on earth are you blathering about? And now you say that she is not even Sabatani, but Ratosi. How the devil can you draw such a conclusion?'

'I once arrested Ratosi, sir.'

'But that was well over a year ago. You remember her?'

'Yes, sir. I do.'

'Hm. But as I remember, you could not prove anything against her.'

'I was prevented from proving anything, sir, by the intervention of the Countess von Widerstand.'

'Ah, yes. Of course.'

'And now she is back again, using a false name, and again trying to contact the countess.'

'What makes you think that?'

Werter looked close to an explosion. 'She asked for her, sir. She came here, seeking her. Do you not find that suspicious?'

'Well, you know what these women are like.'

'Sir?'

'You are an innocent, Herr Werter. The Countess von Widerstand and the woman Ratosi had an, ah . . . relationship. This was observed by the monitors in the apartment she was then using.'

'A relationship?' Werter was scandalized.

'It is one of the countess's weaknesses. Indeed, it is her only one, that I know of. Now Ratosi has returned to renew this relationship. I have no idea why she should choose to use another name . . .'

'Complete with another passport, sir? Is *that* not suspicious?'

'Well, she's an Italian, you know. They do some very odd things.'

'With respect, sir, she was an Italian as Ratosi, now she is a Swiss as Sabatini. Do you not find *that* suspicious?'

'In view of what is happening in Italy right now, I don't blame her for claiming Swiss nationality. As we don't know how long the countess will be away, I think your best bet would be to return this woman to Switzerland as rapidly as possible.'

Werter stared at his superior in consternation. 'You mean we are not to hold her?'

'Certainly not. She is here to see the countess, presumably at the countess's invitation. As the countess did not know she was being sent on this tour until a few days before she left, she presumably could not let her, ah, friend, know that she would not be here at the appointed date. They will have to arrange another meeting later on, eh? You send her back to Switzerland, Werter. I hope you have not roughed her up.'

'Well . . .'

'In that case, you had better get down to your cell and make it up to her. I am sure you do not want to get into the countess's bad books. Again. That would be a very dangerous thing to do.' He held up the ring. 'And return this with your apologies.'

Werter continued to stare at him for several moments, then he clicked his heels. 'I will endeavour to make it up to Fraulein "Sabatini", Herr Reichsführer. Heil Hitler!'

Incident in Warsaw

'Come in, Comrade Commissar.' Marshal Rokossovsky was a powerfully built man; he seemed to be all shoulders and jaw. 'I have something that may interest you.'

Nikolai Tserchenko entered the room cautiously, as he did most things cautiously.

Rokossovsky held up a sheet of paper. 'I have here a report from one of our spies, behind the German lines, at −' he glanced at the paper − 'Lodz. He says that the German troops there have been visited by the newly appointed Minister of Morale, better known as the Countess von Widerstand.'

'What?' Tserchenko shouted, suddenly animated, and ran to the huge map of Poland and Eastern Germany pinned against the wall. 'Lodz! Marshal . . .' He turned to face his superior, cheeks aflame.

'I thought she had to be the woman in whom you are interested,' Rokossovsky said.

'But if she is there, just a short distance away . . .'

'The distance is longer than it looks on the map, and there happen to be well over a hundred thousand German soldiers still between us and Lodz.' 'And in any event, this report is dated four days ago. The lady seems to be on a tour. She will not be there now. However, this man does go on to report that her next destination is Warsaw. She could well be *there* by now.'

'Warsaw!' Tserchenko went to the window. The current headquarters were in the suburb of Praga, situated on the east bank of the Vistula. In the afternoon sunlight the city was clearly visible across the water, the smoke rising above it; even with an easterly breeze the sounds of gunfire and explosions were audible. 'Then we must cross the river now, sir. Frankly—' He changed his mind about what he would have said.

'You do not understand why we have not already done so, while the Germans have their hands full with this Polish uprising? That is because you do not understand high strategy, Comrade Tserchenko. Those men over there are not Communists. They are Poles, the most recalcitrant people on the face of the earth. For the last five hundred years they have been virtually ungovernable, and we have no evidence that they have changed. They wish to free Poland of Nazi rule, but they are not prepared to accept any other rule. And of course, because they are fighting the Nazis, they have become instant heroes to the British and the Americans, who have no concept of the true aim of politics, and stumble from one emotional crisis to another. We will ignore all these hysterical appeals for help, for permission for Allied aircraft to land and refuel on our airfields after dropping supplies to these abominable people. If we go in now, and "rescue" this Polish Home Army, what then? We will be left with a large number of men, with arms in their hands, who hate us and will do everything they can to obstruct our plans for Europe. So we will have to destroy them ourselves. Think of the wail of protest that would rise from the Allies were that to happen.'

'So we sit here and do nothing.'

'We continue issuing statements that our troops are not yet strong enough to cross the river and attack the city. We will wait for the Germans and the Poles to destroy each other, and then will, as they say, pick up the pieces.'

'My orders, Comrade Marshal, given to me by Comrade Beria personally, are to secure this woman at the first opportunity and no matter what the risk.'

'And my orders, Comrade Commissar, given to me personally by Premier Stalin, are not to attack Warsaw until the scenario I have outlined is attained.'

The two men stared at each other, then Tserchenko said, 'Have I your permission to cross the river.'

'Are you out of your mind?'

'If I miss this opportunity, I may never have another.'

Rokossovsky considered for a few moments. 'You cannot do it on you own. She is undoubtedly protected, and you would not even get to her. See if you can recruit a squad. I would say twelve men. They must all be volunteers. Secure the necessary uniforms from our prisoners; they should be available in all sizes. Be sure that you also wear German equipment. Do you speak the language?'

'Yes, I do.'

'It would be helpful if some of your men did too, otherwise you will have to do all the talking. Be ready by tomorrow night and we will ferry you across the river, north of the city. There is little fighting going on there at the moment, and you should have no difficulty. Then you are on your own. You say that you are required to capture this woman alive?'

'If that is possible. Do you suppose she will still be there, tomorrow night?'

'Judging by this report, she seems to spend several days in each place, so there is no reason why she will not be. Now, when you have obtained your objective, supposing you do, return with her to your landing place, signal us with your torch, and we will fetch you. Do you understand all this?'

'Yes,' Tserchenko said.

'What will you do if you do manage to secure her person, but are overtaken by the Germans before we can rescue you?'

'In that eventuality, Comrade Marshal, I am instructed to kill her.'

'It might be safest to do that anyway.'

'Having killed her,' Terschenko said, 'I am instructed to cut off her head and take it to Moscow. I will of course need adequate transport. And a suitable container.'

Rokossovsky regarded him for several seconds. 'Well, then, Comrade Commissar, I will wish you good fortune. And, Comrade Commissar, if you do not return, I will inform Comrade Beria that you died carrying out his orders.'

'My God!' Anna remarked. 'What a shambles.'

Berlin could equally be described as a shambles, but Warsaw almost defied description. Whole blocks had been razed to the ground – Hitler's orders, she remembered – others were burning; the stench of charred wood and human bodies was revolting. And there was still firing going on, mostly in the distance, but some from close at hand as the Waffen – the Fighting – SS roamed through the destruction, armed with tommy guns, dogs and flame-throwers, seeking and destroying. 'You mean these people are still fighting?'

'There are a stubborn lot,' General Greiff agreed. 'They prefer to die than surrender. Of course, if they surrender they die anyway, but it is done in a more civilized manner. People with that point of view are very difficult to overcome.' He appeared to be genuinely irritated by this. 'Now, here is where you will stay while you are in Warsaw.'

The car, having at her request driven through the heart of the city, slowly and with difficulty because of the rubble and the craters, stopped outside a house in one of the suburbs, where the air was reasonably clean. The door was opened and Anna got out. As required by Hitler she was wearing her flamboyant best, a pink dress with a hem just below her knees and a deep neckline, with a matching pink straw hat, silk stockings and pink shoes and gloves, as well as all her best jewellery; her hair was loose and fluttered in the breeze. The general obviously felt like a million dollars to be her escort. But . . . 'There is no roof.'

'Oh, there is half a roof. Over the wing you will occupy. The building was struck by a Russian shell, you see.'

Anna turned to look across the street. There were two blocks between her and the river, but she could glimpse it through the houses and the shattered trees, and then the far bank. 'And is it not likely to be struck again?'

'No, no. It is perfectly safe for the time being. The Ivans have not fired a shot for the last fortnight.'

'Do you know why that is?'

'There are several theories. One is that they have outrun their supplies, and are waiting for them to catch up.'

'In which case they could resume the offensive at any moment.'

'Should that happen we would immediately move you. I have my orders. But a more likely scenario is that they are afraid to bombard us because that would mean bombarding their allies, the Poles who are fighting for the city.'

'But you say the uprising is virtually over.'

'It is, but the Russians do not know that.'

'Hm.' Anna watched the other two cars draw to a stop behind them. Katherine was also dressed as if for a party, in a pale blue dress, also with a matching hat and accessories. Anna had given her some pieces of good jewellery to wear and if she would never be as striking as her sister she was certainly worth a second glance. Behind her, Birgit, in a severe black dress with a white collar, looked exactly what she was, a servant, and she was also very obviously terrified, unlike Katherine, who gazed at the house and decrepit garden and remarked, 'What a dump.'

'It is very comfortable inside, Fraulein,' the general insisted.

'In you go,' Gutemann commanded the orderlies who were carrying their bags.

'I will show you around,' the general volunteered.

Actually, the wing in which they were to stay was undamaged and had obviously just been subjected to a thorough cleaning. The drawing room was well furnished, and the kitchen well-appointed. 'I was told that you would not need staff,' the general said, anxiously.

'I have my own staff,' Anna assured him. 'As you can see.'

'Well, the bedrooms are up here.'

There were four bedrooms and two bathrooms on the first

floor, which seemed very civilized. 'Whose house is this?' Anna asked.

'Oh, it once belonged to some Polish businessman. We requisitioned it when we occupied the city, five years ago.'

'Where did the family go?'

'We discovered that they had Jewish blood. They went to a resettlement area.'

Anna wondered if he honestly believed that. 'I will have this room, Major,' she told Gutemann. It was at the back of the house, overlooking the garden, and had a large double bed.

'That is an excellent choice, Countess,' he said enthusiastically, eyeing the bed. They had been travelling, and meeting the troops, at such a rate that he had not yet achieved his ambition. But they had been told they would be in Warsaw for several days.

'Now, Countess,' the general said. 'I am sure you are tired and need a rest, and an early night. I would be delighted if you would have an informal supper with my wife and I tonight. And your sister, of course.'

'Your wife is in Warsaw?'

'Oh, indeed. We actually have a villa outside the city. It is more salubrious. You told me,' he hurried on, again anxiously, 'that you would prefer to be in the city during your visit.'

'I did. I am required to report to the Führer on actual conditions where I visit. As long as it is safe.'

'I can assure you of that. Tomorrow I will take you on a tour of the city . . . well, those parts of it, where we have regained full control, and then I would very much like you to meet my officers at a reception in the evening.'

'Certainly, General. And the troops?'

'Ah. We will start on them the next day. You understand that owing to the situation this will have to be done in small groups, as so many of them are always on duty. But they will prefer that, eh? More intimate.'

'Absolutely.'

'Well, then, my car will call for you at six this evening.'

'Thank you. One thing: is there water?'

'Oh, yes, Countess. Water has been laid on.'

'Very civilized. Then I will see you tonight.'

*　　*　　*

Anna took off her hat, surveyed herself in the mirror. She half expected to see her hair turning white. But she looked exactly as always, the face calm and confident, that of a very young and totally innocent girl. Preaching victory to a horde of monsters. If she could not help but feel a certain sympathy for the line soldiers, grey-faced and haggard, who were only doing what their Führer commanded them to do with that blind obedience required of every professional soldier, she could feel none for the SS, who were trained to fight less than to kill, mercilessly and without reason. Which was not to deny that they were the best soldiers in the German Army, and perhaps in any army in the world . . . because they had also been trained to die, willingly and without question.

And she was one of them!

Birgit hurried in to unpack. 'Are we safe here, Countess?'

'Should we not be?' Anna undressed; it was a hot September afternoon and she intended to have a nap before bathing and dressing for the evening.

'Well, with the Russians just over there . . .'

'They are apparently unlikely to trouble us. Is your room comfortable?'

'Oh, yes, Countess.'

'And there is food in the larder?'

'Oh, yes, Countess.'

'Then prepare lunch. I will have mine here.'

'Of course, Countess.' She scurried off.

Anna lay on the bed, naked, stretching her arms and legs to their widest. What she was doing, travelling almost every day, talking to the men, being so obviously admired by them, having most of them so clearly lusting after her, was, she supposed, sustaining her. It meant that she was living always in the here and now. And right now, to contemplate next month, next week, or even tomorrow, was not a sensible thing to do. She was completely cut off, still without any idea of Clive's, or Laurent's, reaction to her non-return to Switzerland. Experience and common sense told her that they would understand that something had happened to prevent her carrying out her plan. But that streak of insecurity that lurked behind the facade of total confidence, total control, kept telling her that by now they would know of her new position, and of what she was doing . . . might they not have determined that she had decided to stick with her Nazi masters to the end?

There was a tap on her door. She hastily rolled beneath the sheet, not quite in time as the door opened.

'Oh!' Gutemann said. 'I apologize, Countess. I did not know you were in bed. May I come in?'

'You appear to have done that,' Anna pointed out. 'I am very tired.'

He closed the door and advanced, hesitantly. 'I just wished to make sure that you were comfortable.'

'At this moment, I am very comfortable, thank you.'

He had reached the bed, where he stood even more hesitantly. 'Did you know that Paris has fallen?'

'That happened a fortnight ago. Paris! I suppose it also is now just a mass of rubble. We seem to be determined to destroy civilization.'

'No, no, Countess. Paris was captured intact, virtually undamaged save for a few bullet holes.'

Anna frowned. 'But General Choltitz had orders to destroy the city rather than surrender.'

'He seems to have disobeyed them.'

Hitler must have had one of his fits, Anna thought. But hooray for Choltitz.

Gutemann accepted that he was not going to get anywhere on this occasion either. 'Well, then, I shall . . .'

But suddenly Anna felt like celebrating. She threw back the sheet. 'Is this what you have come for?'

He flushed as he gazed at her, and licked his lips.

'I need to be held in a man's arms. Now.'

His mouth opened and closed. 'Just like . . . ah . . .'

'You are a difficult fellow,' Anna remarked. 'I wish to have sex, yes. Just like that. I am tense and it relaxes me. Why don't you take off your clothes and get to know me?'

'Countess! It has been a great honour.'

The officers in turn bowed over Anna's glove. She had no doubt that they had been overwhelmed. She was wearing a pale blue sheath with no shoulders and a deep décolletage. As there were no straps visible, either round her neck or on her bare back, they had to suppose that the garment was sustained by flesh alone. Her crucifix nestled in the midst of that valley that so fascinated them, and she was again wearing the best of her jewellery.

She had spoken individually with every one of the twenty men present, rested her gloved hand on his arm in a gesture of warmth and even intimacy, told them about the irresistible new weapons that were coming out of the factories and would soon be with their army, suggested that when they returned to Germany, victorious, she would be delighted to meet them again, perhaps to dine with them, and then . . . who could tell?

She was watched, from the side of the room, by Gutemann, eyes glowing with a mixture of admiration, jealousy, and, she supposed, the pride of possession. Well, he had certainly possessed her that afternoon and last night, despite being very obviously piqued at having not been invited to General Greiff's intimate supper party. That had largely been because she had wanted to be possessed, for a brief while, but she had never denied to herself – or to anyone else – that when the mood took her, sensuality was all that mattered. Just as when she was carrying out an assignment, however dangerous or disgusting, successful completion was all that mattered. That single-minded, concentrated approach had been responsible for her success. It would be folly to change it now.

Thus Gutemann was a happy man, because, like all men, he could not believe that any woman could give so much of her body, her lips, her smile, her sighs of contentment, without loving. He had never studied the life and words of Liane de Puchy, France's most famous courtesan of the century, who had said, 'When you are required to make love to a man, you must love the man.' Afterwards was a different matter.

But he was definitely contemplating afterwards now, and moved forward as the general escorted her to the door. 'You were magnificent, Countess,' Greiff said. 'There is not a man here tonight who will not fight the harder for having met you.'

'You say the sweetest things.'

'And you, Fraulein,' he assured Katherine. She also was in a low-cut evening gown and had Anna not been present would have dominated the evening. Now she gave a simper in response, well aware that as Anna *had* been present she had been entirely superfluous.

They went down the steps to the waiting car; the September

evening was already dark. Gutemann got into the front beside the driver, the sisters sat together in the back. 'A successful evening, Countess?' the major asked.

'I think so,' Anna said.

'And tomorrow we start on the enlisted men.'

'I wish we didn't have to,' Katherine said.

'You are becoming a snob,' Anna suggested.

'It's just that they never smell clean.'

'Well, they are fighting a war.'

'And they look so hungry. I mean, for us.'

'That's why we're here.'

The car stopped, and they went into the house, where Birgit was waiting, even more anxious than usual. 'Some men were here,' she told them.

'What men?' Anna asked.

'They were soldiers, commanded by a lieutenant.'

'Soldiers? You mean SS men?'

'No, Countess. Soldiers. They wore ordinary uniforms.'

'What did they want?'

'They were looking for you, Countess. They asked if this was the residence you were using while in Warsaw.'

Anna looked at Gutemann.

'Did they say why they wanted to see the countess?'

'No, sir. I told them she wasn't here, so they asked when she would be back, and I said, very late.' She looked at the clock on the mantelpiece; it was just coming up to ten.

'And they decided not to wait,' Anna commented. 'Thank God for that.'

'Yes. But the lieutenant said a funny thing as they left.'

'What funny thing?'

'He asked, "She *is* coming back?"'

'And you told him yes.'

'Well . . . shouldn't I have?'

'Of course you should. I am back, aren't I? Do you think we should do something about this, Gutemann? Or do you suppose they just wanted a private audience?'

'Whatever they wanted, it is very irregular. I will report it to the general tomorrow morning.'

'The price of fame,' Katherine remarked, going into the drawing room and sitting down. 'I feel like another glass of champagne.'

'Oh, really?' Anna asked. 'Haven't you had enough?'

'No,' Katherine said.

Anna regarded her for some seconds, but she was obviously in a recalcitrant mood, almost certainly brought on by jealousy: Anna had been watching her throughout the evening. Well, she thought, if the silly girl wants to have a head tomorrow, so be it. 'Is there any champagne, Birgit?'

'Oh, yes, Countess. There are several bottles.'

'Then open one and bring it to Fraulein Fehrbach, with a glass. Good night.'

She went up the stairs, and found Gutemann at her elbow. 'Don't you wish some more champagne?' she asked.

'I wish some more of you.'

She paused in her doorway. 'Not tonight, Gunther.'

'Oh!' His face fell. 'I thought we . . .'

'Yes, we do. But not to the extent that it becomes boring.'

'Then when . . .?'

She shrugged. 'Who knows? Maybe tomorrow?'

She undressed. The night was very close and hot, accentuated by the heat drifting their way from the many burning buildings. I am sleeping where I belong, she thought: in Hell. But even her hair felt hot. She went into the bathroom, and found a shower cap. Into this she scooped her hair, exposing her neck and shoulders, and then got into bed.

But she knew she wasn't going to sleep. She was, in fact, feeling just as recalcitrant as her sister, for an entirely different reason. She had been the belle of the ball, as always. But the situation, all those eager men, the ones she had met on her previous stops, the ones she had met tonight . . . all were going to die, perhaps quite soon. As she had thought earlier, they no doubt deserved to die for their crimes. But they were so eager. As for those who had called here tonight . . .!

Her eyes opened and she stared at the darkened ceiling. That was what was keeping her awake. Whatever her hatred for the Nazi regime, she had never been able to fault the discipline of the German soldier. Throughout her tour so far, although more often than not surrounded by men most of whom could not have had a woman in weeks, perhaps months, not one had ever attempted to take a liberty, not even a hand 'inadvertently' brushed against her bottom. But twelve men, apparently including an officer, had called at this house tonight . . . seeking what?

In any event, she would have supposed that just about every soldier in Warsaw who was interested would have known that tonight she was being entertained by their officers. So what had they been after? If they were would-be deserters out for what they could get, surely they would have taken whatever was available, Birgit and such food or money they could find? But when the maid had told them her mistress was not available, they had simply gone away again.

After ascertaining that she *would* be there tomorrow. Or later tonight? They had to expect that she would report the incident to General Greiff, when they would almost certainly be rounded up. And they had not been SS! But the only German troops in Warsaw were all SS!

She got out of bed and went to the window. The curtains were drawn, but she parted them sufficiently to look down at the deserted street. But it was not deserted. There was no light down there, but she could make out a command car parked beside the pavement and several shadowy figures, covering this house.

She went to her door and pulled on her dressing gown, then opened her shoulder bag and took out her pistol and the two spare clips: Birgit had said there were a dozen of them.

She put the clips in her pocket, stepped into the hall, listened. The light was still on in the drawing room, although there was no sound from there; Katherine must have fallen asleep with her bottle. She went along the hall to Gutemann's room, listened to him snoring. She did not turn on the light, waited for her eyes to become accustomed to the gloom, and then went to the bed, and squeezed his arm.

'Eh? Ah . . . Anna!' His arm went round her thighs. 'You have changed your mind.'

'Get up and put something on,' she said. 'Find your weapon.'

'What? What?' But he sat up.

'And hurry. Shit!' She had turned back to the open door, and now heard a crash from downstairs. 'Follow me,' she snapped. She ran into the hall, and heard a scream. Katherine! She reached the landing and looked down. A man stood there, armed with a tommy gun, and looking up. He saw her shadowy figure and levelled the gun. But where she was a shadow, he was illuminated by the light from the drawing room; Anna shot him through the head.

Another man emerged from the drawing room, just as a third, who must have been on guard outside the front door, came inside. Both were armed, and Anna shot them both before they could fire.

Gutemann was at her shoulder, wearing a pair of pants. 'Jesus!' he muttered. He had never seen her in action before.

But now several more men came out of the drawing room. Two were carrying a struggling, kicking woman who had to be Katherine – they had dropped a hood over her head – and Anna hesitated for a moment; they had switched off the light and were indistinct, and she had to be sure of not hitting her sister.

Birgit emerged from her bedroom, screaming. 'Countess . . .!'

'Get back,' Anna shouted. Several of the kidnappers were firing up the stairs; in the gloom their shots were wild, but they were ricocheting to and fro.

'Countess!' Gutemann also wanted to get back.

The men had got Katherine to the door. Anna took careful aim and fired again, and another man went down. Then the door was open and they were dragging Katherine through.

'Shit,' Anna said. She still couldn't go down the stairs as two men remained, spraying their tommy guns upwards. But they were now exposed, and she shot them both, aiming for the leg of the second man.

The house was suddenly quiet, save for the reverberations of the shots and the groans of one of the stricken man. And the sound of a car engine being gunned on the street. 'Shit,' Anna said again. 'Shit, shit, shit!'

Gutemann came forward to stand at her side. 'Countess?'

'They got away,' Anna pointed out, 'with my sister. We must hurry.'

She ran down the stairs, switched on the hall light. Gutemann followed, gazed at the bodies. 'My God!' he muttered. 'You shot six men. With six shots. Six men shot dead.'

'This one isn't dead.' Anna nudged the wounded man with her toe; he had stopped groaning and appeared to have lost consciousness.

'How do you know he is not dead?' Gutemann asked, his voice trembling. 'He looks dead to me.'

'He is not dead,' Anna pointed out, 'because I did not shoot to kill him. I shot him in the thigh, because I wanted one of them alive.'

'You . . .' Gutemann seemed on the edge of a nervous breakdown. 'You could make such a decision, in the dark, at such a time?'

'I could see him,' Anna reminded him. 'But he may well die, if we do not stop this bleeding. Birgit,' she called. 'Stop that caterwauling and bring your first aid kit down here. You, Gutemann, get some proper clothes on and go sound the alarm. That car must be found, quickly.'

'Yes, Countess. But you—'

'I am going to patch this fellow up, and then ask him a few questions.'

Gutemann gulped, his imagination clearly working overtime. Then he hurried back to his room to dress.

'What a terrible thing,' General Greiff remarked. 'German soldiers, *SS men*, behaving like that?' He gazed across his desk at Anna.

It was broad daylight, and she was fully dressed, as immaculately as always, a splash of magnificent colour in her pink dress and hat. 'They were not SS, Herr General, they wore the uniforms of line soldiers, but they were not German soldiers, either,' she said. 'They were Russians, wearing German uniforms.'

'What? Good heavens! How do you know this?'

'I was able to interrogate one of them before he died. I'm afraid he was more badly hurt than I had supposed. I intended to hit him in the thigh, but I actually hit him in the groin, and must have ruptured his stomach. It was dark,' she added apologetically. 'But before he died he gabbled a few words. And they were Russian. I speak Russian, although I could not understand what he was saying.'

Greiff did not appear to be listening. 'You shot this man? You, Countess?'

'She shot six of them,' Gutemann said. He was seated beside her. 'The other five were killed instantly.'

Greiff looked at Anna.

'It's what I do,' she explained.

'My God!' the general commented.

Anna was getting tired of his apparent inability to concentrate. 'The point is, Herr General, that there were several of these Russians, wearing German uniforms and driving a

German car, who have kidnapped my sister. I think you need to find out how they managed this.'

'I have checked,' Gutemann said. 'The car was stolen from outside the Officers' Mess, last night. As you may remember, Herr General, there was a fair amount of merriment, and it does not appear to have been missed.'

'But the alarm was raised several hours ago,' Anna said, 'Surely . . .'

As she spoke, the telephone rang. General Greiff took the receiver from its hook. 'Yes? Ah. I see. Yes. That is all you can do.' He replaced the receiver. 'The car has been found, abandoned, twenty-five kilometres north of the city.'

'Are there no checkpoints?' Anna asked.

'Oh, indeed. To get that far they would have had to pass through three checkpoints.'

'May I ask how they managed that?'

Gutemann swallowed. He had heard Anna use that softly menacing voice before.

'Well, you know,' the general said, 'they were wearing German uniforms, and one of them was dressed as an officer. He apparently spoke perfect German, and, well . . .'

'They were allowed through. Tell me, Herr General, what would have been the situation had they been the spearhead of a Russian advance coming down from the north to attack Warsaw?'

'Ah, well, that would have been impossible. Had the Russians got across the river in any force, we would have known about it and all entrances and exits from the city would have been fortified and reinforced. You see, Countess, these people were *leaving* the city, not attempting to enter it. There was no reason for the checkpoints to stop them.'

Anna sighed. 'Very well, Herr General. But now we know where they left the car. They can't have gone far on foot. I assume a search is being mounted?'

'Ah. Well . . .'

'Yes?'

'A search was mounted immediately, in the vicinity where the car was found. But it was on the river bank, and our people have found evidence of a boat having been brought into the bank at that very place, so I am very much afraid—'

'Are you saying that it is possible for the Russians to cross the river as and when they choose?'

The general produced a handkerchief to wipe his brow. 'In small numbers, I suppose it is. It is quite impossible for us to patrol every metre of the river bank. We simply do not have enough men. If they attempt to cross in any numbers, now, well, we would know about it.'

'As you knew about their crossing the river south of Warsaw, in force, two months ago. But they still crossed.'

'Yes, they did. I was not in command there.' Anna did not look the least convinced, and he hurried on. 'What I find it impossible to understand is why they would have mounted an operation, in which the risk factor is very high, and in which indeed they lost six men, simply to kidnap your sister.' He looked at her, eyebrows arched, his expression suggesting, now you try answering a question.

'Herr General,' Anna said, as patiently as she could, 'they came to kidnap me, not my sister. In the dark, they made a mistake.'

'Good Heavens! I never thought of that. What are we to do?'

'If they have got her across the river, there is nothing we can do.' Katherine, she thought. In the hands of thugs who were sworn to execute the Countess von Widerstand, even if they would hardly know that it was not her; it was four years since she had been in Moscow, and the only person she could remember who had known her at all well, and had lived to tell the tale, had been the young female gaoler in the women's section of the Lubianka Prison. Her first name had been Olga; Anna had never learned her last name. Olga had tortured her with jets of water, sending them into her face and every orifice of her body until she could hardly breathe, with never a change of expression. When Joe Andrews had come for her, armed with that precious order of release issued by Beria, and it had been questioned by that ghastly woman Tserchenka, who had ordered the water torture, and she had killed both her and Commissar Chalyapov, she had fully intended to kill Olga as well, but had been persuaded not to by Andrews, appalled by the carnage that had already been committed, and anxious only to get out of the prison while he, and she, could. But it was very unlikely that Olga was still around, three years later.

Even so, that was going to be Katherine's fate, until they executed her. All because she had wanted to be like her big sister in everything. And there was nothing Anna could do about it. She felt quite sick.

'Countess?' Greiff had been watching her expression, and was anxious. 'Would you like to return to Berlin?'

'Am I not required to speak with your troops today?'

'Well, yes. But in the circumstances . . .'

'I will speak with your troops, Herr General. Otherwise I, and my sister, should not have been here at all.'

'Comrade Tserchenko,' Lavrenty Beria said. 'Welcome home. I understand that your mission has been completed.'

'Yes, sir.' Tserchenko spoke proudly.

'And you had no difficulty?'

'Well, Comrade Commissar, it was not easy. We lost six men.'

'I told you it might not be easy. But six men?'

'The woman was well protected. She gave us no trouble, herself, beyond a lot of screaming, and we soon put a stop to that. She was alone in the downstairs of the house, you see, and I suppose we took her by surprise. But her bodyguard was quite deadly. He opened fire from the top of the stairs, and as I reported, shot six of my people before we could get out of the house. With the woman.'

'You mean he had a tommy gun, and opened fire indiscriminately while you were carrying the countess?'

'No, sir. There was no tommy gun. It sounded like a pistol. He fired six shots, and killed six of my men. I have never seen such speed and accuracy. I think we need to be thankful that the Germans do not have many marksmen like that in their army.'

Beria was frowning. 'And this man was not hit himself?'

'Well, no, Comrade Commissar. It was dark and we could not see him clearly . . .'

'But he seems to have been able to see you. You will be telling me next that the Germans feed their troops on raw carrots. Anyway, you got the woman.'

'Yes, sir.'

'She is not hurt, I hope? I gave orders that if taken alive she should be brought here unharmed, to face trial.'

'She is not harmed,' Tserchenko said. 'Nothing that shows,

anyway. At least while she is wearing clothes. It was necessary to restrain her from time to time.'

'And to amuse yourself, no doubt.'

'Well, sir, it is a long way from Warsaw to Moscow.'

'And did she say anything?'

'Oh, she kept insisting that she was not the countess, but her sister. Frankly, I had expected something more.'

Beria stood up. 'Where is she now?'

'I handed her over to Major Morosova in the Women's Section.'

'Then let us go down and see this monster.'

They took the elevator to the ground floor, and the guard on the door of the Women's Section opened it for them. The commandant, having been warned by phone, was waiting, a small, pretty young woman who wore her black hair cut short and was immaculate in her green uniform. 'Comrade Commissar!'

'Good morning, Olga. You have a prisoner for me.'

'Of course, sir. You wish to see her?'

'That is why I am here.'

Olga hurried in front of the two men, waving subordinate female warders out of the way. They went down various corridors between locked doors, into a world of women, both audibly and odorously, and finally stopped before a cell in the ultra security section. Olga slipped the panel over the window to one side, looked in, and then stepped aside.

Beria took her place. 'She is certainly a beauty.'

'Yes, sir. She is not so beautiful as her sister, of course.'

Beria turned, slowly. 'What did you say?'

'That is what she kept saying,' Tserchenko complained.

Beria ignored him. 'What makes you think this is the countess's sister?'

'I once had the countess in this very cell, Comrade Commissar.'

'Three years ago. She has undoubtedly changed.'

'Not that much, sir. Besides, the countess had a vivid blue scar on her right rib cage. I believe it was caused by a bullet wound. This woman has no such scar.'

Beria looked at Tserchenko.

'But –' the colonel stuttered – 'I had the photograph. A tall, very handsome woman, with yellow hair . . .'

'Who when you approached her did nothing but scream. While

her "bodyguard" picked off six of your people in rapid succession,' Beria observed. 'I knew there was something familiar about your story, and I have just remembered what it is. In the summer of 1941 we discovered that the countess was in Washington, and gave orders that she was to be arrested and brought to Moscow for trial. So she was seized by six of our people. And do you know what she did? She shot all six of them dead. Does that not sound familiar to you?'

'But . . .' Tserchenko looked at Olga for support, and found none.

'Six appears to be her favourite number, when it comes to killing our people,' Beria observed. 'So, Comrade, you have not succeeded in your mission. One could say that you have not even started your mission, as you had the opportunity and let it slip through your fingers.'

Tserchenko swallowed. 'I shall return to Warsaw, Comrade Commissar. I shall—'

'You require a more realistic approach to the matter. Do you suppose that time stands still? It is a fortnight since you were in Warsaw. Yesterday Bór-Komorowski surrendered what was left of his so-called Home Army to avoid total annihilation. The news arrived this morning. So Marshal Rokossovsky is about to launch his assault on the city.'

'Well, then . . .'

'Do you seriously suppose that the countess is still there? She is probably back in Berlin by now.'

Tserchenko looked dumbfounded.

'What do you wish done with this one, Comrade Commissar?' Olga asked.

'Oh, tell your successor to keep her locked up. She may come in handy.'

'My successor, sir?'

'I am relieving you of your position.'

'But . . .' Olga looked flabbergasted; Tserchenko's mistake had had nothing to do with her.

'I am appointing you to be Colonel Tserchenko's aide in this mission.'

Olga's jaw dropped as she looked at Tserchenko.

'You,' Beria said, 'at least know what the Countess von Widerstand looks like.'

The Sentence

'Welcome to England, sir.' Joseph Andrews shook hands with his boss as he stepped from the just landed aircraft.

Wild Bill Donovan did not look convinced. The October rain was chill, and the clouds showed no sign of breaking. 'I didn't even know where the goddamned place was, until we touched down.' He was not a big man, but he exuded both personality and energy to an extent that occasionally could be overwhelming, and which had earned him his soubriquet. Today he looked tired, as he sat in the back of the car to be driven to the London headquarters of the OSS, discreetly tucked away down a quiet side street where it could be totally inconspicuous. 'You know why I'm here?'

'Actually, I can think of several reasons,' Joe said. 'Although . . .'

'There is one in particular that is top of the current list. Who is your driver? One of our people?'

'Recruited locally, sir.'

'A Limey?'

'Yes, sir. But he's a good man, very reliable. And he's signed all the forms.'

'Maybe. But this is between you and me. Nobody else.'

'That figures. Close the glass, will you, Harry.'

'Yes, sir.' Harry slid the glass partition into place.

Donovan looked out of his window at the widespread bomb damage. 'I guess you understand that I don't like what I am going to have to say.'

'I appreciate that. I don't think I am going to like it either.'

'So I guess you read that report?'

'She's still our agent, sir. Even if nebulously. I try to keep tabs on her.'

'But she doesn't communicate with you.'

'Not recently. But then, I gather that even MI6 have lost contact.'

'Or they say they have, right? I have to tell you, Joe, that the prevailing opinion in Washington is that they sold us a pup. Whether that was inadvertent or not, whether she's proved a pup to them also, doesn't alter the fact that what was turning out to be an embarrassment is now setting up to be a disaster. Countess von Widerstand shoots dead six Russian soldiers. That ring a bell?'

'Yes, sir, it does.'

'It is ringing a bell in the White House as well, although not so loud as in the Kremlin. Yet. You realize that the Reds still do not know how Anna got away with killing six of their people in Washington back in '41. But they're suspicious. For Christ's sake, they're suspicious about everything. But FDR feels that they are essential to winning the war. Now the rub is, that next month the country goes to the polls, with FDR running for an unprecedented fourth term. Now I happen to think, and I hope you agree, that he is more important to our winning the war than the Soviets. Well now, their ambassador in Washington is asking all kinds of questions and threatening to blow the whole Anna business sky high.'

'They can't possibly know that Anna works for us,' Andrews objected.

'They're not as stupid as some people think, Joe, and like I said, suspicion is their middle name. At the very least they regard her escape from Washington as total incompetence on our part, together with total non-cooperation. Well, we can't argue with that. But they also seem to be remembering that only a couple of months before that junket Anna also made a spectacular escape from Russia, from the Lubianka, no less, again after killing a couple of their people. You wouldn't care to remind me who engineered *that* little coup. The Soviets certainly haven't forgotten.'

Andrews gulped.

'You persuaded me she was the goods,' Donovan said, 'and on that basis I told Hoover to get out of the ball park and take the Soviet people with him. FDR went along with that, but now he has come to the conclusion that if Moscow goes public on this, as they are threatening to do, it could blow his chances of re-election. President lies to Soviet allies, blah, blah, blah.'

Andrews swallowed again. 'So . . .'

'There is also the fact, of which he is aware, that we gave her a big, a vital job to do, and she didn't do it.'

'With respect, sir. The bomb didn't go off.'

'The second one did. And she put the kybosh on the impending coup.'

'I've explained all that,' Andrews protested. 'She had no choice.'

'She had a choice, Joe. Between risking all, as she is reputed to do when necessary, to push the coup through, whether Adolf was alive or dead, or get out of the hot seat and back the regime. She chose. Minister of Morale! Shit!'

'That's not how MI6 sees it.'

'Fuck MI6. I have an idea that they're paddling their own canoe. We know for sure that Churchill doesn't go along with FDR's view of the Soviets. He seems to regard them with more suspicion than they regard us. So you stay away from them, Joe, except socially. We have to handle this on our own.'

'Will you be explicit?'

Donovan drew a deep breath. 'The President has told the Soviet ambassador that we will take care of the lady, providing they keep their mouths shut. The ambassador accepted the deal on behalf of his government.'

'You can't be serious,' Joe protested.

'I wish I wasn't, believe me.'

Andrews stared out of the window, and Donovan allowed him a few moments, then he asked, 'Have we any means of reaching her?'

Andrews sighed. 'We have one man who is known to her, and has contacted her before. He gave her the bomb.'

'Name?'

'Lars Johannsson. He's a Swede, and as such can come and go in and out of Germany almost as he pleases.'

'And you reckon she trusts him?'

'Well, like I said, she's dealt with him before. I would say she trusts him. But if you're thinking of him getting her out of the country so that she can be arrested, that's a tall order. Certainly where Anna is concerned.'

'I wasn't thinking of getting her out of any country, Joe.'

Andrews stared at him. 'Now I know you can't be serious.'

'To paraphrase the Good Book, those that live by the sword,

have got to reckon on dying by the sword. Or the Luger, or whatever.'

'But . . . Anna?'

'So you once shared a bed with her. Believe me, I envy you. What you need to remember is that you are damn nearly as much on the line as her.'

'Shit!' Andrews muttered.

'The attitude in Washington is, you brought her in, so it's your business to take her back out. And you know, you would probably be saving her a lot of grief. Whether or not we take her out right now, or when the war ends, which can only be a month or two away, she is going to be arrested and indicted as a war criminal. The Soviets are going to insist upon it. That means that after a lot of unpleasantness, she is going to wind up being hanged. And in the meantime, her very presence is going to do an immense amount of damage, to us, for having condoned a mass murderess –' he held up a finger as Andrews would have spoken – 'I know. She would say, and you and I believe, that it was self-defence. A lot of people would consider killing six people at one time in self-defence was going over the top. The point is that the President of the United States was involved in letting her off the hook and now he has given his word that the business will be sorted out. It has to be done, Joe. Anna came to us as your baby. I'm giving her back to you to put to bed. I'm sorry, but that's how the cookie crumbles. Sometimes.'

Andrews was silent for a few moments. Then he said, 'You understand that while she's touring Europe as this Minister of Morale, she's going to be damned difficult to catch up with. We don't have any idea where she's going to turn up next. We only know where she's been.'

'But she's running out of places, Joe. She did Poland. Now the Russians have taken Budapest and are linking up with Tito's lot, I don't see Berlin risking her in that theatre. Italy is a shambles. And the West is pretty much of a shambles as well. The Krauts have got nothing left to oppose us. My bet is that she's going to be back in Berlin for Christmas. Get your man Johannsson there to wait for her. I am assuming that he is trained in executive action?'

'Yes, sir. So is the countess.'

'We know that, Joe. But we also know that she trusts us,

and you say that she has cause to trust Johannsson as one of us. That should give him sufficient advantage, providing he keeps his mind on the job.'

The two men gazed at each other for several seconds, then Andrews asked, 'You reckon either you or I are ever going to sleep again, sir?'

'Sit down,' Baxter instructed, and Clive obeyed. 'How is Belinda?'

'Still in a state of total mystification. As am I. I had promised her there was no possible chance of her meeting anyone she knew, apart from Anna, of course. So she runs slap bang into that fellow Werter, the chap who roughed her up in Lubeck last year. She reckoned she was in deep trouble, certainly when she was carted off to another Gestapo cell.'

'Where presumably she was roughed up again.'

'Well, she had to submit to another strip search.'

'She must be getting used to that by now.'

'Do you seriously suppose, Billy, that anyone, much less a refined woman, can ever get used to being stretched naked on a table and have some lout put his fingers up her ass?'

'Probably not. But they didn't find anything. Not even her capsule.'

'She wasn't carrying a capsule.'

'What?'

'She didn't reckon she'd need it. She had no doubt that Anna would protect her. And thank God she didn't have it.'

'But Anna wasn't there. She was in Poland bumping off a few dozen Russians or whatever.'

'Your sense of humour does you no credit,' Clive pointed out. 'But that is the oddest thing of all, which neither Belinda nor I can understand. As you say, Anna was nowhere around. But after only a few hours in her cell, Belinda was released by Werter himself. He apologized for having arrested her in error, gave her her clothes, and told her she was free to go. He did suggest that she leave Germany just as rapidly as possible, but she was happy to do that. He even gave her a ticket to the Swiss border and a reserved place on the train.'

'As you say, very odd. The point is that she did not make contact with Anna.'

'As you have just pointed out, Billy, Anna wasn't there.'

'Quite. I am not blaming Belinda. I am merely stating a fact. A rather vital fact.'

'Say again?'

'Did you know that Donovan is in England?'

'No, I did not know that. What's on his mind?'

'I'm sure he has a great number of things on his mind. But there is one in particular.'

Clive frowned. 'How do you know this?'

Baxter commenced to fill his pipe. 'I have a man in the OSS set-up.'

'You, have a man in the American secret service?'

'He's not on the staff. He's a chauffeur. We had him apply for the job when your friend Andrews was setting up their office over here, provided him with impeccable references and what have you.'

'You know, Billy, there are times when I hate working for you. But there are other times when I am damned glad that the security of this country is in your hands. These people are our allies.'

'You mean,' Billy said, striking a match and puffing, 'we are their allies. There is a difference. And while I am fully aware that we could not exist without them, certainly right now, I am even more aware, as I have reminded you more than once, that the Yanks are inclined to do their own thing, and fuck everybody else. Like right now. Harry was on duty two days ago when Donovan landed. He drove Andrews to Hendon to pick the boss up, and then drove them back to the OSS headquarters in SW8. Donovan had something of such importance to say that he couldn't wait to get to the office to start telling Andrews what was top of his list.'

'And he said it in front of your man?'

'Not so far as he knew. All those cars of course have a glass screen, and that was closed. But Harry had long fixed that, and was able to overhear most of what was said. You know, of course that that business in Warsaw which Goebbels so happily publicized to the world was an attempt to snatch Anna. When it misfired, leaving six dead, the Kremlin apparently remembered that when last they had attempted to snatch her, in Washington, it also cost them six lives. That business has always rankled, the way Anna managed to get out of the States and back to Germany without being arrested, much less brought to trial. They damn well know there had to be connivance at a very high level. Now they're threatening to blow the story. Worse, when they get hold of Anna, as they intend to do, they are going to put her on trial with the maximum publicity, and spill every bean they have on her. And there are quite a few, beginning with how she got out of the Lubianka. Now, they may not be certain that the authorization not to charge her with the Washington deaths came from the President, but the threat sure has put the wind up the White House. It could blow Roosevelt's credibility. And as you know, they are also unhappy that she failed to carry out their assignment to get rid of Hitler, and they are even starting to buy Goebbels' version of events, that it was Anna who effectively quashed the coup d'état before it could take off.'

'So they would like to nab her and put her on trial themselves. We know that, Billy. But I think we have time to get to her and warn her as soon as she ceases her travels, and to get her out of Germany before anyone else.'

'You're missing the point,' Baxter said. 'They've changed their minds about putting her on trial. They reckon that might be far too dangerous.'

Clive frowned. 'So what is their solution?'

'What do you think?'

'And Joe went along with that? I can't believe that.'

'Because he once had something going for her? I suspect the operative word is once. Anyway, Harry didn't hear Joe decline the job. Well, he couldn't. He's an employee of the US Government just as we are employees of HM Government. We do what we're told, even if we don't like it.'

'If he thinks he can get rid of Anna just like that he's liable to wind up in a morgue along with half a dozen of *his* pals.'

'Delightful thought. Unfortunately, they reckon they have a trump. Anna still believes she is working for them. And they have an agent, that bloke Johannsson, who has been their go-between in the past, and who they reckon she trusts absolutely. All he has to do is get up close and personal.'

'What a shitting mess,' Clive said. 'I've a mind to . . .'

'Do what? If push comes to shove, these people have clout which we lack. All we can do is warn Anna.'

'For God's sake, Billy, that's what we've been trying to do for the past four months.'

'Well, now it has to be top priority. So . . . Belinda?'

'I'm not sure she'll go for it again, certainly if we can't guarantee that Anna will be there to field her. To ask her to go through that ordeal a third time is a bit much. And her trouble is, she doesn't know why they let her go the last time. If they've changed their minds, she could really be up the creek. Or in the nearest concentration camp.'

'If we can't use Belinda, who have we got?'

Clive considered. Then snapped his fingers. 'Laurent!'

'Who?'

'That Swiss chap who was going to help her escape. He seems devoted to her.'

'Just what do you mean by that?'

'I shudder to think. But he certainly wants to help. And he can go in and out of Germany as he pleases.'

Baxter knocked out his pipe. 'How much does he know about her?'

'Well, he knows she killed those two Gestapo thugs in Geneva. And thanks to Dr Goebbels, he now must know that she did for those Russians in Warsaw.'

'So he's a glutton for punishment. I meant, how much does he know about Anna's relations with us?'

'He knows she works for us, and thus he must know that she has been a double agent for some time.'

'But if he met her when she was acting as a courier for Himmler, he must be in cahoots with the Nazis.'

'I don't know the truth about that,' Clive admitted. 'He wouldn't tell me what he actually does for Himmler. But I can tell you what he does for a living: he's a banker. So it's quite possible that he's handling Himmler's investments, outside of Germany. That's what makes me feel that he can go and come without interference.'

'But you can't be sure where his loyalties actually lie, apart from, you hope, to Anna.'

'Isn't that what is important? Billy, he's our only hope. Don't let's forget that Johannsson, who masquerades as a Swedish journalist, can also come and go as he pleases. And the Americans are inclined to look for instant action.'

'I don't like it. It seems to me that just too many people who shouldn't are finding out just too much about how we work. I mean, you'll have to put him in the picture about the Americans. And if he were to turn out to be a rotten apple . . .'

'He's all we've *got*,' Clive shouted. 'And anyway, I don't think I need to mention that Johannsson works for the Americans. Wherever Laurent's sympathies lie, he has to be against the Russians.'

'You'd better wear your thermal underwear,' Baxter recommended. 'It's snowing in Switzerland.'

Laurent listened to what Clive had to say, his face expressionless. 'You'll forgive me for being confused,' he admitted. 'I thought that Great Britain and the United States are allied with Soviet Russia against Nazi Germany?'

'We are.'

'Yet you are saying that Soviet Russia wish to execute Anna. Your number one agent in Germany.'

'I don't blame you for being confused, Herr Laurent. The point is that the Russians do not know that Anna is our agent, and I don't think it would make a lot of difference if they did. It so happens that three years ago, on the orders of her Nazi masters, Anna made an attempt on the life of Marshal Stalin. Obviously she didn't succeed, but she managed to escape the country. They have been after her ever since, and their feelings have been rather accentuated by her habit of killing, virtually on sight, all of the people they send to arrest her.'

Laurent regarded him for some seconds without speaking, so Clive went on. 'Had you known that when you and she, ah, first got together, would it have made a difference?'

'To wishing to get close to Anna? I don't think so. I already knew that she killed those two men in Geneva. But despite the fact that she seems to kill people who are actually your allies, you continue to employ her, and indeed, you are prepared to go to any lengths to preserve her.'

'Wouldn't you?'

'Touché. Tell me, you have no doubts that she is working for you, and not the Nazis?'

'For God's sake, Laurent, you know the score. She works, or she appears to work, for the Nazis because they hold her family.'

'I know this is what she has always claimed.'

Clive frowned at him. 'She was bringing her family to you, when something went wrong.'

'That is the assumption we have made, yes.'

'Well,' Clive said. 'I seem to have made a serious mistake. And so has Anna.'

Laurent smiled. 'You do not know all the facts.'

'Oh, yes?'

'As I told you when last we met, Anna has been visiting me, on an irregular basis for more than a year, bringing certain instructions from Herr Himmler. I am not at liberty to discuss these with you. But Herr Himmler apparently has no more use for my services. He sent Anna to me last July to terminate our relationship.'

'My God! And . . .?'

'I am still here? That is because she did not carry out her assignment, and indeed told me of it. In exchange for which she asked me to help her get her parents out of Nazi hands. As you know, I agreed to this. However, the plan did not work, for whatever reason we do not know. The point I am making is, we also do not know what she told Himmler. That she did not carry out her orders? In which case he would hardly have agreed to her being made Minister of Morale. Or that she did carry out her orders, in which case he must think I am dead.'

'Shit! You mean, if you were to turn up in Berlin . . .'

'I very much doubt Herr Himmler will suppose that I am a ghost. Although he may resume his interest in making me one.'

'Shit!' Clive said again.

'However, I have a colleague who might be prepared to carry your warning.' He studied Clive's expression; there could be no doubt what was going through his mind; he was a secret service agent, who was being asked more and more to forget about the secret part in order to save the life of *his* chief agent. A woman with whom there equally could be no doubt that he was in love. That was a problem which would have to be dealt with in due course. But was it a problem? On the one hand a man who was clearly about twice Anna's age, by no means good-looking, and a no doubt underpaid civil servant even if he had a glamorous sounding job, and on the other a man only a few years older than her, handsome and sophisticated, with a bulging portfolio – even if she did not know that yet – with whom she had shared what had to be some of the most passionate moments of even her life. There could surely be no comparison. So, back to the question: apart from the thrill of the chase, the pleasure of beating another man to the winning post . . . was she worth the risk?

But she was certainly worth preserving, if it could be done *without* risk, at least to himself. And it was an intriguing situation. 'You say this man Johannsson is known to Anna. Do you mean that they have worked together?'

'No. She does know of him professionally. But we are afraid that she may trust him as a friend.'

'And you believe that he has been commissioned to murder her. Anna has always given me the impression that she is very capable of looking after herself.'

'She is. But she is also inclined to trust those she regards as her friends. As you seem to have found out, Herr Laurent.'

'Again, touché. And this man, this Johannsson, is employed by whom? The Russians?'

'We agreed that you should know nothing more than the essentials. All that is required is that a message be got to Anna that Johannsson has been assigned to kill her. I think, as you have said, that we can leave the rest to her.'

'As I will be unable to deliver this message personally, will she believe my messenger?'

Clive drew a deep breath. He was breaking every rule in the book. 'He should tell her that he comes from Belinda.'

'Anna!' Himmler embraced her. This was now becoming an increasingly nauseating familiarity, overshadowed, in her experience, by the fact that men who embraced her usually had bed in mind. After three years? Then he must be overcoming his subconscious fear of her. 'It is so good to see you.' He held her at arm's length, retaining his grasp on her shoulders. 'You are like a breath of fresh air. No, no. Like the sun, rising out of my office floor.'

She supposed he could be right. She had taken off her sable and its matching hat on entering the room, and today she was wearing her pink frock, with her hair loose on her shoulders.

'Come, sit down.' He gestured her to the chair before his desk, then seated himself behind it, rested his elbows on the blotting paper. 'You have heard the news?'

'Roosevelt's re-election? Yes.'

'The Americans seem to be intent upon making him dictator

for life. It is very disturbing. Had he been replaced by someone not so friendly with Churchill, as should have happened, it would have had to be to our advantage.'

'How is the Führer taking it?'

'Surprisingly calmly. He holds the opinion that Roosevelt is a mental defective in any event, as a result of his polio. Anyway, he is more concerned with events closer to home. As should we all be. We were so distressed to hear about your sister. Those swine. Do you think she is dead? They have made no announcement about it.'

'That is because they made a mistake in taking her instead of me. To announce it would make them look like fools.' As for whether she is dead, she wondered, would that not be preferable to a lifetime of torture at the hands of someone like that little bitch Olga, supposing she was still around? *She* had determined that she had to write Katherine off in her endeavour to rescue her parents, but she had still held a vague hope of being able to get her too out, at the end. Now . . .

'But you are bearing up magnificently, as one would expect. You have proved a true heroine of the Reich, eh? We have had nothing but glowing reports of your tour.'

'Thank you, Herr Reichsführer. I don't think I did all that much good. The men I spoke with may have been pleased to see me, but almost without exception they were exhausted, and their morale was non-existent. They do nothing but retreat, retreat, retreat. And always there are more and more enemy soldiers coming after them, more and more tanks, more and more aircraft. The aircraft are the worst. Their fighter-bombers attack everything that moves, all day.'

'You almost sound as if you have personal experience of these attacks.'

'I do have personal experiences of these attacks, sir.'

'What? You were told not to expose yourself to enemy action.'

'That is the point I am making, Herr Reichsführer. It is not possible for anyone to be within a hundred miles of the front line, in either France or Poland, without being constantly exposed to attack.'

'My God! But you are not hurt?' He peered across his desk in search of bandages.

'No, sir. I am not hurt, thanks to the unfailing gallantry of the men protecting me. But I knew I was coming home, whenever I had had enough. Those men know they are not coming home. If only they could look up and see the Luftwaffe taking on the Spitfires and the Typhoons and the Mustangs . . . but there are never any German planes to be seen.'

Himmler was studying her, frowning. 'You have not, I hope, revealed these . . . observations to anyone else?'

'No, sir. I have not.'

'Very wise. The Führer wishes to see you.'

Oh, lord, Anna thought. It must have registered in her expression, because Himmler added, 'I do not think he will wish sex with you. I do not think he is capable at this moment; he has still not fully recovered from that explosion in July, and he has a lot on his mind. I know that he is planning some huge operation which he believes will alter the course of the war in our favour, although he has not told me the details. All of which means that his moods are uncertain. So please be careful what you say to him, and please do not attempt to contradict anything he may say to you.'

'I understand, sir. May I ask if I am now to resume my duties here?'

'Yes, indeed. We shall have to find you a new secretary, eh? But first, I would like you to undertake a little trip for me.'

'Sir?' Her heart leapt. But he could not possibly be sending her back to Switzerland as he obviously believed that she had carried out his orders as regards Laurent.

'I know,' he said sympathetically. 'You have just returned from an arduous tour and would like to put your feet up, eh? And so you shall, as soon as you come back from Stockholm.'

'Stockholm?' Anna's heart was doing handsprings again. The last time she had been sent to Stockholm she had been able to contact MI6, and although Clive had been unavailable, she had had that amusing meeting with Baxter. The important thing was that she would be able to re-open contact, bring them up to date with what had happened in July, and find out what they wanted her to do next. Of course, that visit had also included her encounter with three over-eager Gestapo agents who had attempted to arrest her on suspicion that she was fleeing the Reich. They had been thoroughly unpleasant men, and she had had no compunction about sending them to hell, even had they not been Gestapo, a force for which she held an in-built hatred at all times. But that situation was extremely unlikely to arise again.

'I know,' Himmler said, more sympathetically yet. 'I am again sending you to the North Pole in the dead of winter. Still, you survived the last trip, did you not? And it is urgently necessary for you to deliver a letter to Count Bernadotte. You liked him, didn't you?'

'Yes, sir.' She had indeed liked the handsome middle-aged man who had entertained her with such studied elegance the previous January, had been unfailingly polite, and, whatever his private feelings, had shown neither an overt interest in her as a sex object nor criticism of her as a representative of the Nazi Government. But that she had made an impression had been revealed at their second luncheon, when, before saying goodbye, he had indicated that if she ever needed his help in the collapse he could clearly see ahead, he would be happy to respond. If only she could take advantage of that.

'As before,' Himmler went on, 'it will be necessary for you to wait for his reply.'

'Of course, sir.' At least two, perhaps three, days in the peaceful sanity of Sweden!

'There is, however, a problem,' Himmler said.

Shit! she thought. 'Sir?'

'You will not yet be aware of it, but the Swedes have closed their ports to our shipping. Rats, eh, deserting the sinking ship, after appearing to be our friends for so long. These measures include the Malmo–Lubeck ferry.'

Anna could not restrain herself from asking, innocently, 'Are we a sinking ship, Herr Reichsführer?'

He gazed at her for several moments, then said, 'That is how some people view the situation, certainly. They are entitled to have their opinions, however erroneous, providing they do not air them publicly, at least here in Germany. The point is that this move creates certain obstacles to our people getting in or out of the country. These obstacles are not insuperable; they merely involve certain delays. You will have to travel by a Finnish vessel. This actually is something of an advantage, in that it will deliver you to Stockholm itself, after a pleasant overnight voyage.'

Surrounded by Soviet submarines and aircraft, Anna thought. But she said, 'That does indeed sound very nice, sir.'

'I knew you would be pleased. I have booked a room for you at the Falcon Hotel. You enjoyed that the last time, did you not?'

'It was very comfortable,' Anna acknowledged.

He handed her an envelope of Swedish money, an open return ticket on the Finnish ferry, and a passport. 'It will be necessary to use a false identity.'

'With respect, sir, I am known both to Count Bernadotte and at the Falcon as the Countess von Widerstand.'

'Oh, quite. The Finnish passport is simply to get you in and out of the country without any questions being asked. Once you are in, you can revert to your true identity, certainly when you are with people who already know you.'

Anna flicked open the little booklet, looked at her photograph, and read the details. 'Anna Halfden. Well, that is quite a pleasant name.'

'I thought so. Well, the Führer is waiting. There is a car to take you to the Chancellery. I would like you to report to me tomorrow morning to receive the letter for Bernadotte before you leave for the journey to Rostock.'

'Of course, sir.' Anna got up. 'Heil Hitler!'

'Heil. Ah . . . Anna?'

She had reached the door, here she paused. 'Herr Reichsführer?'

'You, ah . . . never discuss with the Führer any of our private arrangements?'

He had asked her this so often before. She suspected that he was close to being a nervous wreck. 'Of course I do not, sir.'

'Not even when in, ah . . . the throes of passion?'

The man has got to be joking, she thought. Throes of passion, with Hitler? 'No, sir. Not even then.'

'Because you keep yourself under such perfect control at all times, eh? It is one of your great assets. But then, you have so many great assets. You are a treasure. Oh, by the way, during your absence you had a visitor.'

'Sir?'

'That Italian woman you became, ah, friendly with last year, after you had interrogated her.'

'Bel— Claudia was here?'

Clive must indeed be desperate to find out what happened, she thought. But here?

'Bold as brass,' Himmler confirmed. 'Just walked up the steps out there and asked to see you. You know, Anna, while I am prepared to overlook your, ah, peccadilloes in view of your multiple talents, I really cannot condone them if they are, well, displayed too publicly.'

'I assure you, sir, that I really never expected to see Signorina Ratosi again.'

'I think that is a very wise decision. I mean, suppose the Führer were to find out? You know how he feels about, well . . .'

'Homosexuality,' Anna suggested, helpfully.

'Absolutely.'

'May I ask, sir, when she discovered that I was not here . . .?'

'Oh, she was arrested.'

'Sir?'

'She had the misfortune to run into her old friend Werter. Now I would not like you to get worked up about this, Anna. He recognized her, and for some obscure reason she was travelling under an assumed name. Ah . . . Valentina Sabatini. Apparently she was claiming to be a relative of the novelist. I suppose she was trying to be discreet. Well, you see, you can't blame Werter for being suspicious. I mean, he remembered her from last year.'

'Yes, sir.' Anna kept her emotions under control with an effort. 'So where is she now?'

'I imagine she is back in Italy, or Switzerland, or wherever it is she comes from.'

Breath rushed through Anna's nostrils. 'You mean . . .?'

'I told him to let her go.'

'Thank you, sir. May I ask, for how long she was in Werter's custody?'

'I'm afraid, a few hours. You know what Werter is like. But I am assured that she was not harmed. Well, not in any permanent fashion.'

'I see,' Anna said, grimly.

'So there you are. As I said, you really have to keep your personal, ah, weaknesses separate from your job. I will see you tomorrow.'

'Inspector Martine is here, Monsieur Laurent, ' said the male secretary. 'He telephoned for an appointment.'

'Of course,' Laurent said. 'Inspector. Come in.' He shook hands. 'Have a seat and tell me what I can do for you.' He was watchful, but not concerned; in Switzerland, top bankers, provided they broke no Swiss laws, were very seldom troubled by the police.

'It is good of you to see me, monsieur.' The inspector, a little man with grotesquely long bushy eyebrows, settled himself. 'It is rather a delicate matter.'

'Feel free.'

'Well, sir, I believe a few weeks ago you released from your service a Mademoiselle Essene.'

A little alarm bell tinkled in Laurent's brain. 'That is correct.'

'The lady seems to have been upset by this.'

'I am sure she was. She had been with us for some time, and had always proved reliable. But then, I think it was something to do with an unhappy relationship, she began to drink, very heavily. This was obvious from her breath. Well, as I am sure you understand, Inspector, my business relies absolutely on confidentiality. I simply cannot afford to employ anyone who might be indiscreet.'

'I entirely understand, monsieur, which is why I said it is a delicate matter. But she claims to have information on a police matter, in which you might possibly be involved.'

Damnation! Laurent thought. The bitch! But his face remained calm. 'And she has apparently forgotten that when she came to work for us, she signed a confidentiality agreement.'

'I know, monsieur. It is very embarrassing. But what am I to do? The information she has lodged has to do with our ongoing investigation into a peculiarly vicious crime that took place here in Geneva nearly eighteen months ago.'

Laurent needed time to think. 'And you are still investigating it?'

'Well, monsieur, it was a murder. A double murder. The files on murder cases are never closed.'

Laurent came to a decision as to how this had to be handled. It was very regrettable, but then, he had just about made his final decision as regards Anna anyway. This was the decisive development: there was no way he intended to become embroiled with the police. 'And I am supposed to be involved? You will have to tell me about it, Inspector.'

'The murders took place in a bedroom in the Gustav Hotel. The bodies of two men were found by the chambermaid when she entered the room in the morning. All identification had been removed. The bodies, as I say, were found just after nine in the morning, but medical examination indicated that they had been dead for some twelve hours. Now, just before nine that morning, the occupant of that room, registered as Mademoiselle Anna O'Brien, bearer of an Irish passport, checked out. It seems obvious that she was the murderess, but from the nature of the crime and the way it was carried out, it also seems certain that this young woman was a highly professional assassin. But having left the hotel she disappeared into thin air. We had a description of her, but it was of no great value: tall, good-looking, in general fair although she seems to have kept her hair concealed, and carrying what seemed to be a heavy attaché case.' He paused.

'And now,' Laurent said, 'a year and a half later, Mademoiselle Essene has come to you and told you that a woman answering that very rough description, and carrying such a case, called at this office on the morning after the murder. At nine o'clock.'

'Well, monsieur . . .'

'Of course you had no choice but to follow it up. And you were entirely correct. The woman who came here that morning was the Countess von Widerstand.'

Martine's jaw dropped. 'The woman from Warsaw?'

'That is one way of putting it, certainly.'

'Good God! And you knew this when . . .?'

'No, I did not know this when she came to me. I only knew that she was an agent for Herr Himmler, bringing me certain items that he wished me to dispose of for him. As you will understand, Inspector, I am not at liberty to reveal these confidential items to you, or anyone. But I had absolutely no idea that she had just killed two men. Nor would I have considered it possible, in such an attractive and apparently innocent young woman. You see, while she was here she changed her clothing, and her appearance, entirely, and just left as soon as our business was completed.'

'You did not find this suspicious?'

'I'm afraid not. I knew that she was a German courier, and I assumed that she had her reasons for wishing to change her appearance. It is not my business to be inquisitive about my customers, only such of their affairs as they bring to my notice.'

'But when you heard of the murders . . . we publicized the description of the woman we were looking for.'

'I'm afraid, Inspector, that unlike, it seems, my erstwhile receptionist, I simply do not have the time to follow criminal matters, certainly when they are not connected to me. I have said, it would never have crossed my mind that such a woman would be capable of killing anyone.'

'And now we know that she has eight deaths to her credit.'

How little you know, Laurent thought, and remarked, 'Incredible.'

'Yes. Tell me, sir. Have you seen this woman since? I mean, here in Switzerland.'

'Yes, I have.'

'Sir?'

'We have met, let me see, it would have been twice, I think, in Lucerne, again when she was bringing certain items from Herr Himmler for deposit in my bank.'

'Would either of these meetings have been after her exploits in Warsaw?'

'Certainly not. Had I known about that, well . . .'

'You would have come to us, of course. But do you think there is any chance of her returning again?'

'I have no idea.'

'But you will bear in mind that, regardless of anything that might have happened in Poland, which I suppose we could put down to the exigencies of warfare, she is wanted for murder here in Switzerland.'

'Inspector, you have my assurance that should the Countess von Widerstand appear in Switzerland again, I will immediately contact you.'

'Thank you, sir. And thank you for your time. Good morning to you.'

Laurent allowed him five minutes, then summoned his secretary. 'Send Gregoire to me.' The young man appeared five minutes later. 'All ready for your trip?'

'Yes, sir. I am looking forward to it.'

'Well, I am sorry to say, it's off.'

'Sir?'

'Circumstances have changed, Gregoire. The young lady no longer needs a warning.'

'Oh.' He was crestfallen. 'Yes, sir.'

'But thank you anyway for volunteering.' Laurent watched the door close and leaned back in his chair. I am doing her a kindness, he thought. A quick death at the hands of a Russian assassin is surely preferable to a long, drawn out and highly publicized trial, with certain conviction at the end of it.

But what a waste.

Incident in Stockholm

'What a climate!' Joseph Andrews stood at the window of the Embassy, and looked out at the snow clouding over Stockholm. 'And you have to live here all the year.'

'Does it not snow in America, sir?' Lars Johannsson asked.

'Sure it does. But not too often in Virginia, which is where I come from.'

'It is very pleasant here in the summer,' Johannsson suggested.

Andrews studied him. Johannsson was a big man, over six feet tall, with bland features and a shock of yellow hair. The ultimate Aryan, he supposed. And he did not look like a killer, nor, he equally supposed, did he so regard himself. But he had been lethally trained, and as an agent his record could not be faulted. 'So. Tell me what you feel about it.'

He returned to sit behind the desk he had been allotted together with this private office. Johannsson was already seated before it. 'I think it is a great tragedy, sir. She is such a beautiful and charming woman.'

'How well do you know her?'

'I have only met her three times.'

'Did you ever make advances to her?'

Johannsson flushed. 'I did suggest, at our last meeting, that I would like to know her better.'

'And what did she reply?'

'I can remember exactly, sir. She said: "Business before pleasure, Herr Johannsson."'

'That sounds like Anna.'

'I must admit, I did not take that as a final refusal, sir.'

'Few men do. So she is beautiful, charming, and she turned you on. That is par for the course. Will you do it?'

'If you tell me that it is essential, sir, and order me to do it, I will do it.'

'It is essential, and I do order you to do it.'

'Very good, sir.'

'But there is another question. *Can* you do it?'

'Sir?'

'I know that you are considered an expert, Mr Johannsson. But do you actually know anything about the countess? Do you suppose that it will be a simple matter of a bullet or a knife in the heart, or a cord round the neck?'

'I will let the circumstances decide which is the most appropriate, sir. But I have an idea how it can be done, while arousing the minimum of suspicion, at least before a post-mortem.'

Andrews frowned. 'You are thinking of poison. That *would* require getting up close and personal. What poison would be virtually undetectable?'

Johannsson felt in his pocket and produced a bottle. 'I am never without this. Or the hypodermic.'

Andrews' frown deepened as he took the bottle. 'Good God! I never knew you were a diabetic. And you reckon . . .?'

'Yes, sir. An overdose of insulin, taken by a non-diabetic, is lethal and has the added advantage of being painless. The subject merely collapses.'

'Hm.' Andrews handed the bottle back. 'Do you know in what capacity the countess is employed by the Germans?'

'She is Herr Himmler's personal assistant, sir.'

'She is Herr Himmler's private killer, Mr Johannsson.'

Johannsson frowned. 'You mean because of that business in Warsaw? I do not believe that story. It is Nazi propaganda. I mean, she is a woman, sir.'

'There are some cases where male chauvinism can be as fatal as an overdose of insulin,' Andrews pointed out. 'I have been privileged to see the countess at work, briefly. It is always, very brief. She could shoot a finger off your hand at twenty-five yards while you were still levelling your weapon. I have also seen her break a neck with a single blow. And I know that she has accounted for more than thirty people in her short life.'

Johannsson stared at him.

'If you disbelieve me,' Andrews said, 'I am sending you to your death. If you undertake this mission, you must believe everything I have just said. You have one very great advantage. The countess knows that you work for us, and at the present time she believes that she also is working for us. Therefore you should be able to get very close to her, as you plan to do. But if you make any move she regards as sinister, she will kill you without a moment's hesitation. Believe me, her greatest asset is that she never hesitates.'

Johannsson licked his lips.

'So?' Andrews asked.

'I will carry out this mission, sir. And I will remember what you have told me.'

Andrews nodded. 'Very good. Now how are you going to get to her?'

'It will not be difficult, once I am in Berlin. I know where she lives, and I know her habits.'

'I meant, how are you going to get to Berlin, now that there is no ferry traffic between your countries?'

'That is not a problem, sir. This closing of our ports to German shipping is a diplomatic exercise designed to convince the Allies that we are really on their side. There is still a good deal of traffic between Sweden and Germany. For example, there are Finnish ships out of Stockholm all the time. And a number of them visit Rostock. I will simply take passage on one of them.'

'Very good. Well, then . . . it only remains for me to wish you good fortune and a safe return.'

They did not shake hands.

'Anna!' Hitler's left arm was apparently still not usable; he carried it mostly behind his back, where the constant twitching could not be seen. He squeezed her fingers with his right hand. 'Seeing you is like inhaling a breath of fresh air. And you have been such a success. The reports are glowing.'

'I tried to do my duty, my Führer.' How are the mighty fallen, she reflected. Like her, like just about everyone in Berlin, Hitler had been forced to take to the cellars, even if on a more elaborate scale than anyone else had been able either to afford or achieve. The area beneath the Chancellery had been turned into an underground palace, two floors of communications, conference halls, bedrooms, and of course, an elaborate suite for the Führer himself, on the lower level, beyond the reach of any bombs.

He gestured her to a settee, and sat beside her. Even Bormann had been excluded from the room. 'As you always do. Having you back is like a ray of sunshine coming into my office.'

Another would-be poet, she thought.

'Now tell me what observations you have made on your journeys? Apart from killing Russians left, right and centre, eh? But the swine got away with your sister. That is a tragedy. And I never even met her.'

'That is a shame, sir. You would have liked her. Now . . .'

'She can only be avenged. This will be done, Anna. I give you my word. Your observations.'

'Yes, sir. I am bound to report that I found morale disturbingly low.'

Hitler nodded. 'I know.'

'And then, the news of *Tirpitz* . . .'

'Ha! All that time, and money, and above all, steel, poured into *Bismarck* and *Tirpitz,* and where are they now? At the bottom of the sea. I had my doubts from the beginning, you know. Battleships are obsolete. If there is anything that this war has proved, it is that simple fact. But that fool Raeder talked me into it. Possess the two most powerful warships in the world, he said, and even the Royal Navy will be afraid of us. So what happens? *Bismarck* goes off to prove how good she is, and is sunk in a week. *Tirpitz* spends almost the entire war trapped in her Norwegian fjord, because she is too valuable to be risked at sea, so the RAF sink her at her moorings. Doenitz knew from the start they were colossal white elephants. U-boats, he said. There is the key to victory at sea. Put all our naval resources into U-boats. And he was right.'

His voice had been steadily rising, as his face had been taking on that familiar mottled appearance, and Anna braced herself for one of his terrifying explosions, but suddenly he calmed again.

'Morale,' he said. 'Yes. Morale. It is suffering here as well. I blame Josef.'

'Sir?' She knew he regarded Goebbels as his most faithful aide.

'You know that I gave him command of the home front so that I could concentrate on the war?'

'Yes, sir. He told me that himself.'

Hitler regarded her for several seconds, and she wondered if she had said too much. But he had to know that she had had sex with the doctor, more than once.

'He is too inclined to go to extreme measures,' the Führer grumbled.

Talk about the pot calling the kettle black, Anna thought.

'Almost the first thing he did with his new powers,' Hitler went on, 'was to close and ban all cinemas, all theatres, and even the opera. I think that was a mistake. Nothing relaxes people more than a good film, or uplifts them more than a piece of rousing music. Now he is calling for the formation of a Home Guard. He points out that this is what the English did in 1940. Well, do we want to start copying our enemies? And it is a defeatist strategy. These old men and young boys, armed with obsolete rifles, where they can be armed at all, and wearing arm bands instead of uniforms, they cannot be used in any offensive military sense. Thus it stands to reason that they can only be used to defend the Fatherland, after an enemy has *entered* the Fatherland. But I have declared that this will never happen. Woolly thinking.'

'Yes, sir.' Anna could think of no reason to defend Goebbels, even if she realized that these measures were but a continuation of the plans he had outlined to her back in July, to make every German, man, woman and child, understand that they were fighting for their lives.

'But it is the Wehrmacht that matters,' Hitler said. 'Aren't they happy about Arnhem? You know about that?'

'I have been told of it, sir. I was in Poland when the battle took place.'

'It was a great victory. Montgomery tried to get into Germany itself by means of an airborne invasion. One has to admit that it was a bold plan. It involved an entire army. But we were ready for him, and smashed him. I believe it is the first time he has ever been defeated. I should have thought that would have boosted morale.'

'Yes, sir. When I visited the area a few weeks ago I found

those troops in better spirits than any others.' Which was not saying a great deal, because their version of events had been somewhat different from Hitler's. Montgomery himself had not personally been in command of the Allied troops at Arnhem, simply because it had not been an army but a division, and everyone knew that the attempt to seize the Rhine bridgehead had failed because, simply by chance, an entire SS division had been placed in that area a couple of weeks before the attack, to rest and recuperate after serving on the Russian front, something of which the Allied planners had been totally unaware.

'Now,' Hitler went on, 'I intend to bring the war in the west to an end.'

'Sir?' Anna was taken aback. Was he going to seek peace? No wonder Himmler had been confused.

'Do you realize, Anna, that with Normandy far behind them, all the Allied logistical supplies, from ammunition to oil, have to come through Antwerp? It is the only port big enough to handle the required volume of traffic. Seize Antwerp, and the Allied advance will come to a halt. More, they will not even be able to sustain themselves where they are. They will have to fall back, and it is a well-known military maxim that when an army is forced to retreat after a series of advances, it falls apart. That is what happened to Napoleon's Grande Armée in 1812, after he had captured Moscow. That is what happened to Rommel's Afrika Corps in North Africa in 1942. And that is what is going to happen to Eisenhower and Montgomery in Flanders in 1944.'

Anna's brain was reeling. 'But . . . can you do it, my Führer?'

'Of course. I am not going to tell you the plan, not even you, Anna. But I can tell you that I have assembled ten Panzer divisions, the pick of the German Army, to do the job. It will be 1940 all over again. We shall smash them as we did then. It will be the greatest battle in history.'

'I am sure of it,' Anna murmured. Was she going to get to Sweden in time to warn the British? Even if she had to feel that the idea was crazy. If Hitler really did still possess ten crack Panzer divisions, surely they should be deployed in the East, against the Russians. 'May I ask when this offensive will begin, my Führer?'

'Ha ha. I am not going to tell you that either, Anna. Not even you.' He was like a small boy with a new toy. 'But it will be before Christmas. And when it is over, when we have won, I shall send for you. I will be well again then. And we shall celebrate.'

Bormann waited in the ante-chamber. 'Have you made the Führer as happy as always, Countess?' he asked.

'You will have to ask him that, Herr Bormann,' she replied.

'Perhaps one day you will be able to spare the time to make me happy as well,' he suggested.

Anna was surprised. He had not shown the least interest in her when they had previously met. But perhaps that had been because of the Warsaw crisis. As she knew he was married and had several children, there had to be a libido somewhere inside that lifeless façade. Although making love with him would have to be like embracing an over-ripe cheese. 'You will have to ask your wife about *that*,' she said, and left the room.

Presumably, Anna thought, as she took the train to Rostock, she had made another enemy. But she was more concerned with Hitler's plans. Or were they just dreams? To believe one's own propaganda had to the greatest weakness a man could have. But there was always the possibility that it was not just pie in the sky. Certainly the Allies had to be warned that such a blow was impending. But she was on her way to do that.

And to find out about Belinda. The poor woman had undoubtedly undergone yet another horrendous experience. Five hours in the custody of Werter! When she would have been anticipating . . . Anna remembered the curious, but fascinating, mixture of sophistication and innocence, the uncertainty and then the willing complicity she had revealed to the passion that had suddenly flowed over her. Anna wondered if she had ever told Clive? Because she knew that a great deal of what she had done had been with at least a subconscious desire to drive a wedge into a relationship she regarded as the only real threat to her future. Not that she hadn't enjoyed it.

And that future still had to be reached. She slipped her hand into her shoulder bag to finger the envelope which lay beside her Luger. Himmler's hand had trembled as he had given it to her, as his voice had been anxious as he had reminded her that it was to be delivered to no one except Count Bernadotte, and that no one was to know the contents except the count, that she was to defend its secrecy by whatever means she considered necessary.

These were the instructions that he gave her whenever she was on a mission for him, whether it had involved delivering money to Laurent or on her previous visit to Stockholm in January, and so far it had cost, directly, five lives. As they had all been Gestapo agents they did not lie on her conscience, but it was a relief to feel that on this trip there should be no necessity for bloodshed. And there was the possibility that within forty-eight hours she might be in Clive's arms.

Or would Baxter himself come again? She remembered how absolutely terrified he had been, in January, at finding himself alone in a bedroom with her. That had not been fear of her as an assassin, but as a woman. She wondered what Mrs Baxter was like, supposing there was a Mrs Baxter? Perhaps one day she'd find out.

The ship was buzzed from time to time by Russian aircraft, but as she was flying the Finnish flag she was not attacked. If the Finns had fought on the German side during Barbarossa, the utter collapse of the invasion over the last year had involved them in a humiliating peace. Anna had a good dinner and was early in her bunk, to be on deck the following morning to watch the ship negotiating its ways through the ice floes into Stockholm; icebreakers constantly roamed up and down to keep the passage open.

But as she remembered from her last visit, this was a country of peace and tranquillity, of undamaged buildings and un-cratered streets, of people who, if genetically serious – no doubt because of their climate – were also unafraid of what each day might bring . . . and were also capable of letting their hair down and enjoying themselves with an almost innocent pleasure that was so sadly lacking in cities like Berlin or Paris, or even Vienna.

Customs formalities were brief and brisk, then she was in the main hall of the building, carrying her valise – she had no heavy luggage as she was only going to be here for a few days – and passing the long, orderly line of passengers waiting to board the vessel for its return trip.

And pausing in surprise as a tall man left the line and came towards her; he also carried only a valise. 'Countess?'

'Sssh,' she said, and hugged him; it was such a splendid and reassuring encounter, actually to run into both a friend and a colleague so unexpectedly. 'I am Anna Halfden, a Finnish journalist. But it is so good to see you, Lars. Listen, we have to talk. Where are you going?'

'Nowhere, now.'

She pulled her head back. 'Explain.'

'I was going to Berlin, to see you. But as you are here . . .'

'What a magnificent coincidence. And we could have so easily missed each other.'

'Yes,' he said, thoughtfully.

'But things always turn out for the best. Well, nearly always.' She tucked her arm through his as they left the building. 'You mean, Joe sent you? Thank God for that. I had nearly given him, and you, up. What is he after now?'

'Tell me first what you are doing in Sweden?'

'The usual thing, acting as Himmler's messenger girl. But I have information for you. I was going to try to contact Belinda, but it will be even quicker through you.'

'Of course.' He ushered her through the outer doors into the freezing morning. 'You should cover up.'

Anna unwound her silk scarf and wrapped it round her nose and mouth before again securing it. With her hair concealed beneath her fur hat, this left only her eyes exposed, and these she now covered with her dark glasses; the glare from the snow was startling. 'I really am not known to anyone here, you know,' she said. 'Well, with one or two exceptions, and we are hardly likely to bump into them.'

'I was thinking of your complexion, Countess.' He waved a taxi to a halt.

'Anna, please,' she reminded him. 'Where can we go, to talk?'

'My apartment.' He waited for her to get into the car, then gave the address to the driver. 'You do not mind this?'

'I am booked into the Falcon, but as long as I am there for lunch. I have some calls to make.'

'To London?'

'Yes.' She rested her glove on his and squeezed. 'They are still my number one employers, Lars. And I must make contact whenever I have the opportunity. But I also have to call the people I am here to see, and set up a meeting.'

'Who are these people?'

'I'm sorry, Lars. I don't think I should tell you that.'

He considered for a moment. 'But you will give London this information you have.'

'Of course. But I am quite happy to give it to you first. It is as important to Washington as it is to London.'

'We are here,' he said.

Slipping and sliding on the compressed snow, chains clinking, the taxi had turned down several streets and now came to a halt before a block of flats. Relaxed in the company of such an old friend, Anna had not kept track of the route.

'Cover up,' Johannsson reminded her.

She had allowed the scarf to slip down to her chin; now she reinstalled it, and he held the door for her, then paid the driver. He unlocked the front door and ushered her into a very clean hallway; to one side there was a staircase. 'I'm afraid it's a walk-up,' he apologized. 'But it's only two floors.'

'I think I can mange that.' Anna went first, and reached the second landing. Johannsson unlocked the door and she entered a spacious bed-sit. 'Cosy,' she remarked, regarding the bed. 'You wouldn't have designs, I suppose?'

'Now, you know that I have had designs from the moment we met.' He closed the door, and made sure that the latch had clicked into place.

The apartment was centrally heated. Anna took off her scarf and hat, fluffed out her hair, then laid her sable across a chair; she was wearing a high-necked green woollen dress. 'But you know that it always has to be, business before pleasure.'

'But after the business?'

She had no desire to get together with anyone save Clive, but she didn't want to upset him. 'Who knows?' She sat in one of the two armchairs. 'Tell me what Joe wants.'

'Would you like a cup of coffee?'

'You mean, real coffee? Oh, yes, please.'

There was a small stove to one side, close to the dining table; there was also a sink and a cupboard. He turned his back on her as he lit the gas and filled the kettle, but asked over his shoulder, 'How do you like it?'

'If it's the real thing, I believe in the Brazilian motto: coffee should be as hot as hell, as black as night, and as sweet as sin.'

'Absolutely.' He fussed, his back still turned to her, while the kettle began to boil. 'So, no milk. But do you mind if we do not use sugar?'

'How can it be sweet without sugar?''

'It is simply that I am not allowed to take sugar. I am a diabetic.'

'Oh, I'm sorry to hear that. You mean you have to inject yourself every day, and that sort of thing?'

'I'm afraid so.'

'That must be ghastly. But then, how do you make your coffee sweet?'

He turned, holding up the little jar. 'It's a sweetener. It has the same effect as sugar. Well, nearly. I use it all the time.'

Anna shrugged. 'I'll try anything once. Actually, I have an idea that I use too much sugar, anyway.' She smiled. 'If I am not careful I may wind up a diabetic like you.'

Johannsson dropped little tablets into the cup, and then poured and stirred. 'Which no doubt accounts for your sweetness.' He handed her the cup and saucer.

'As you say the sweetest things. But we really need to get on. What was Joe's message?'

He sat in the chair opposite her. 'Do you like the coffee?'

Anna lifted the cup to her lips, replaced it in the saucer. 'It needs to cool.'

'I thought you liked it as hot as possible?'

'I do, when it is poured. Heat brings out the flavour. But burning my lips and mouth does not. You were saying?'

'Well . . . you know that the war will soon be ending. With Germany's defeat.'

'That depends on who you listen to.'

'That is our opinion, anyway,' Johannsson said. 'Joe is anxious to know your plans. So am I,' he added. 'I mean, you know you cannot risk being taken by the Russians.'

'I do know that,' she agreed.

He watched her raise the cup again, and this time she sipped.

'How much do you know of my situation?' she asked.

'That the Nazis hold your parents as security for your loyalty?'

'Ah. Joe told you that, did he?' This time she drank, and made a face.

'Don't you like it?' He was anxious.

'It's bitter.'

'The sweetener always tastes like that at first. You'll get used to it.'

Anna drained the cup. 'Fortunately, I don't have to. At least, yet.'

'You mean you would not like another cup?'

'Frankly, no. I think I'll stick to sugar. So. Joe . . .'

Her mouth closed and he watched her face seem to freeze at the same time as her eyes glazed. She stared at him as she tried to focus. 'You unutterable bastard,' she muttered, and then her entire body sagged, her head lolling against the back of the chair, the cup and saucer falling to the floor.

Johannsson remained staring at her for several seconds, taking in the utter beauty that was so suddenly and completely at his mercy. For the moment it was utterly modest, but the bodice of the dress rose and fell with a fascinating rhythm, and her legs, which she had crossed when she sat down, were now drifting apart, and he looked at flawless stocking-clad calves. While the face, so relaxed, seemed more beautiful than ever, with her mouth slightly open as she breathed. Only the glory of her eyes was for the moment absent.

He realized that he could just stare at her for ever and after some minutes had to force himself to move. He picked up the cup and saucer and put them in the sink, then lifted her left arm, pushed the sleeve of her dress away from her wrist, and took her pulse. It was only slightly slower than he would have expected. So, all he had to do was inject her with the insulin overdose he had planned. And that would be that. It was quite incredible that it should have turned out this way, that he should be able to complete his mission, so easily and with absolutely no risk to himself.

Then he remembered that she had not told him what her important information was. Well, it was too late now. And he did not suppose it had been that important. Not compared with the completion of his mission. He went to the bedside table, took out the bottle and the hypodermic needle. He had used a needle every day throughout his adult life. Carefully he filled it to the limit. That was way above the danger level, but he thought that to make sure he would have to do it twice.

Needle in hand, he turned back to her, again stared at her. In five minutes, all of that consummate femininity would become only a memory. But . . . a memory! Was it not

possible to have an even greater memory, a memory to carry
with him for the rest of his life? She was out cold, and was
surely not going to come round for at least an hour. And in
that time . . .

He laid down the needle, knelt at her feet, slowly took off
her shoes, placing them neatly together at one side. Then he
slid his hands up her calves, over her knees, and up her thighs,
carrying her dress with them, aware of feeling almost sick
with desire, with the knowledge of what he wanted to do,
what he *could* do, because there was absolutely nothing to
stop him.

He stood up, put his hands in her armpits, and lifted her,
grunting with the effort: she was heavier than he had expected
in so slender a body. But that had to be because she was so
completely inert. Panting, he dragged her across the room and
laid her on the bed, lifting her legs to stretch them out. He
contemplated her for another few moments, then rolled her
on her face, turning her head to one side to make sure that
her nostrils and mouth could reach the air.

He wanted her to be fully dressed with no evidence of any
sexual assault when found, so he unbuttoned the dress with
great care, and then with even greater care extracted her arms,
one by one, from the sleeves. That done, he rolled her on her
back again, straightened her arms at her sides, and slowly
drew the dress down her body, scooping her hips from the
bed to slide the material past, before removing it altogether,
and laying it carefully across one of the chairs.

Time for another contemplation of his victim, committing
her to memory for the rest of his life. He wished he had a
camera, but he knew that would have been too dangerous
in any event. No trace of what had happened here today
could ever be found by the police; only the fact, as would
be established by the post-mortem, that when he had left
her alone for a few minutes to go out, she had taken an
overdose of insulin. No one would know whether it had
been deliberate – he would tell them that she was a depres-
sive and had been in a disturbed state, which was why he
had gone out to buy some alcohol to cheer her up – or
whether she supposed the bottle she had found in his bedside
drawer had been heroin.

He got her arms through the straps for her camiknickers,

eased them down with the same care as he had her dress, although this time he paused as he uncovered her breasts, and then her stomach, and then her groin. Now she was *there*, waiting for him. But not quite ready. He unclipped her suspender belt, rolled down the stockings, laid them on the table beside the camiknickers.

She was entirely his, a sight he did not suppose he would ever forget. Or would ever want to forget. To destroy such perfection would be a far greater crime than merely carrying out an execution. If only there was some way to keep her alive, a perpetual prisoner. But there wasn't. And after all, she wasn't *quite* perfect. He knelt on the bed beside her, peered at the blue stain on her flesh, then tentatively touched it with his forefinger. It felt as smooth as the rest of her, but he estimated that it was a bullet wound. Someone before him had sought to destroy her. He wondered who it was, and what had been his fate?

It was time. If he didn't do it now he never would. He undressed, rapidly, scattering his clothes about the room. He wanted to lie on her, naked, feel her naked body against his. So it would not be pulsing with life, but nothing was ever truly ideal. He knelt again, between her legs, holding them up to gain his entry, having to force his way in. To his disappointment he was spent in seconds.

He pushed himself off her, sat up beside her, panting. So that was it. Now . . . he turned his head and looked into her eyes. Her open eyes! He drew a deep breath and was struck a paralysing blow over the kidneys.

Johannsson fell off the bed on to his hands and knees on the floor, coughing and almost choking. He had never felt such pain.

Anna sat up in turn, and swung her legs off the bed. Her brain was still groggy as she had only just woken up; she had acted instinctively, as she had been taught, and even when lying down had managed to get nearly all of her hundred and thirty pounds into the blow.

She put her bare foot in the centre of his back and pressed. His knees gave way and he collapsed on his face, but he was breathing more evenly.

'If it interests you,' Anna remarked, 'that kidney punch was taught me at SS training school, by someone called Cleiner.

A thoroughly detestable fellow, but you must admit that he knew his stuff. It doesn't kill, of course, just paralyses for a few minutes. But I could have killed you, by a blow to the neck. Again taught me by Dr Cleiner.'

'Why didn't you?' Johannsson groaned.

'Don't tell me you wish to die?'

'I deserve to.'

'A hit man with a conscience? Do you think you deserve to die for raping me, or because you intended to kill me? You did intend to kill me, didn't you? When you had finished enjoying yourself?'

Johannsson licked his lips. He was twice her size, but he was not going to risk trying to get up while she was in a position to deliver another blow like that.

'I really would like to know,' Anna said.

Johannsson drew a deep breath. 'I thought, as you were going to die anyway, it didn't matter what I did to you. And . . . well . . .'

'You have always wanted to get your hands on me,' she agreed, sympathetically. 'Well, now you have achieved your lifetime ambition. How were you proposing to do it? Kill me, I mean?'

He didn't reply, so she moved her foot. 'Don't get up,' she advised, 'or I will hurt you *very* badly.' She went to the table, picked up the bottle of insulin, and then the full hypodermic. 'Of course. How simple. Now tell me who you are working for. I imagine the Soviets have got to you.'

Johannsson drew another deep breath and pushed himself up with all his strength. But he was too slow. Anna crossed the room in two strides and swinging her right leg with the speed and precision of a champion footballer, crashed her bare toes into the side of his head. 'Ow!' she remarked.

Johannsson had gone down without a sound, and lay on his back, arms outflung, again gasping for breath.

Anna stood above him. 'I did warn you,' she pointed out. 'You were going to tell me something.'

Slowly he raised his head. Blood dribbled from his cut mouth.

'You are making life very difficult for yourself,' Anna told him. 'Try to remember not to move.' She went to her shoulder bag, took out the Luger and the silencer, screwed it into place.

Johannsson had by now got his eyes back into focus, and

now he rolled on to his side. Anna returned to him, put her foot on his shoulder, and pushed him on to his back again. He stared at the pistol. 'I'm quite good with this thing,' she said, and knelt, grasped his penis, and held the muzzle of the silencer against it. 'If you don't tell me, now, I will blow this off and leave you to bleed to death. That would be both painful and humiliating, don't you think?'

To her surprise, he was actually reacting to her fingers. But that was probably because he had got his brain working. 'Andrews,' he muttered.

'*What* did you say?'

'Joe Andrews,' he gasped. 'He didn't want to do it. I didn't want to do it. But it was orders from Washington.'

Anna released him and sat on the bed. Her knees felt quite weak, and she could feel her stomach solidifying into a vast lump. 'Am I allowed to know why?'

'They think you have betrayed them. Hitler did not die. And now, the Russians are claiming that they, the Americans, have been protecting you. They say you have killed fourteen Russians. The Russians are America's allies . . .'

'And they regard that alliance as more important than me,' Anna mused. 'Well, I suppose that is logical, if, in my opinion, mistaken. Thank you for your cooperation, Lars.'

His eyes were enormous. 'What are you going to do?'

'I always take one step at a time. But there is something I would like to explain to you. I hate being raped.'

'I accept that. I behaved terribly. I was so overwhelmed with your beauty . . .' He looked into her eyes. 'I will make it up to you, I swear it.'

'You won't, you know. You are begging for your life. But the other eight of the nine people who have raped me are dead. And the ninth is going to die, some time soon. And then, I hate people who try to kill me. All of those are dead. And most of all, I hate people who I have believed to be my friends, who have said that they are my friends, who then betray me.'

He licked his lips. 'Anna . . . I . . .'

'So, I will see you in hell.' She shot him between the eyes.

Anna unscrewed the silencer and replaced it and the gun in her bag, along with the spent cartridge. There was a small bathroom at the back of the apartment; she had a shower and douched herself, then dressed. She put on her gloves, washed the cups and saucers, carefully dried them, and replaced them in the cupboard. She had not touched anything else, save the bottle of insulin. This she also washed and dried, and replaced it and the hypodermic in the bedside drawer. Then she put on her coat and hat, her dark glasses, and wrapped her scarf around her face, slung her shoulder bag and picked up her valise. She left the apartment and went down the stairs.

As she reached the lobby, the street door opened and a woman came in, carrying a shopping bag. She smiled at Anna and made a remark, but as Anna did not speak Swedish she could only assume that it was good morning, so she grunted in reply and went outside. She had no clear idea where she was, but the breeze was off the harbour, so she walked towards it and soon found herself on a busy street. She hailed a taxi and uttered the two words, 'Falcon Hotel.'

A few minutes later she was in her room and able to take off her outer clothes. She had refused to think while making the brief journey, nor did she want to now. But it was becoming very necessary.

She kicked off her shoes and threw herself on to the bed, lying on her face across it, absolutely still. As she had told Johannsson, she was very angry. But she knew she was also suffering from shock. Joe Andrews, she thought. Acting on orders from Washington, which could only be Donovan. Who took *his* orders from the very top. Well, fuck them, she thought. But did that very top also control the British attitude? Although the room was pleasantly warm, she was still chilled from the outside temperature, but now she suddenly felt very hot.

If that were so, she had nowhere to turn, nowhere to run, nowhere to hide, except Laurent. She rolled on to her back. It couldn't be so. Clive had known about the failure of the attempt on Hitler's life when she had spoken with him in July. He had been as supportive and loving as ever. And if the Warsaw incident had not then happened, he had always known all about Chalyapov and Colonel Tserchenka, and about the six NKVD agents in Washington.

But so had Joe Andrews and Wild Bill Donovan! The sudden atmosphere of mistrust with which she was surrounded would have been amusing had it not been so desperate. When she considered that the only people she was betraying, as she had done for the past five years, were the Nazis, who trusted her absolutely, while the Americans, for whom she had tried to do her best, wanted her killed! Joe Andrews, to whom she had once given her all – admittedly only out of gratitude for his help, in getting her out of the Lubianka – who had welcomed her to his home in Virginia, who had once told her he loved her more than life itself, and who had now, when the chips were down, decided that his loyalty to his job and his superiors were more important than any promises he might have made to her.

She realized that her fists were so tightly clenched her nails were eating into her palms. This was getting her nowhere. She had a lot to do, a lot to find out, and it had to be done now. Firstly, Bernadotte. He would at least bring a breath of sanity to her world.

She placed the call, remembering that the last time she had been here she had been unable to contact him right away. But this time, the moment she mentioned the name Countess von Widerstand she was put through.

'Countess?' Bernadotte was obviously surprised. 'It is good to hear your voice. But where are you calling from?'

'The Falcon.'

'But . . .'

'I know. I should not have been allowed in. Are you going to have me deported?'

'Of course I will not do that. Am I to suppose . . .?'

'I have something for you from the Reichsführer, yes.'

Bernadotte was silent.

'Don't you want to receive it?' she asked.

'Frankly, Countess, no.'

'Oh!'

'That is because I am quite unable to accomplish any of the things he desires. But I would very much like to see you again, and so I will accept the letter. Will you lunch with me?'

'I would like that very much.'

'Excellent. Then . . .' She gathered he was either looking at his diary himself, or was silently communicating with his secretary. 'Unfortunately, as I received no warning of your coming, I have an engagement today. Will you still be in Stockholm tomorrow?'

'I shall be in Stockholm until I can deliver the letter to you, and until I receive your reply.'

'My car will pick you up at twelve tomorrow.'

'Thank you, sir. I look forward to that.'

She hung up, then put through a long distance call to London. 'Good morning, Amy.'

'Good . . . oh! Countess?'

'I need to speak with Mr Bartley.'

'Yes, ma'am.'

A moment later Clive was on the line. 'Anna? Oh, my dearest, dearest girl.'

The words that above all she wanted to hear.

'Are you all right?' he asked.

'Shouldn't I be?'

'Well . . . that Warsaw business . . .'

'Do you condemn me for that?'

'Of course I do not. Those bastards had it coming. But now . . . we've been moving heaven and earth to get in touch with you.'

'So I understand. Is Belinda all right?'

'Mention the name Werter to her and she is inclined to start breaking the furniture. But listen, you haven't been in touch with anyone else, have you?'

She had to be absolutely sure. 'Who did you have in mind?'

'Well, your friend Laurent was going to try to get a message to you.'

'I have heard nothing from Laurent.'

'Hm. And, ah, nothing from the OSS?'

'I need to speak with you, Clive, very urgently.'

'Oh, shit! You mean . . .?'

'It is not something that I can discuss over the telephone. Listen. I am in Stockholm, and I can stay here for two days after today. Can you come to me?'

'I'll be with you tomorrow.'

'Thank God for that. I am having lunch with someone, but I should be back here by four at the outside. May I assume that you will be staying the night?'

'If you'd like me to.'

'I want that more than anything else in the world.'

'So do I. Anna . . . are you all right?'

'I will be all right, Clive. After I have seen you.'

Friends

At last she could relax. Clive knew something about the OSS. But then, so did she. That would be sorted out. And he had been trying to reach her. Poor Belinda, she thought again. As for Henri, she had no idea what was going on there; he surely would not dare show his face in Germany, much less Berlin. But they would be able to sort that out as well. And they would be together. And she would be able to tell him about Hitler's offensive. And about Joe! She wondered what his reaction would be to that. And now she had thirty-eight deaths on her conscience. No, never on her conscience. With the exception of those three British agents in Prague four years ago, everyone had been an enemy. And she was fighting a war. As she had thought on several occasions before, if she had been a fighter pilot she would have been decorated.

She undressed and went to bed. Although she had slept soundly on the voyage, her experiences this morning had left her exhausted, and she was also feeling some discomfort from Johannsson's forced and unassisted entry. She knew that would wear off, but she had no desire for any company, had a room service dinner, and again slept heavily. The knowledge that tomorrow she would see Clive took away all the stress.

But first, there was Bernadotte. She wore the same dress as the previous day – no one save Johannsson had seen it beneath her coat – and tucked her hair out of sight as before. His car was punctual, as always in the past, and then she was in the restaurant, which she remembered very well; it was apparently his favourite.

He bent over her glove, a tall, very distinguished looking man in early middle-age, wearing uniform; she knew that he was a descendant of the Napoleonic general, who had been chosen King of Sweden, and had founded the present dynasty.

He had been waiting for her in the lobby, and regarded her with a quizzical expression as she divested herself of her coat, hat and gloves, handed them to the waiting maitre d', took off her dark glasses, and fluffed out her hair. 'You do not change,' he remarked.

'Would you like me to change?'

'I personally would hate you to change, Countess. However . . .' He escorted her to their table, set in a discreet alcove.

'I don't think you can stop there, Count,' she suggested as she sat down.

He spoke to the waiter in Swedish, and champagne cocktails were brought. 'Shall we order?'

'I am in your hands. Linguistically.'

He gave a little smile and instructed the maitre d'. Then they gazed at each other for a few moments. 'May I ask you a question?'

'Of course,' she agreed.

'How long have you been in Sweden?'

'I arrived yesterday morning. By Finnish ferry.'

'Of course. Using a false name. You had no trouble with Customs or Immigration?'

'None.' Little alarm bells were beginning to tinkle. 'Should I have?'

'Well, you see, since last you were here . . . was it really last January? You have become a rather high profile figure. Oh, I know that you have always been a high profile figure in Germany, and I suppose, after the Bordman business, in England as well . . . Do you regret any of that?'

Anna sipped her cocktail. 'As I am sure you understand, Count, I serve the Reich. I cannot afford to have regrets. If it will make you happier, while I was married to Ballantine Bordman I was a good and compliant wife. In every way.'

His flush faded rapidly. 'But you were betraying him.'

'I was betraying his government,' Anna said carefully. Because that was not entirely true; she had still been married to Bordman when she had had that unforgettable encounter with Clive. How she wished that she could explain that to this so honourable and upright man. But as she couldn't . . . 'Are you saying that my reputation has spread to Sweden?'

'It could hardly avoid doing so, after the splash Dr Goebbels made about your exploit in Warsaw.'

'I would have preferred it had that not happened.'

'The incident, or the splash?'

'Count Bernadotte, those men tried to kidnap me.'

'Why should they do that?'

Anna grimaced. But he now knew sufficient about her to make further concealment absurd. 'I was once sent to Moscow to assassinate Stalin.'

He stared at her. 'You?'

Anna finished her cocktail, and the first course was served. The waiter poured the wine, and she drank that as well.

'I'm sorry.' Bernadotte said, signalling the waiter to refill her glass. 'I did not mean to upset you.'

'I was thinking that I had upset you.'

'You surprised me. I mean . . .'

'I don't look like a professional assassin. I suppose that is my greatest asset.'

'But . . . ah . . . Stalin . . .'

'Is obviously still very much alive.'

'So you don't always carry out your assignments.'

'In his case, I was betrayed before I could do so. So the NKVD got to me first.'

It was Bernadotte's turn to finish his wine. He signalled the waiter to refill them both. 'You were arrested by the NKVD? And you are sitting opposite me now, apparently in the best of health?'

Anna made a moue. 'They're still looking for me.'

'You know, Countess . . . or may I call you Anna?'

'Oh, please.'

'I realized last January, when we first met, that you were quite an exceptional young lady. I thought, how lucky Himmler is to have such a treasure working for him.'

'And now you've changed your mind,' Anna suggested.

'Now . . . I would like to spend about a week talking with you. But I suppose that's not possible.'

'I'm afraid not.'

Their main course was served, and the wine changed.

'Then may I ask one or two more questions now?'

'You may not like the answers.'

'I'd still like to hear them.'

Anna shrugged.

'This assignment, to, ah, eliminate Marshal Stalin. Was it . . .?'

'It was not my first such assignment, no.'

'And you are still here. You must be very, very good.'

'I am the best,' Anna said, simply.

'It is difficult to doubt that. Now for the big one. Why? Are you that dedicated a Nazi?'

Anna gazed into his eyes. 'I do what it is necessary for me to do, Count Bernadotte.'

He returned her gaze for several seconds. Then he said, 'That relieves me greatly. But I'm afraid I am also a little confused. Perhaps you can help me. You may remember that we last lunched here on the seventh of January.'

'I remember it very well.' She began to anticipate what was coming next.

'Then you'll remember that although it was already dark when you left the restaurant, and very cold, you elected to walk back to your hotel. You said you wanted to *feel* the true Stockholm.'

'I am flattered that you should remember the conversation so well.'

'My memory has been stimulated. You told me you were catching the early train to Malmo the following day. I assume you did this?'

'Yes, I did.'

'That morning three German businessmen were found dead in the office they shared. They were apparently operating an import–export business.' His eyes never left her face. 'There was not a single clue as to why they had died. They had all been shot, with a single pistol, although there was another gun that had been fired. The pistols were still there, regulation issue Luger automatics. It appeared as if they had had a fight and exchanged fire, although the bullet extracted from the brain of one of the men came from the gun he was still holding, which suggested that having killed his two compatriots he then shot himself. It was quite a cause célèbre for a few weeks, but the case was never solved. I believe the police contacted the German Embassy to see if they could shed any light on the matter, but they did not appear to be interested.'

Anna sipped her wine.

'Of course,' Bernadotte went on, 'there could be no possible connection between the beautiful, glamorous, Countess von Widerstand, on a hurried visit to Stockholm, and this rather sordid event in a dingy office.'

'But you were . . . interested.'

'No. Not in that event. I mean, I thought of you only as a beautiful and glamorous woman. Until I read about Warsaw. But even then the idea was immediately rejected. Until, well . . . Have you read this morning's newspaper?'

Oh, shit, Anna thought. This man is too bright for his own good. 'I'm afraid I don't read Swedish,' she confessed.

'Of course you do not. Well, it appears that we could be facing another mysterious murder case. A man was found dead in his apartment yesterday afternoon. He was a Swede, named Lars Johannsson, and he appears to have been rather a strange fellow, who kept very much to himself. He was reputed to be a journalist, but no paper has admitted employing him. He also appears to have been fairly well-to-do, but no one has any idea where his income arose. And to cap it all, he was naked when he was found, and he had been killed by a single shot through the head. There is to be a post-mortem today, but the police are fairly sure that the bullet in his head came from a Luger automatic pistol, and also that he had had a sexual discharge shortly before his death. I hope you do not mind my mentioning these rather indelicate matters.'

'I do not mind in the least. All of this is in the newspaper? Your police must be very cooperative with the press.'

'Very little was in the newspaper,' Bernadotte said. 'I spoke with the detective in charge of the case. Would you like a cup of coffee?'

'I would love a cup of coffee.'

'And a brandy, perhaps?'

'Thank you.'

He signalled the waiter. 'I have ordered Hine Antique,' he said. 'Only the best for the best. You would not care to comment on what I have just said?'

'Would you care to comment on why you called the police in this matter? Am I about to be arrested?'

'Why should you be arrested?'

They gazed at each other, and the coffee and brandy was brought.

'My interest was aroused,' Bernadotte said, 'because of the extreme professionalism of the case. The police think it was a love affair that had turned sour. But of course their horizon is limited. And even they are surprised by the fact that there is no sign of anyone else having been in the apartment. Not a fingerprint, not a trace of who might have been there. If that was a crime of passion, the lady seems to have got over it very rapidly and very efficiently. Almost as if she had done that sort of thing before.'

Anna drank coffee. 'And you are certain it was a lady? Could it not have been a homosexual lover?'

'I suppose it could. But the police do have a lead.'

Anna put down her cup.

'One of the other tenants in the building, returning from her morning's shopping, encountered a woman just leaving. According to the police surgeon, this would have been very soon after Johannsson was killed.'

'So they have a description of a possible suspect?'

'Unfortunately not, from their point of view. This woman's face was entirely concealed behind dark glasses and a scarf, and her hair was out of sight beneath her hat. All they have is that she was unusually tall, and was wearing a full length dark coat and a matching hat. The witness thinks these were both genuine fur, but she cannot be sure. So they do not feel they are any further ahead.'

'And you did not offer an opinion?'

'I preferred not to. I would appreciate hearing your opinion, though.'

Anna finished her coffee and regarded the balloon of brandy. She understood that she could be in very deep trouble indeed. But this man had struck her from their very first meeting as genuinely wanting to be her friend. And nothing more than that. For her, this was unique. Of course he had been attracted to her by her looks and her personality, her charisma, but the attraction had been that of one outstanding human being for another, not of a man for a woman. If that was genuine, he could prove to be the most valuable friend she had.

Did she dare? But in view of the almost entirely accurate deductions he had already made, did she have any choice? She drew a deep breath. 'The three men that were killed last year were Gestapo agents.'

'And you shot them all, with three bullets?'

'I fired four shots, actually.'

'I see. Please forgive my innocence, but if you work for Himmler, aren't you Gestapo yourself?'

'No, sir. I am SD. I do not like the Gestapo.'

'I'm glad you said that. But . . .'

'The SD is even worse? I can't deny that, in certain directions. But we do not usually go in for torture.'

'Only for killing. Forgive me. But whether you like the Gestapo or not, you are basically on the same side. So weren't you, well . . . stepping out of line?'

'They arrested me when I left the restaurant that afternoon, and took me to their office. They wanted to know what was in the letter you had just given me. The Reichsführer had instructed me that no one was to read that letter. But they also intended to amuse themselves. I did not like that.'

'And they had no idea who you were, and more important, what you are. That was clearly unfortunate for them. And Johannsson? Was he also Gestapo?'

'No.'

Bernadotte waited.

'I'm sorry,' Anna said. 'I would prefer not to go into that.'

'Because he was your lover?'

'Johannsson was not my lover, Count Bernadotte. I thought he was my friend, and I was under the impression that he had some important information for me. So I accompanied him to his apartment, whereupon he drugged and raped me. I regard that as the lowest form of human behaviour. He also informed me that he had been sent to kill me.'

'And he also had no idea of who or what you were.'

'He should have had. A lot of men make the mistake of seeing me only as a woman.'

'Well, you can't really blame them. I would be very interested in knowing exactly what part he played in your life, before you ended his.' He gazed at her, but she merely sipped her brandy. 'Not possible?'

'I'm afraid not, sir. You know too much about me already. May I ask what use you intend to make of your knowledge?'

'I intend to make no use of it, except in so far that it may enable me to help you.'

'Why should you wish to do that? I am a self-confessed

murderess, and I serve the most wholly bestial regime that has ever existed.'

'The fact that you can say that is reason enough. But at the same time it distresses me in equal measure, that someone like you should find herself in such a position. I told you in January that if I could ever help you, I would like to do so. I will repeat that now.'

'I will remember those words with gratitude, sir. But I do not think it is possible.'

'Well, you know, I have an idea about that. You have a communication for me.'

Anna opened her bag and handed him the envelope.

'Would you forgive me if I read this immediately?'

'I would like you to.'

She sipped her brandy very slowly as she watched him slit the envelope with his unused butter knife, extract the two sheets of paper, and scan them. Then he folded them again, replaced them in the envelope, and put it in his breast pocket. 'As before, I assume that you have no knowledge of what he says?'

'None.'

'Well, I think you should know, that your master is endeavouring to arrange a separate peace with the Western Allies. If they are prepared to negotiate, he is prepared to overthrow Hitler and seize power before the Russians get into Germany.' He gazed at her. 'You do not appear to be shocked.'

'I have suspected that that is what he has had in mind for a long time. Do you think the Allies will be prepared to negotiate? With him?'

'Frankly, no. But he is virtually begging for my assistance. He wishes me to visit him in Germany so that we can discuss the matter. I would say that he is a very frightened man.'

'You would be right.'

'Is he your lover?'

'Himmler? Good God, no.'

'Yet you work for him, with utter loyalty.'

Can I tell him the truth? Anna wondered. But however much she liked this man, that would be an unacceptable risk. Certainly until she had seen Clive. 'I have no choice.'

He studied her. 'Another brandy?'

'No, thank you.' She looked at her watch. Three o'clock.

'I must be going. Thank you for a lovely lunch. I hope my company wasn't too indigestible.' She stood up. 'May I assume that you will have an answer for me in the next couple of days?'

'Your company was, as always, unforgettable, and I will give you my answer now. Tell Herr Himmler that if he will give me a place and a date, I will come to Germany to meet him. But I need him to give me a few weeks to sound out various Allied contacts of mine.'

'I'm sure he will be delighted with that answer.'

'Good. Now you must tell me the hold he has on you.'

'I cannot do that.'

'Yes, you can, Anna. If I am going to help you, I need that information.'

'I have told you that you cannot help me.'

'And I know that I can. Listen to me. We are both agreed that Herr Himmler is a very frightened man. He wants only to save his own skin. And he believes that I am the only man who can help him accomplish that. This letter is couched in terms of desperation. Well, I have absolutely no desire to help him. I believe he deserves everything he might be going to get. But if I tell him I will do everything I can, well . . . quid pro quo, would you not say?'

'And you would do that for me? Why? Do you wish . . .?' her eyes were enormous.

He smiled. 'Much as it might be desirable, I think it would be a mistake, for both of us, were we to sleep together. I am more interested in preserving a unique personality, for as long as is possible.'

Anna continued to stare at him for several seconds. Then she sat down again.

Bernadotte's car dropped Anna in the hotel forecourt. She thanked the driver, went into the lobby, and to the desk for her key. She had drunk more than she had intended for lunch, and that, combined with what had happened, had her feeling quite light-headed. Not for the first time she had placed the fate of her family, her future, her life, in the hands of a man she felt she could trust. But she had done that with Joe Andrews.

'There is a gentleman to see you, Countess,' the clerk said.

Anna turned, her right hand instinctively dropping to the catch for her shoulder bag . . . and gazed at Clive, who had been sitting on the far side of the room, and now stood up. Her knees felt weak as she went towards him: it was well over a year since last she had seen him.

He held her arms and kissed her on the forehead. 'You said four o'clock.'

Anna looked at her watch; it was nearly five. 'My God! I'm sorry. Lunch took longer than I expected.'

'Lunch being with whom?'

'Let's go upstairs.'

There was a lift attendant, and they could do no more than gaze at each other, although Clive did say, 'You grow more beautiful every time I see you.'

She blew him a kiss, and a moment later they were in her bedroom and she was in his arms. He took off his hat and then hers and kissed her forehead, her eyes, her nose, her chin, each ear. Then he kissed her mouth, slowly and deeply. 'I thought I had lost you.'

'I'm not that easy to lose.'

'You don't know the truth.'

Anna released him and took off her coat and scarf, then her gloves. 'I'm finding it out, the hard way.'

Clive also removed his coat. 'Will you tell me?'

'I have an awful lot to tell you.' She sat on the settee. 'But I'd like you to tell me first. Like what exactly our American partners are up to.'

He frowned as he sat beside her. 'You know about that?'

'Isn't that why you put Belinda through the wringer again, so that she could warn me?'

'But she never got to you.'

'True.'

He held her hands. 'But at least the bloody Yanks didn't get to you, either. Let me put you in the picture.'

'Would you like a cup of tea?'

'I'd love a cup of tea. But . . .'

Anna got up and rang room service. 'I seem to remember they do a very nice currant bun,' she said, and ordered some with the teas. 'I had rather a boozy lunch,' she explained.

'But –' he scratched his head – 'Anna, your life is in danger. Aren't you interested in that?'

Anna sat beside him again. 'I am very interested in that. But it is yesterday's news, literally. At least for the time being.'

'You've lost me. You mean you've heard from Joe? And he managed to warn you?'

'I have heard from Joe,' Anna said. 'Indirectly. Through Johannsson.'

'Johannsson? But he was sent to kill you.'

'I know. He told me.'

'Good lord! But he didn't. Thank God there are some decent people left in the world.'

There was a knock on the door. Anna got up and opened it, and the maid placed the tray on the table. 'Thank you,' Anna said, and closed the door again. 'I don't suppose she understood me. Very few of these people speak English. I've forgotten: one lump or two?'

'Two. Anna—'

'And you must try one of these buns.' She handed him the cup and saucer and a plate.

'For God's sake, Anna, this is serious. Deadly serious.'

'I know,' she agreed, again sitting beside him with her own cup and plate. 'We have to decide what we are going to do about it. What *you* are going to do about it.'

'Yes. I think I need to know, firstly, exactly what Johannsson told you.'

'Eat some of your bun,' Anna recommended. 'You'll love it. Johannsson didn't tell me a lot. He did a lot, though. He drugged me, and when I was unconscious, he raped me. Unfortunately for him, he spent so much time enjoying himself that the drug wore off sooner than he had expected. He was about to start killing me when I woke up.'

Clive appeared to be choking on a currant.

'Drink some tea,' Anna recommended.

He did so.

'He was going to shoot me full of insulin,' Anna explained. 'That is difficult to tell from natural causes at first sight.'

'But . . . oh, Jesus!'

'Yes,' Anna said. 'I shot him. I would probably have shot him even if he had not been about to poison me.'

'The police . . .'

'Know that a tall woman in a dark coat and hat was seen leaving Johannsson's apartment shortly after he died. The woman's face was concealed behind a scarf and dark glasses, and her hair was also concealed by her hat. They also apparently have no idea what Johannsson does, or did, for a living. So they are a little short of a motive.'

'How do you know all this?'

'I have friends apart from MI6 or the OSS. Now, you knew this was going to happen.'

'Yes,' Clive said, miserably. 'We knew some months ago that Washington had come to the conclusion that you had sold us all down the river. That's why we sent Belinda to warn you. But at that time they were talking only of arresting you when the war is over.'

'How do you know that?'

'Joe told me.'

'And you accepted that?'

'I said, Billy and I felt we had ample time to warn you not to surrender to the Americans. But then back in October, we discovered they actually intended to eliminate you to prevent you being put on trial and revealing things the Administration felt would be embarrassing.'

Anna refilled their cups. 'Joe told you this, did he?'

'No he did not. He knew we wouldn't accept it. We have a man in the OSS headquarters in London.'

'With friends like your two lots, enemies really are superfluous. And you say this was in October?'

'We've been busting a gut ever since trying to get to you. As I told you, we even got your friend Laurent into the act. He felt it would be too dangerous for him to enter Germany, but he said he had an absolutely reliable man who would contact you.'

'You told Henri that the Americans were out to kill me?'

'No. We couldn't risk being that trusting. The message was that you should not, under any circumstances, allow Johannsson to get too close. We didn't identify Johansson's employers.'

'I wonder what he made of that? Not that it matters. As I said, his man, whoever he was, never showed. So tell me what happens now.'

'I can understand that you're unhappy with the situation . . .'

'I think you should say that again,' Anna suggested. 'So that we can both die laughing.'

'We can sort it out.'

'Tell me about it.'

'The important thing is that the Yanks must not find out that we know what they have in mind. Now, who knows that you are in Stockholm?'

'This hotel staff, obviously. And Folke Bernadotte.'

'Would he be the friend you mentioned?'

'Yes. And he is a very good, very faithful friend.'

'You seem to have one of those stashed in every country in Europe.'

'If you are going to be juvenile about this, Clive, I think the best thing you can do is catch your plane back to England.'

'I'm sorry.' He put down his cup to hold her hands. For a moment her fingers remained tense, so much so that he almost thought she would pull away from him. Then they relaxed. 'I've been beside myself with worry these last two months. I imagine you have too.'

'Not in the same way. I didn't know what was happening. Now I need to know what happens next. You're my controller.'

'Right. So . . . we can't confront the Yanks. They hold all the high cards. But if your friend Bernadotte is as reliable as you claim, and the Stockholm police really do not have any idea what Johannsson did for a living, it's going to take them a while to find out what happened to their boy. Obviously he belongs to a branch of the OSS here, and they'll start making enquiries when they don't hear from him, but if they don't know you were here when he died they can't make the connection. By definition, secret agents have secrets about their personal life.' He grinned. 'I should know. I'm one of them, remember?'

And he doesn't know half of mine, she reflected.

'So it's difficult to see how they can relate Johannsson's death, here in Stockholm, with you, when you're supposed to be in Berlin.'

'I suspect they will eventually,' Anna said. 'But that doesn't solve the overall problem. When they discover that Johannsson is dead, whether or not they have any idea why he died or who did it, they'll have to realize that he didn't complete his mission. And send somebody else.'

They gazed at each other.

'OK,' she agreed. 'I can probably take him out as well. But

what happens when the shooting stops? How long do you think we have?'

'Well, everything is snowed up at the moment. But come the spring . . .'

'Shit!'

'That's still four months away,' he protested.

'No, no. We've been so caught up in my problems that we haven't got around to the big one.' She told him of Hitler's plans.

'Wow! Before Christmas? Today's the fifteenth.'

'Will you be in time to warn them?'

'I'll be in London tomorrow morning. But . . . Shit!'

'I know. You really should go now. Is your plane standing by?'

'Yes. But Anna—'

'I want you too. But this is too big.' She looked at the window; the curtains were drawn, but it was obviously dark outside. 'Can you take off in the dark? And in sub-zero temperatures?'

'No problem. Well . . . what a fuck-up. And your problem is still on hold.'

'Not entirely.' She told him of Himmler's plans and hopes.

'That's a non-starter.'

'Which is Bernadotte's opinion as well. However, he's prepared to do what he can.'

'So he would like to end the war. I don't think he can do it any sooner than military action, certainly if we can nip this latest plan in the bud.'

'He's doing it to help me, Clive. He reckons he can bargain with Himmler: his help in exchange for my parents.'

'I really must meet this character. But hold on a moment. If he does that, Himmler will know you have confided in him.'

'Yes. But he is confident that Himmler is so desperate for his help he'll go for it, if he can be made to understand that unless he releases me, there isn't going to *be* any help. It's a risk But it's a way out. And I have a big trump of my own.'

'Which is?'

'I'm Hitler's favourite woman, right now. If I were to tell the Führer that Himmler is negotiating for a separate peace under his leadership, that would be the end of him.'

'Can't you do that anyway?'

'It wouldn't do me much good if Hitler doesn't know where my parents are. In any event, I don't think the Führer intends to let me go any more than Himmler does. Threatening to tell him about Bernadotte is a bluff, but Himmler is in such a nervous state, and is so terrified of his Führer, I think it would work.'

'It never ceases to amaze me,' he said, 'what a remarkable woman you are. You seem able to cut your way to the core of every problem, instantly, no matter how deep your emotional involvement.'

'You say the sweetest things. Or perhaps you don't mean it that way. Now listen. There is no way I can contact you until this is over. If it works, I will make for Switzerland, with Mama and Papa, and contact you from there.'

'You mean you will go to Laurent.'

'Now, Clive . . .'

'No histrionics. And I won't argue that I may be slightly prejudiced. But I must tell you that I was a little disappointed when I saw him in September and asked for his help in warning you of the situation.'

'Because he wouldn't risk coming to me himself?'

'Not just that. There was a . . . hesitancy in his commitment to you.'

'As you say, you're prejudiced. I know what you mean. I have observed it myself. But he is a banker by profession. Bankers are by definition men of cautious attitudes, not instant decisions, and even less, instant action.'

'Will you tell me exactly what he does, for Himmler?'

Anna considered, then nodded. 'I take large sums of money from Himmler to Laurent, and he places it in a number account for future reference.'

Clive gave a low whistle. 'Now that is very interesting.'

'You can't use that information, Clive. As I said, he is still my safest route out of Germany.'

'And you trust him.'

'Yes, Clive, I trust him.' Her mouth twisted. 'If only because there is no one else I can trust. Except you. And, I hope, Billy.'

'On those last two you can rely.'

'Even with Uncle Sam breathing heavily down your neck?'

'Even with the Devil himself sitting on our laps. You tell

us when you are ready to come out, my dearest girl, and we will look after you. You have my sacred oath. Now –' he sighed, and kissed her – 'I suppose I had better be on my way.'

Anna held his hands. 'Is fifteen minutes going to make that much difference?'

The Lysander droned into the darkness. Ice was forming on the cabin windows, but the de-icers were keeping the wings from being over-burdened. Clive looked at the luminous dial of his watch. 1930. The pilot had said they'd be down by 2030. So just an hour to go.

An hour to think? Or to remember? He would far rather remember. Because he never knew when there was going to be a next time. She was the most compelling woman he had ever known, or could ever imagine. And she lived her life on a constant knife-edge, which he accepted was the only way of life she had ever known. So, supposing he extricated her, what was he going to do with her? He knew what he wanted to do with her: place her somewhere no one else would ever reach her, save only himself.

But to attain that happy state . . . he could only hope Billy would have some ideas, because he knew enough about the Americans to understand that they had very long memories, and if they had determined that Anna was an enemy, and when the war ended they would be, as seemed inevitable, the greatest power in the world, and a power on which Britain would have to depend for her survival, much less recovery, in a post-war world with the threat of Russia looming perhaps just across the English Channel . . .

And the problem was already in his lap. What he had to tell Baxter the moment he landed, could only have come from Anna. They could claim that she was not the only agent they had in Germany, but anyone who knew anything approaching the reality of the situation, which certainly included the OSS, had to know there was only one source in Germany from which such secret information could have come. One would have supposed they should be grateful, if they were able to check the German onslaught. But the OSS also knew that MI6 had lost normal contact with Anna, and thus the information had to have been passed verbally, face to face. Once their thoughts took that road, they would know it could only have been either Switzerland or Sweden, as Anna had no access to any other neutral country. And when they discovered that the agent they had sent to eliminate her had mysteriously been murdered in Sweden . . . well, they weren't that dumb. In fact they weren't dumb at all.

Yet the warning had to be delivered. He looked at his watch; 2020, and they were descending. He looked out of his window again, and gulped. What he had thought was thickening ice was, he realized, actually thickening cloud. He leaned forward and tapped the pilot on the shoulder. 'Can we get down?'

'Ground control says not at Hendon: visibility is down to a hundred feet.'

'So do you have an alternative?'

'They say to try Biggin. It's a bit clearer there. We don't have too much choice.' He indicated his fuel gauge; the needle was hovering above empty.

'Shit!' Clive muttered.

'Ah, we'll get down, Mr Bartley.' The voice was reassuring. 'We always do.'

Clive remembered being shot down over the Mediterranean, on his way to Anna rather than on his way back. That pilot had said something similarly reassuring minutes before the Italian fighter had opened fire.

The seat-belt light came on, and he thrust the steel tongue into the buckle socket. He still could not see a thing, even by peering forward over the pilot's shoulder and past the propeller; he was not even sure he could see the propeller.

The pilot was chattering into his radio, but with the mike against his mouth Clive could not make out what he was saying. Then he turned his head. 'No go. We're out of fuel.'

As he spoke the engine died. 'So what do you recommend?' Clive asked, pleased with the steadiness of his voice; the air was not his natural environment. 'Do we jump?'

'We're too low. But they have us on radar. They tell me we're over some open country. I'm going to bring her down there. Don't worry; we don't have enough fuel left to catch fire. Just sit tight until we stop bumping.'

The pain was in the background, almost obscured by the waves of the analgesic drug drifting through his mind. But that was not strong enough to take away his sense of urgency.

Clive blinked at the ceiling and realized it was daylight. Holy shit! he thought.

But he must have said it aloud, because a face peered at him. It was a female face, exposed because whatever hair it possessed was tucked out of sight beneath its starched white hat. He supposed it could be an attractive face, in the right circumstances, but these were conspicuously absent. The face was also looking severe. 'Mr Bartley?'

'Where am I?'

'You are in Reading General Hospital.'

Clive could remember nothing of the crash. And now he realized that a far greater pain than that in his leg was the pain in his head; he must have hit it a colossal whack. 'How long have I been here?'

'You were brought in at nine thirty last night.'

'My God! You mean I have lain here for . . .?'

'You were severely concussed, as well as physically injured. Now, you must not agitate yourself, or I shall give you another sedative.'

'Fuck it!'

'Really, Mr Bartley, that simply will not do.'

'How do you know my name?'

'Your effects are over there.'

He glanced at the table on the far side of the private ward, and then down at himself, realized he was wearing a bed gown. 'You did all of this?'

A faint flush appeared. 'There were three of us. You were . . . restless.'

'Where is Pilot Officer Brian?'

'I'm afraid Pilot Officer Brian was dead on arrival, sir.'

'Shit, shit, shit!'

'*Sir!* Dr Close . . .'

The doctor, all little moustache and large horn-rimmed glasses, who had been passing the open door, hurried over. 'What seems to be the trouble?'

'I have to get out of here,' Clive told him. 'I have to get out of here, and this woman is being difficult.'

'*I* am being difficult?' the nurse remarked.

The doctor assumed a benevolent expression. 'My dear Mr . . . ah . . .?'

'Bartley,' the nurse muttered.

'Mr Bartley, apart from a severe concussion, your leg is broken in two places. You cannot possibly leave that bed for at least a week. As for leaving hospital . . . we are talking of probably a month.'

Clive glared at him. 'Then you had better get me a telephone.'

'Your next of kin are being informed . . .'

'I have no next of kin,' Clive said. 'And I must make a telephone call.'

'I'm afraid there are no facilities for telephones in the wards . . .'

'Holy Jesus Christ!'

'Really, sir! In front of a nurse! I must protest!'

'Now you listen to me very carefully,' Clive said. 'Because if you do not do exactly as I tell you, and do it *now*, you are going to be locked up and tried for treason, and very likely hanged. In my wallet over there you will find a card with a telephone number on it. Telephone that number and ask for Mr Baxter. If there is any query, tell them that you are calling on behalf of Clive. When you get Baxter on the phone tell him that I have got to see him immediately. Tell him it is a matter of life and death. Go.'

The doctor looked at the nurse, who shrugged. Then he went to the table, found the card, and looked at Clive again.

'A matter of life and death,' Clive reminded him, 'And we are talking about the nation, not me.'

Dr Close hurried from the room, and Clive turned to the nurse. 'Now you,' he said. 'I need a bed pan.'

'What a dump,' Baxter commented. 'They say I can't smoke. Bloody little Hitlers.' He surveyed his aide, sceptically. 'Do you realize that you have a lump on your forehead the size of a hen's egg?'

'I hit my head when we crashed,' Clive explained.

Baxter placed the chair beside the bed and sat down. 'And you have a broken leg and are going to be out of action for God knows how long. So, was a night between the sheets with Anna worth a broken leg? But you didn't spend a night, did you? You must have had a hell of a spat to come charging back at night at this time of year. You could have been killed.'

'Poor Brian *was* killed,' Clive pointed out.

'Well, there you go. You need your head examined.'

'I came back last night, Billy, because Anna gave me an absolutely vital piece of info. Now will you be quiet and listen?'

Baxter listened. 'The bit about Antwerp will be very useful,' he acknowledged.

'Billy, the whole front is about to go up.'

Billy nodded. 'The whole front went up four hours ago.'

'*What?*'

'News is still coming in. The Yanks are in a panic. They had no idea that anything like this could happen, so they don't have much in the Ardennes area, and those that are there seem to have been caught with their pants round their ankles. They're being scattered in every direction.'

'So Jerry is through.'

'Early days,' Baxter remarked. 'He seems to be doing pretty well at the moment. But he has a long way to go, and we seem to be hampered by the same weather you ran into last night, which limits our air activity. But we have our own people on the northern flank of the push, and reinforcements are being rushed up from everywhere. Best of all, Montgomery is being placed in overall command of both the Yanks and us. I should think we'll stop them. But as I said, knowing that their target is Antwerp will be very useful. I'd better get back and see the boss.'

'Hold on one moment. How are you proposing to tell him?'

Baxter raised his eyebrows. 'Exactly as you told me. It's a godsend for us as regards Anna. We'll be able to put a spoke in the Yanks' wheel.'

'No we won't.'

Baxter raised his eyebrows, and then sat down again as Clive outlined the situation. 'That girl does pose us some problems,' he remarked.

'You mean you think she should have lain there and let Johannsson get on with it?'

'You mean that bastard actually raped her while she was unconscious? He should be castrated.'

'Anna considers that her way of dealing with these things is more effective. I think she was more annoyed that he had done it when she was out than that he did it at all; she does like to know what's going on. The point is, Billy, that no one except you and I can ever know that Anna was in Stockholm on the day Johannsson was killed. Ergo, no one except you and I can ever know that I was in Stockholm either, as Joe Andrews would have no doubt that the only reason I would go there would be to see Anna.'

'Hm. Won't the Stockholm police make the link?'

'Anna says not. She was travelling on a Finnish vessel and as a Finnish journalist. No one seems to have queried this. She reckons no one knows she was there save for the chap she went to meet.'

'Who is?'

'Folke Bernadotte.'

'What? The Red Cross johnnie? What on earth—?'

'Listen.'

Again Baxter listened. 'Well, well, well,' he commented. 'Now that is very interesting.'

'You can't use it without blowing Anna's position vis-à-vis Himmler.'

'It may still come in handy. And you don't think this chap Bernadotte is going to go to the police when he finds out about Johannsson? That Anna is guilty of murder?'

'Bernadotte knows everything about Anna.'

'*What*?'

'Keep you hair on. Not that she works for us, or that she is connected with the OSS. Only that she is a member of the SD and does what Himmler tells her to because of her parents. She says he is trying to help her to get out.'

'Why should he want to do that?'

'She says he is one of her closest friends.'

'I see.'

'I thought I did too, at first. But she swears their friendship is strictly platonic.'

Baxter pulled his nose, and got up again. 'I have to rush and unload this info.' He held up his hand. 'Relax. I'll be discreet. Anna isn't our only agent in Germany. It'll be information received from an impeccable source.' He went to the door, paused. 'What do I tell Belinda?'

'If you really think she'll be interested, tell her I got in a car smash.'

The Task

Anna slept badly. The sex had not been good. This had been at least partly because she was still uncomfortable from Johannsson's efforts – a discomfort she had determinedly concealed from Clive – but also because of the shortage of time. Hurried sex was never good. They had both also had too much on their minds. Was the end really in sight? She had thought so before, and had all her plans collapse. But before had not included Count Bernadotte!

As soon as she had breakfasted she telephoned the ferry company and discovered that there was a boat leaving that afternoon. She booked a cabin and then it was just a matter of waiting, which she did in her room, as despite her confidence that there was almost no risk of her being connected with Johannsson's death, at least as things stood, she knew that her striking looks were liable to stay in people's minds, and she had no desire for anyone outside of the hotel to remember her being here at all.

After lunch she wrapped herself up, using her scarf and her dark glasses for maximum concealment, took a taxi to the docks, boarded, and again went straight to her cabin, where she remained until dinner, by which time they were well out to sea. There was no temptation to go on deck; at sea the cold was even more bitter than on land.

She smiled at the other passengers but did not join them for after dinner brandies and coffees, preferring to return to her cabin. This time she slept soundly, but awoke with a start. She sat up, looked at her watch; it was eight o'clock, but seemed to be still dark; her porthole was closed. She switched on the cabin light, and was nearly thrown out of her bunk by a violent explosion. Then she heard the ship's tannoy, first in Finnish, which she didn't understand, and then in German, summoning all passengers on deck with their lifejackets.

Anna found that she was panting. If she was used to risking life and limb on land, the sea was foreign territory. She had crossed the Atlantic twice in 1941, but on each occasion she had known that Admiral Doenitz had been informed of the name and description of her ship, and had issued orders to his U-boats that she was not to be attacked. But she could still remember the utter relief with which she had sighted the hills of Portugal rising out of the eastern horizon on her return journey.

The cabin door burst open and a steward looked in. 'Hurry Fraulein!' he said. 'The ship is sinking.'

'Oh, my God!' Anna said, and threw back the blankets. The steward stared at her naked body in consternation, but she ignored him. There seemed no time to dress properly, so she dropped her green dress over her shoulders, wrapped herself in her sable, and grabbed her shoulder bag, sweeping her jewellery from the dressing table into it.

The steward was holding her lifejacket. 'Let me help you, Fraulein.'

Anna slung the bag and then allowed herself to be inserted into the kapok vest, and he tied the cords. Then he half pushed her into the corridor, which was already sloping downwards. He was holding her arm now to move her up the slope and to the ladder leading to the deck; it was only when she stubbed her toe that she realized she had no shoes.

The steward dragged her up the ladder into the midst of a crowd of people. There was a lot of chatter and a few shrieks but no real panic. One boat had already been lowered and two more were swung out and waiting.

'In you go, Fraulein,' the steward said.

Anna cast a hasty glance around her. Dawn was just breaking, over a calm sea but a leaden sky. There was land astern of them, but a very long way away; she guessed it must be Gotland. The ferry itself was well down by the head; water was slurping over the bows and flooding the well-deck behind the forecastle. And as she hesitated, the lights went out.

'Come *on*, Fraulein,' the officer in the boat shouted, and she clambered over the rail.

'Aren't you coming?' she asked the steward.

'I'll be along later,' he assured her, and stepped back.

Then they were going down very rapidly, past the cabin

deck to land heavily on the sea, which produced another chorus of muted shrieks. The boat settled, and the oars went out; there were three seamen to a side and they pulled steadily away from the sinking ship. This clearly had only a few minutes to live, and there were still people on the sloping deck.

'Will they all get off?' Anna asked. She didn't think they'd have much chance if they entered the near-freezing water.

'There's a boat for them,' someone said.

She was sitting next to a woman who was huddled up, shivering. 'Do you know what happened?' she asked.

The woman muttered something in Finnish.

'I think we were torpedoed,' said the man on the other side, in German.

'But Finland is not at war. Is it?'

'Do you think that matters to the Russians?'

The woman was still talking.

'What is she saying?' Anna asked.

'She wants to know what is so important about that bag you have. She says no other woman has a bag.'

'As she should be able to see,' Anna pointed out, 'I was wearing this bag before my lifejacket was put on. I do not propose to take either off right this minute.'

The woman continued to grumble, but Anna ignored her. She had problems of her own, principally the cold. Her sable was keeping her body warm, but she had lost all feeling in her feet, so that she wondered if she was suffering from frostbite. What a calamitous trip this had turned out to be.

And now she realized that the distant land was dwindling. 'Why are we going the wrong way?' she asked the man, her teeth chattering. 'The land is back there.'

'It is very far away,' he explained. 'The captain got off a mayday, and there is a ship close by.'

So that she also can be torpedoed, Anna thought, and we'll have to go through this trauma all over again. She hugged herself over her lifejacket, and made herself work her toes, even if she had no idea if they were responding. There had been so much promise, from Bernadotte, so much support, from Clive, so much to be angry about, at the way Joe Andrews had forsaken her, all so meaningless right this minute.

Then she mentally squared her shoulders. She was alive.

Supposing she didn't lose a couple of toes, she was as fit and strong as ever, and she had a lot to do. And suddenly there was a stir in the boat, heads turning, people who had been almost somnolent from a combination of shock and cold beginning to chatter animatedly. Anna turned her own head and saw a destroyer approaching them at speed. If that is Russian, she thought . . . she would have to get rid of her bag and the incriminating identification she was carrying. Even so the outlook was grim.

She squinted into the misty morning, and saw the Swastika ensign.

'Countess von Widerstand?' The captain was clearly dumbfounded as he gazed at the bedraggled figure in the chair in his cabin. Anna was still wearing her dress and sable, but her bare feet had been encased in thick woollen stockings, and were extremely painful as circulation returned, but at least she seemed still to have all her toes. 'Are you all right?'

'I am very cold,' Anna said, eyeing her shoulder bag, the contents of which had been emptied on to the captain's desk. But if he had no doubt been taken aback by the Luger and the spare magazines, not to mention the expensive jewellery, he had also discovered the carte blanche issued by Himmler that gave her authority over just about every German soldier or sailor she was likely to meet. The questions that had to be bubbling in his brain would only be asked if he dared, and answered if she chose.

'Of course.' He signalled his orderly, who was hovering in the background, and a cup of steaming coffee was produced. 'It is laced with brandy,' he said reassuringly.

'Thank you.' Anna sipped, and felt the heat tracing its way down inside her chest. Beneath and around her the little ship shuddered and bounced from wave to wave; it was travelling at full speed.

'It is a great honour, to have been able to rescue such a lady as yourself,' the captain ventured.

'But you would like to know how I managed to be on a Finnish ship in the middle of the Baltic Sea being torpedoed by a Russian submarine. I'm assuming that it was a Russian submarine?'

'We think so, yes.'

'I'm afraid I cannot answer any of your questions. I was on a secret mission for the Reich.'

'Of course I understand that, Countess. I am just happy to be of service. Have you breakfasted?'

'No.'

'Then . . .'

Anna finished her coffee and held out her cup for a refill. 'I would rather not eat right now, Herr Captain. If I could lie down for a little while . . .'

'Of course, Countess. You shall use my bunk.' He indicated the small sleeping cabin that lay through the doorway.

'Thank you.' She commenced sipping her second cup of coffee. 'I would like my bag back, please.'

'Of course.' Hastily he replaced all the items he had taken out. 'You understand that I had to discover who you were.'

'Why? Have you found out who all the other passengers are?'

'Well, no. Not yet.' He was embarrassed. 'The captain of the Finnish ferry felt that there was something . . . unusual, about you.'

'I see.'

'And then, that is a very expensive coat you are wearing. And that jewellery . . . and then, the pistol . . .'

'I see,' Anna said again. 'Tell me, now that you have discovered that I am not an international jewel thief, what are you going to do with your knowledge?'

'Believe me, Countess, my only wish is to help you in any way possible. If you have been inconvenienced, I most humbly apologize.'

'I do regard being torpedoed as an inconvenience, Captain. But that was not your fault. And I am most grateful for being rescued. I will make sure that you are commended.'

'Thank you, Countess.'

Anna finished her second cup of coffee. 'Now, I really must lie down before I fall down. What time do you expect to reach Rostock?'

'Rostock, Countess?'

Anna had a sudden pang of indigestion. 'Isn't that where we're going, Rostock?'

'No, no, Countess. We are going to Königsberg.'

'Would you mind saying that again?' Anna requested. 'Königsberg?' That was at the eastern end of East Prussia, virtually on the far side of Poland. 'I need to get to Berlin, as quickly as possible.'

'I am most terribly sorry, Countess. There is no way we can possibly make Rostock, both because there is too much Russian naval activity in that area and because we lack the fuel. There is not a lot available,' he added, ingenuously.

'But you were out here.'

'We were only a hundred kilometres from Königsberg when we heard your mayday call. That was the limit of our permitted patrol area. We should be in port in a couple of hours.'

Anna finished her coffee. She felt like another but getting drunk, however desirable, would not be a good idea. 'So what happens when I get to Königsberg?'

'I am sure that General von Hotten will see what can be done. Unfortunately, communications with Germany proper are tenuous at this time. The Russians, you see.'

'I would like another cup of coffee,' Anna said.

'Countess!' General von Hotten was clearly an old school professional soldier, tall and stiff-backed, with haughty features which for this occasion he had arranged into a benevolent smile, and a breastful of medal ribbons, dominated by the Knight's Cross. 'This is a great pleasure.'

'I'm sure, in any other circumstances, it would be for me also,' Anna conceded. 'But you understand that I should not be here at all.'

'The fortunes of war,' the general suggested.

'And you must also understand that I am required to be back in Berlin just as rapidly as possibly.'

He nodded. 'Commander Roeder did say that you were in a great hurry. But, ah, well . . . you understand that Marshal Rokossovsky's army is all around us.'

'You mean you are surrounded, and therefore cut off?'

'We are not yet surrounded. But it is going to happen within a week or so. They are steadily closing in.'

'Then shouldn't you abandon the city now, while you have the chance, and fight your way out?'

'We cannot do that.'

'May I ask why?'

'We have been commanded by the Führer, personally, that we are to hold Königsberg to the last bullet and the last man.'

Anna stared at him. 'Does that make any military sense, when you are bound to be overwhelmed?'

Hotten's features remained urbane. 'It may not to you, dear lady. It may not, even to me. But we must accept that we have no concept of the overall situation. Tying up Rokossovsky's front for even a few weeks may well allow us to gain a victory elsewhere, certainly if our offensive on the Western Front is as successful as seems apparent. Besides, as I have said, it was a personal command from the Führer himself.'

'Did you say, offensive in the West?'

'It commenced yesterday. The plan was kept so secret that no one knew of it. But our panzers are running riot just as they did in 1940. The Americans are shattered. It is the greatest victory of the war.'

And I failed to get the news to England in time, Anna thought. But as Clive would have landed two nights ago, the news *had* to have got there in time. Could it be possible that her warning had not been believed?

'So you see, Countess,' Hotten went on, 'it is our duty to obey our orders to the letter, confident as we are that the Führer's military genius will take us to ultimate victory.'

Anna realized that the general's professional loyalty was not something she could argue with. 'I am sure you will do your duty, Herr General,' she said. 'But just as you must obey your orders, so must I obey mine, which are to return to Berlin with all possible haste. So if you will provide me with transport and an escort . . .'

'That will not be possible, Countess. To get from here to the Oder you would need a brigade.'

Anna kept her cool. 'Well, then, surely you can fly me out.'

'The only planes I have left are half a dozen single-seater fighters for which I have hardly any fuel. I am sorry, but as you are here . . . my wife will make you as comfortable as possible, and –' he peered at her decidedly bedraggled appearance – 'find you some clothes to wear.'

'You wife is here with you?'

'Of course.'

'And you are prepared to have her stay here until she is captured and raped and murdered by the Russians?'

'My wife understands her duty as a German,' he said stiffly.

'I look forward to meeting her,' Anna said. 'But I also understand my duty, to the Reich. I accept that you are not in a position to help me with what you have here. So you must allow me to seek outside assistance. I assume you are in radio contact with Berlin?'

'Of course.'

'Well, will you send a personal message from me to the Reichsführer? Tell him that I am here with no means of leaving, and that I wish to know what he intends to do about it.'

He regarded her for several moments. Then he said, 'You wish me to send that message to the *Reichsführer*?'

'Yes,' Anna said. 'Immediately, if you will.'

'Countess!' Frau von Hotten held Anna's hands. 'This is such an honour, and a pleasure.'

'And for me, Frau,' Anna conceded. 'I must apologize for my appearance.'

'But you have been sunk!' Hilda von Hotten was a plump middle-aged woman with red cheeks and a thrusting bosom. 'Imagine! The freezing sea! I am amazed that you survived.'

'I did not actually get wet,' Anna pointed out. 'But as you can see . . .'

She was still wearing her thick woollen socks, now sadly discoloured.

'And your clothes . . .?'

'Are all at the bottom of the Baltic.'

'Oh, my dear girl. But we will take care of it.'

'Ah . . .' Anna eyed her hostess; she did not relish the thought of attempting any of these shapeless garments.

'Oh, yes,' Hilda said. 'I will send to the shops and have a selection brought in for you to try.'

'You still have shops?'

She had been allowed only a brief glimpse of the city on her way here from Military Headquarters, but it had struck her as being almost as badly damaged as Berlin itself.

'Oh, yes.' Hilda giggled. 'A few have escaped destruction.' She rang a bell and when a uniformed maid appeared gave the necessary instructions. 'Now, you must relax and try to forget your ordeal. The Russians never come over until dark. So we can have a cup of tea and you must tell me all about Berlin – it's months since I have been there – and tomorrow night I will have a supper party for our senior officers –' she gave

Anna a roguish smile – 'and a few of the more handsome younger ones, to be sure. I'm afraid we will have to eat in the cellar . . .' her gaze became anxious. 'You will not mind this?'

'For the last year, Frau, I have lived in a cellar.'

Hilda clapped her hands. 'Well, then you see, you will feel perfectly at home.'

Was it possible that she did not understand the fate that was hanging over her? Anna decided that she was too intelligent for that, in which case she had to be a woman of frightening courage. What was truly frightening was the thought that there were millions of German women who had to know that their futures were bleak, where a future was attainable at all, but who were continuing to go about their lives.

So, at least as long as she was acting the part of a German woman, she had to match them. She secured a pink evening gown with matching gloves as well as a couple of new dresses and most important, some underwear, and when at dusk the air raid sirens went off she and Hilda retired to the cellars with a bottle of schnapps, where they were shortly joined by Hotten, looking hot and bothered.

'We haven't lost another post, dear?' his wife asked solicitously.

'No, no.' He gazed at Anna. 'I sent your message to Berlin, and have received a reply.'

Anna sipped her drink while she waited.

Hotten took the sheet of paper from his breast pocket and unfolded it. 'I shall read it to you. It says: "Thank God you are safe. A plane will arrive for you tonight. Always yours. Heinrich."'

He raised his head, and his wife said, 'Oh, my!'

'I had no idea that you were . . . well . . .'

'The Reichsführer is my closest friend,' Anna explained.

Frau Hotten looked scandalized. Her husband cleared his throat. 'How he expects to get a plane in tonight . . . those bombers are escorted by fighters, and there are hundreds of them.'

'Don't remind me,' Anna said. 'But I suppose we should get to the airfield. Will you excuse me, Hilda?'

'But . . . we were going to have a party, tomorrow night.'

'We will have one, when next you are in Berlin.' She actually meant that, supposing they could ever be in Berlin again, together. 'I can't thank you enough for all you have done for me.'

The airfield was utterly dark, save for the searchlights criss-crossing the sky and the flashing lights from the explosions of the bombs. Anna, wrapped in her sable, sat in the command car alongside Hotten, watching the patterns. 'Are you afraid?' he asked.

'Should I be?'

He considered. 'I suppose not, if what they say of you is correct.'

She squeezed his arm. 'I am human, General. Therefore I am afraid. But I have often been afraid in the past, and I am still here.'

'To be afraid, and still carry out your orders or your duty, is the highest form of courage.'

'You say the sweetest things.'

An officer appeared beside the window. 'A signal from the Luftwaffe pilot, Herr General. He will be down in five minutes, and requests that the landing lights be switched on. It should be safe: the raid is over.'

Behind them the All Clear was wailing.

The general got out of the car, as did Anna. 'I see nothing,' Hotten remarked.

'Well, I suppose he isn't showing lights,' Anna ventured.

She stared into the darkness, but there seemed nothing there, and then . . . wumpff. She saw the parachute ballooning behind the aircraft before she saw the plane itself, a blacker image than the darkness, identified only by the sparks issuing from its wheels as the brakes were applied.

'What in the name of God is that?' Hotten enquired at large.

Anna felt inclined to ask the same question as the machine taxied towards them, only a low rumble, while in the distance there was another rolling rumble, like thunder.

The machine stopped, the engine was quiet, and the pilot swung himself from the cockpit. Anna stared in consternation; she had never seen anything like it in her life.

'Repack that chute,' the pilot said. 'We must be out of here in fifteen minutes.' He stood to attention in front of the general. 'Heil Hitler! I am to take the Countess von Widerstand to

Berlin.' He bowed to Anna. 'Countess! Captain Joachim Rudent, at your service.'

The name was familiar, although she could not immediately place it. 'Herr Captain. You are going to take me to Berlin in this contraption?'

'That is correct.'

'But . . . it has no propeller. And the wings are too short.'

'It is the 262,' Rudent explained proudly. 'Our latest fighter. You see –' he indicated what looked like two large barrels, one attached to the underside of each wing – 'it is jet propelled. It flies at nine hundred kilometres an hour. That is faster than any other airplane in the world, and so it cannot be caught. You will be in Berlin in forty-five minutes.'

Anna stared at it, and him. If she did not like flying in the first place, the idea of flying without a propeller, and at some unbelievable speed, was terrifying.

'So if you are ready,' Rudent said.

'Well . . .' she turned to Hotten. 'I must thank you again, Herr General, and Frau Hotten, for your assistance.'

'Meeting you, Countess, has been an unforgettable experience. But . . . do you think you will be safe in that machine?'

'No,' Anna said. 'But it seems I have no choice. Tell me how I get on board, Captain.'

'Ah. There is one small problem.'

'Only one?'

'It is a single-seater, you see.'

'I'm afraid I do not see. Where do I sit?'

'Well . . .' He was embarrassed. 'I will get on board first, and you will have to sit on my lap.'

'I see. And you will still be able to fly the machine?'

'Of course. It is very simple. But you must be careful not to touch anything.'

'I don't think I am going to be the one doing the touching. And you say the Reichsführer sent you?'

'The jet is the only way we can guarantee you safe passage to Berlin. The Reichsführer called for a volunteer to make the flight. I was the first to step forward,' he added, again proudly.

'You were prepared to risk your life so that you could have me sitting on your lap for three quarters of an hour?'

'No, no, Countess. So that I may do something for you. I had the great privilege of knowing your sister.'

Of course, Anna remembered: Katherine's boyfriend. She rested her glove on his arm, 'Then you will know . . .'

'That is why I am here, Countess. Now, if you will take off your coat and hat . . .'

'I will freeze.'

'Only for five minutes. The cockpit is heated. And your clothes and your bag can be stored behind the seat.'

Anna sighed, but took off her coat and handed over her shoulder bag and hat; her hair flowed in the breeze and she became a vast shudder. A mechanic clambered on to the wing and put her stuff away, then he came down and fitted a leather helmet over her head and ears. Rudent got in and settled himself. 'Now, Countess.'

The mechanic gave Anna a boost on to the wing. She hitched her skirt to her thighs, got one leg over, and then the other, sat on Rudent's lap.

The mechanic had followed her on to the wing and now he leaned into the cockpit to pass the belt round Anna's waist and over her shoulders. 'This is very tight,' she remarked.

'That is because we are sharing the same belt,' Rudent explained.

Her back was firmly wedged against his front. 'Next you'll be telling me that if something goes wrong, we share the same parachute.'

'Yes, we do.'

'You cannot be serious.'

'But nothing is going to go wrong.' The mechanic withdrew and Rudent closed the canopy; it brushed the top of her head. 'Just enough room. Now, Countess, normally we fly at a minimum of ten thousand metres, but as we have only the one oxygen mask we will make this journey at five thousand. Please do not worry about this; we are still too fast for any enemy interception.'

'Isn't my hair in your face?' His mask had touched the back of her neck as he put it on.

'Yes, it is. But I can see through it. All set?'

'I have a feeling,' Anna said, 'that by the time this flight ends, you and I are going to be very good friends.'

It was the most exhilarating feeling she had ever known. Further conversation was impossible owing to the screaming noise, but the sensation of speed and power was mind-bending. As for the sensation of nearness to the man . . . it came as a surprise for her to realize that she had actually spent very little of even her sexually active life sitting on a man's lap; her partners had invariably been thinking further ahead virtually from the moment of their first meeting.

What made it more interesting was that because of his heavy flying suit she couldn't tell what effect, if any, she was having on him, although from time to time he slightly shifted his position, and while his arms were round her the entire time, his gloved thumbs occasionally touching her breasts as he altered course or adjusted a control, these could not be considered as anything more than inadvertent. But by the time he landed, she felt that she had known him a long time.

Gutemann was waiting for her at Rangsdorf. Since the Warsaw incident he had treated her with almost comical deference, but as he still obviously remained overwhelmed by her beauty and personality, she had allowed him the odd night. As with all the men who claimed to worship her, she could never tell when one of them might be of vital use to her. Rudent had made no such statement, but she had a hunch he might be more useful than anyone else. She held his hand. 'May I thank you for a most enjoyable flight, Herr Captain. Or may I call you Joachim?'

'I would be flattered, Countess. And I would like to apologize for any discomfort.'

'There was no discomfort at all. I think, when next you have leave, you should call on me. I would like to talk about Katherine.'

'Call on you, Countess?'

'You can reach me at Gestapo Headquarters.'

He gulped, and she squeezed his fingers. 'It's in the book.'

Gutemann snorted as he escorted her to the waiting car. 'I hope that lout was not impertinent, or familiar.'

'He was a perfect gentleman,' Anna assured him. 'Now I suppose you are taking me to the Reichsführer?'

'No. He said that if you came in after ten he would see you tomorrow.'

Anna looked at her watch; it was just after midnight. 'There's a relief. Then I will see you also, tomorrow, Gunther.'

'Ah . . . yes, Countess. As you wish.'

A bleary-eyed Birgit emerged from her bedroom as Anna entered the apartment. 'Countess! I didn't expect you back so soon. Did you have a good trip?'

'It was interesting,' Anna said.

'What an experience,' Himmler remarked. 'You have nine lives.'

'I think you mean that I once had nine lives,' Anna pointed out. 'I am not sure how many I have left.'

'Ha ha. Your wit is as sharp as your mind. But I am so very pleased. You say that Bernadotte is prepared to come to Germany to discuss the situation? That is tremendous news. He didn't . . . ah . . .'

'No, sir.' Anna gazed into his eyes. 'The count did not reveal the contents of your letter. I did not expect him to.

'Of course. What was his attitude when he read it?'

'It is difficult to say, sir. He seldom reveals any emotion.'

'Yes, they are a dour people. The important thing is that he is willing to help. Although, of course, it may not really be necessary.'

'Sir?'

'Our campaign in Flanders. Our army there is achieving great things. The Americans have been completely surprised and are falling apart. The war in the West may well be over in the next fortnight.'

Shit, she thought. Shit, shit, shit. She hadn't taken Hotten's ebullient comments all that seriously. Not that the bastards didn't deserve a bloody nose; but it was still essential for them to win in the end, because the alternative was unthinkable.

'So,' Himmler went on, 'we will put the count on hold for the time being. He asked for a week or two, didn't he? Now, Anna, there is a small problem as regards you.'

'Sir?'

'You understand that to extricate you from Königsberg, I had to turn to the Luftwaffe. To obtain a 262, which I was informed was the only machine that could safely bring you home, I had to see Goering himself. He gave permission for one of his aircraft to be used, but . . .'

'Oh, shit!' Anna commented.

Himmler raised his eyebrows, but he said, 'I know exactly how you feel, my dear girl. However, it may not be as bad as you think. He wants you to have Christmas lunch with him.

His wife is apparently at their country estate and has no intention of visiting Berlin at this time. He may just wish the pleasure of your company.'

Anna sighed. 'I am sure you are right, sir.'

'There is, however, another aspect of the situation.'

Oh, lord, Anna thought; what now?

'As you are aware,' Himmler went on, 'it is absolutely essential that no one ever knows of your visits to Stockholm.'

'With respect, sir, the Gestapo agents in Lubeck knew of them when I was using the Malmo ferry. That man Werter, in particular.'

'I will keep my eye on him,' Himmler assured her. 'But you have never mentioned them to anyone of importance, I hope?'

He was thinking of Goebbels, she knew. 'I have never discussed my duties for you with anyone, Herr Reichsführer.' *At least in Germany.*

'And of course it would be disastrous for the Reichsmarshal to learn of them.'

'I appreciate that, sir.'

'So I have told him that as Commander of the Home Army, and with a view to future dispositions, I sent you to Königsberg to find out the actual situation there. Neither you nor I had any idea that you might be trapped by the speed of the Russian advance. So, you made the journey by boat, and you began your return journey by the same means, and you were torpedoed just outside the harbour. I think you should tell him that you were terrified at the experience, and did not feel up to risking it again. Hence the necessity for flying you out.'

'Yes, sir. Actually, I was terrified.'

'You, Anna? Ha ha. Now go and rest up. I have an idea that great things lie ahead of us.'

Almost literally, she supposed. She had only a nodding acquaintance with Reichsmarshal Goering, had never been disturbed by the predatory nature of his eyes when he looked at her; all men who were the least interested in women looked at her like that. But he did not have a great reputation as a womanizer, although one could never be certain with a morphine addict. He did, however, have a reputation as an insatiable accumulator of every object, from paintings to houses, that he considered of value. Did that extend to women?

And could it possibly extend to her? Because she also knew

that if at the beginning of the Nazi movement he had been Hitler's closest associate – his drug habit had been a concomitant of the severe wound he had suffered when walking at the Führer's side during the famous attempted putsch in Munich in 1923, when he had been put on a course of morphine to mask the pain – he had largely fallen from favour since the failure of his Luftwaffe either to defeat the RAF in 1940, or to sustain the garrison at Stalingrad, as he had boasted it would do, in the winter of 1942. On the other hand, she equally knew that he was a man of proven, almost reckless courage, who had been a legitimate fighter ace in World War One, and had, indeed, commanded the famous Richtofen Squadron after that hero had been shot down.

So . . . she wore a deep red woollen dress under the freshly cleaned sable as she presented herself at the door of his Berlin mansion. This was a case of had been, as like almost every other building in Berlin it had been hit by the British bombers, more than once she estimated as she looked at what was left of the sagging roof, the collapsed walls. Thus, like everyone else, the Reichsmarshal had removed himself to the cellars, and again like everyone else who could afford it, had turned them into a subterranean palace; the carpets and decorations excelled even those of the Chancellery. As there was not sufficient wall space for more than a handful of his paintings, the majority were stacked against the walls in the corridors; Anna did not care to speculate on the value of the Old Masters she glimpsed as she was led, by a tail-coated major-domo, to the 'drawing room', situated two flights down from the street.

Here the Reichsmarshal waited for her and, as she had both feared and anticipated, there were no other guests. His uniform was even more gaudy than usual, and his medals presented such a glittering array of gold and silver that she suspected, were he to hug her, he might do her a mortal injury. But for the moment, he preferred to kiss her hand. 'Countess!' he said. 'Anna! It is so good of you to come to see me.'

'I was informed that it was a requirement, Herr Reichsmarshal,' she riposted.

His eyes narrowed for a moment, then he beamed again. 'I was told that your tongue was as sharp as it was sweet. But not so sweet as your twat, eh?'

'Is it to be so immediate, sir? Or may we have lunch first? Or at least a drink?'

Goering snapped his fingers and champagne was brought. 'Merry Christmas!'

'And to you, Herr Reichsmarshal.'

He escorted her to a settee, sat beside her. 'Do your private conversations with the Führer follow these lines?'

'Of course not, sir. The Führer is a gentleman.'

Another long stare. Then he said, 'I would like to tie you naked to a post and whip you till you bleed.'

Anna refused to blink or move her gaze. 'I think that would be very unwise, sir.'

'Because you belong to the Führer. You are a very fortunate young woman. But one should always remember that no fortune lasts for ever.'

'I am sure that is something all of us need to bear in mind, Herr Reichsmarshal.'

He finished his champagne. 'I think we should have lunch.'

'You never did tell me how you got on with Goering,' Himmler remarked, coming into Anna's office.

'Sir?' Anna, sifting through various papers – her current duties consisted in destroying most of the files which could be regarded as incriminating for the SD, a sure sign of the way Himmler's mind was going – looked up in surprise. It was six weeks since Christmas, and he had not raised the subject before.

But equally to her surprise, Himmler, after weeks of depression, was suddenly ebullient, which was difficult to understand, considering the circumstances. In February it was colder and bleaker than ever. Like everything else her office had had to be removed underground, and the true extent of the catastrophe in Flanders was just becoming apparent. After their seemingly immense success at the beginning of the attack the German forces had been shattered. Much of that early promise had been because of the low cloud cover that had prevented the Allied air forces from seeing, much less strafing, the panzer columns. Once the weather had cleared, the Germans had been cut to pieces, and their certainly gallant attempt to hold on to what they had gained had resulted in something close to annihilation. So, ten panzer divisions, the remaining flower of the Wehrmacht, had been squandered to absolutely no purpose.

The last month had been a sombre one in Berlin; Himmler had been the epitome of gloom, and she had not seen Hitler at all. And now this irrelevant question, out of the blue . . . 'Do I have something to tell you, Herr Reichsführer?'

'You had lunch with him on Christmas Day.'

'Yes, sir. I did.'

'What happened?'

'We talked.'

'Now, Anna, please do not play games with me.'

'We talked, Herr Reichsführer. I believe the Reichsmarshal may have had some plans when he invited me, but he found my conversation off-putting.'

'So what did you talk about?'

'Himself, mainly.'

'His plans?' Suddenly his tone was eager.

'Not really. The Luftwaffe. His new planes. He wanted to know what I thought of the 262.'

'Hm. What *did* you think of it?'

'I was very impressed, sir. As I told you at the time,' she remembered.

'Of course. Now, Anna, we have a lot to do. You have a lot to do. I am about to send you on the most important mission of your life.'

He pulled up a chair and sat before her desk, while she tried to anticipate what might be coming next. Was she going back to Sweden? That would be heavenly, whatever the risk of being torpedoed again. Certainly both his tone and his demeanour suggested that he had something very important on his mind.

'What I am going to tell you,' Himmler said, 'is the most secret information you will ever receive. So listen very carefully. The unhappy fact is that the time comes to all of us, when we must look irrefutable facts in the face. As when a doctor tells you that you have a terminal illness, it is no use refusing to believe it. You must accept the situation and make the necessary plans to put what time you have left to its best possible use. So, it is a certainty that the situation cannot be saved.'

'But . . . the Führer—'

'The Führer knows this as well as anyone, even if he will not admit it for public consumption. We must fight to the end. But he is already making plans for that end. And the end, I can tell you, is total destruction. He told us this at a Cabinet meeting the other day. If Germany cannot win this war, he told us, then it is better that the entire country be destroyed, and everyone in it. He has instructed Speer to prepare a plan for the blowing up of every facility in the country the moment we can fight no longer. That is the destruction of every factory, every food producing plant, every electricity station, every water pumping station, every water-retaining dam, every sewerage system . . .'

He paused to stare at her, and she stared back in consternation. 'But—'

'I know. It is pretty apocalyptic. But that is what is going to happen, what we must prepare ourselves for.'

He continued to stare at her. What does he expect me to do, or say? she wondered.

'But you,' he said. 'Your situation is different, is it not? You are not one of us. You have never been one of us. You are not even a German. And you hate us, don't you?'

Shit, she thought; he is about to place me under arrest. She had no doubt that she could dispose of him, but not of the hundred odd members of his staff outside the door. She needed time. 'I do not understand you, Herr Reichsführer. I have served the regime faithfully and well for six years.'

'Because you have had no choice. Oh, come now, Anna, were it not for your parents you would have abandoned us long ago, would you not?'

Anna's heart seemed to have slowed.

'I am prepared to tell you where they are, Anna,' he said. 'And give you carte blanche to take them out of Germany, if you can. I'm afraid I cannot offer you any assistance in this, but you are a resourceful young woman, are you not?'

Am I really hearing this? she wondered. Or . . . she had no doubt that Himmler was as capable of torture, whether mental or physical, as any of the Nazi leaders.

'But before I grant you that reward, there is a service I require of you, a service for which you are uniquely suited.'

Breath hissed through Anna's nostrils.

'As I have said, the Führer is determined that nothing of value in Germany will be left for the Allies or the Russians to appropriate. However, in the vaults beneath the Chancellery the entire gold reserves of the Third Reich. It weighs one hundred tons. There is a figure to conjure with, eh? One hundred tons of solid gold. That cannot be allowed to fall into enemy hands. But how does one destroy bullion? Even supposing all of Berlin was burned to the ground, with a heat so intense that the gold was all melted, it would still be there, and when the heat cooled, it would again harden. So, if it cannot be destroyed, it must be placed where it can never be found. The Führer has selected the salt mines that lie close to Eisenach, and on my recommendation he has selected you to carry out this assignment.'

Anna found that she was holding her breath.

'Now, listen very carefully,' Himmler said. 'There will be a convoy of ten trucks, each carrying ten tons of gold ingots. Each truck will have a single SS driver; he will not know what he is transporting. The trucks will be driven into the shaft to the salt mines at the dead of night, and the moment they are in you will blow the entrance. You will be supplied with sufficient explosive for this purpose.'

'The drivers—'

'Must remain inside. Now we understand that you may need assistance to carry this out, so you will be accompanied by a squad of SD men. None of these men, either, will know what they are escorting, but they also, once the mine is sealed, must be prevented from ever revealing what happened, just in case other people draw certain conclusions.'

'I see, sir. And then?'

'Why, then you return here to Berlin, and I will provide you with the necessary information, as well as the necessary documentation, to get your parents out of their current place of residence and across the border to Switzerland.'

Anna supposed, as she had thought before, that she would never understand how so many men, who considered themselves intellectually superior to ordinary human beings, and who were prepared to accept her as an *extra*ordinary human being, still could not overcome her physical appearance, that of an innocent, slightly dumb, young woman. She almost felt insulted that this man, who certainly had her complete record at his disposal, and was happy to utilize her exceptional talents, should still regard her as being as thick as two short planks. So when she had completed her assignment, just to make sure she did not immediately flee to Switzerland with the knowledge of where the gold was concealed, he would draw her back to Berlin for her parents. And then turn her loose, with the knowledge of where the gold was?

On the other hand, he still held all the high cards. Although it should be possible to adjust that.

He was studying her. 'Can you do it?'

'Of course I can carry out your instructions, sir. But there is one small problem. How do I get back to Berlin? It is approximately two hundred and fifty kilometres from Eisenach.'

Himmler raised his eyebrows. 'You have been to Eisenach before?'

'No, sir, I have not.'

'Then how do you know it is two hundred and fifty kilometres from Berlin?'

'I saw it once on a map, and observed the distance.'

'And you remembered it?'

'Well, of course, sir.'

Himmler regarded her for several seconds. Then he said, 'You will return in your command car. I will provide you with sufficient gasoline coupons and authorization as an officer in the SD to cover your journey.'

'Yes, sir. But who will drive the command car?'

'Why, you will, you silly girl.'

'I do not know how to drive, sir.'

'What? You are a woman of unlimited talent, with the most remarkable memory I have ever known, and you do not know how to drive a car?'

'The SS training school I attended, while they taught me all of the skills they considered I should know, did not consider that I would ever need to drive a car, myself.'

'Good God! I assume that was Dr Cleiner?'

'It was, sir.'

'Well, well. The man is an idiot. And now . . .' He checked what he was going to say.

'Sir?' A sudden wave of inspiration whistled through Anna's mind.

'It is not important. Well, you will have to keep one of your escorts alive to bring you back.'

'That might be difficult, sir. If this man has seen me dispose of his colleagues . . .'

'So tell me how you intend to handle it? I am sure you already have a solution.'

'I would like to take someone who is devoted to me, who I can trust absolutely to do anything I wish.'

'I see. And who is this personal paragon?'

'A Luftwaffe officer.'

'One of your lovers, I presume.'

'He would like to be, sir.'

'And you understand that when he returns you to Berlin he will have to be disposed of?'

'I understand that, sir.'

'I sometimes wonder if you have a heart in there, Anna. Or a lump of ice. Very well. You may recruit your ill-fated lover. The operation is to be carried out next week.'

The Break

'Countess?' Joachim Rudent stood in the doorway of Anna's office.

'Captain. How good to see you again. Come in. Close the door and sit down.'

Rudent advanced, cautiously, sat before her desk.

'You were going to call me,' Anna reminded him.

He flushed. 'I did not feel I could presume.'

'You presumed to make advances to my sister.'

The flush deepened. 'Yes. But, well . . .'

'Are you afraid of me?'

He licked his lips. 'You are . . . well, I am only a pilot in the Luftwaffe. And you . . .'

'I am a woman, to whom you have already been of great assistance. And now you are here.'

'I was told to report here for a special assignment.'

'That is correct. I wish you to accompany me on a mission.'

'*You* wish it?'

'I am acting with the authority of the Reichsführer. As I always do. He told me to recruit someone I could trust absolutely. I selected you.'

'Well, Countess, I am very flattered. I am to fly you some-where?'

'You are to drive me somewhere.'

'Drive?'

'You do drive a car?'

'Yes, I do. But I do not own one.'

'The car will be provided. Now I want you to listen very carefully. This is top secret. We are going to carry out a most important mission for the Reich. I am not going to tell you what it is at this time, but I will require your instant and unquestioning obedience to every command I give, and equally, your instant and unquestioning support in everything I do or require you to do. Will you do this?'

He swallowed. 'If you require it, Countess.'

'I do require it. Now, we leave tomorrow morning. The assignment will only take one day. But I would like you to spend tonight in my apartment downstairs.'

'Countess?'

Anna smiled at him. 'I think we need to get to know each other.'

Easy to say that she needed to use every weapon she possessed to ensure his support. But was she also offering him a farewell gift? She hoped it would not come to that, but for the moment she could only play it by ear. She had already made up her mind how she was going to handle this situation, although it was a disturbing thought that it had to involve the deaths of at least ten more men. But they were SS, she reminded herself.

For seven years, all but, she had been the slave of this ghastly regime. Now they were setting up to dispose of her. She had no intention of allowing that to happen, but she also wished to take her revenge on them . . . and, if everything went according to the plan that had started to take shape in her brain from the moment Himmler had given her her instruc-tions, to take care of her future. But she couldn't do it on her own, mainly because of that fatal weakness in her training, which was something she simply had to rectify, if she could ever find the time.

But meanwhile, one hundred tons of gold! She had no idea of current prices, but she reckoned it could not be less than fifty million dollars. Ten per cent of fifty million . . .

She sent for the necessary guidebooks, and spent two hours studying the Erfurt district, committing to memory every facet of the country around Eisenach, and more particularly the various properties of the two rivers, the Horsel and the Nesse, at the confluence of which the city was situated, and at last finding what she was looking for. She marked it on the largest scale map she possessed, and stowed it in her shoulder bag for the time being; she did not think that the bag itself would be appropriate on this mission. It would be the most desperate, and because of the odds involved, the most dangerous plan she had ever undertaken . . . but she would have the advantage of surprise, and, she hoped, the support of Rudent.

Anna looked at her watch, and nudged the man. 'Anna,' he murmured as he woke up. 'Oh, Anna, Anna. Is this real?'

'Don't you like reality? It's time to get up. I am going to bathe, then we must move.'

He watched her go into the bathroom, then got out of bed himself. Anna had opened the inner door and summoned Birgit, and a few minutes later the maid brought in two steaming mugs of ersatz coffee, giving a little curtsey as she encountered the half-naked pilot.

'Birgit, Joachim,' Anna said from the tub.

'Good morning, sir.'

Rudent had met her the previous evening, but he was still embarrassed.

Anna emerged from the bathroom, towelling. 'The captain and I will be leaving shortly, Birgit, and we will be gone all day. But hopefully we will be back this evening. Have you been upstairs this morning?'

'Yes, Countess. To see if there was any milk.'

'And I gather there wasn't. What about the weather?'

'It is snowing, Countess.'

'Shit!' She put on her red woollen dress – in view of what the day seemed certain to hold it was an appropriate colour – pulled on a pair of fur-lined boots, added her sable and her fur hat, pulled on her gloves. The sable had two very deep pockets. She had already requisitioned a second pistol from the armoury; into this she screwed her silencer, and it and a spare magazine she placed in the left-hand pocket. Her other pistol, again with a spare magazine, she placed in her right-hand pocket, together with her map.

Rudent watched her with sombre eyes. She smiled at him. 'You will remember what I require.'

'Yes.'

'Then remember also that not to do so could cost you your life.'

It was just seven, and utterly dark as well as near freezing, and as Birgit had warned, snowing quite heavily. A car was waiting to drive them to the Chancellery, through streets freshly cratered from the visit of the RAF during the night. In the yard the ten trucks waited in an orderly row, their drivers walking up and down and slapping their gloves together.

Also waiting were three SD men, in plain clothes but armed with tommy guns. The men clicked to attention as Anna got out to inspect them. 'You have brought the explosives?'

'In the boot, Countess.'

'And you know how to set the charges?' She looked from face to face.

'I am a demolitions expert,' one said proudly.

'Excellent. Well then . . .'

'We are not quite ready, Countess.'

'There is no time to waste. We have a long way to go.'

'We must wait for our commander.'

'What commander? I am in charge of this assignment.'

'But I have been placed in command of this detail, Countess,' Werter said, leaving the building to join them.

'You?' A combination of irritation and concern flooded her brain. 'I was not informed of this.'

'I believe it was a last-minute decision by the Reichsführer. It is to make sure that your orders are obeyed.'

'I see. Well, you will have to wait while I check this out.'

'With respect, Countess, I should tell you that the Reichsführer left Berlin last night.'

'To go where?'

'I do not know, Countess. I believe he was driving north, to see conditions up there for himself.'

He is going to meet Bernadotte, she realized. *Without breathing a word to me, the bastard!* Which once again raised the question of how much he trusted her, if at all. And he would trust her less than ever once Bernadotte outlined his terms for helping him. But of course, the fact that Werter of all people had been detailed to accompany her on this mission, merely confirmed that he intended it to be terminal.

Well, she thought, handling this particular problem was something she had always intended to do. 'In that case, Herr Werter, the sooner we complete this mission the better. You know where we are going?'

'No, Countess, I do not. I was told you would inform me of our destination.'

What a devious, twisted world is this Nazi Germany, she thought. Himmler did not seem to be able to bring himself to trust anyone. 'So, do you know what is in these trucks?'

'No, Countess. I am hoping you will tell me that also.'

'It is probably better for you not to know. As for where we are going, I will show you. Captain Rudent and I will lead the way. You will come with us, Herr Werter. The trucks will follow, and I wish the guards to bring up the rear.'

He hesitated, then clicked his heels.

The roads were in such a state it was impossible to proceed faster than twenty kilometres an hour, thus when they stopped for lunch at one they had only reached Wittenberg.

Anna was aware that both her companions were consumed with curiosity, but as she had intended, neither dared pursue the matter in front of the other. Werter did venture, 'Are we bound for Austria, Countess?'

'Not so far,' Anna assured him. 'We shall be at our destination by dusk.'

But soon after they resumed their journey they had to stop and take shelter in a small wood as a squadron of American bombers droned overhead. 'Bastards,' Rudent commented.

It was already dusk when they reached the Horsel River, winding through the north-western foothills of the Thuringer Wald. Anna studied her map by the light of her torch; in the distance she could make out the high tower of the Wartburg, on its hill above the city, so that even if she could not identify many landmarks, she knew where she was.

'Eisenach!' Werter said. 'The salt mines!'

'That is very perceptive of you,' Anna agreed.

They drove for a further hour behind dipped headlights; it

had become very dark. Werter had clearly been brooding on their destination, and now the mine buildings, long abandoned, were in sight in the gloom. He looked over his shoulder at the trucks lumbering along behind. 'You mean this stuff is dangerous?'

'It is most certainly dangerous in the wrong hands. Now, Herr Werter, you understand that this is a top secret exercise?'

'I was told this by the Reichsführer himself,' Werter said proudly.

'Well, then, you see, we are going to blow up the entrance of the mine once the goods have been stowed there. When we stop, while the drivers take their trucks into the mine, your people will set the explosive charges.'

'I understand. But the men in the mine—'

'Will have to stay there.'

Rudent gave a startled exclamation. Werter was silent.

'Those are my orders from the Reichsführer, given by the Führer personally. We should stop here, Joachim; there is the mine entrance.' She turned round and signalled the trucks with her flashlight.

Rudent obeyed, and the trucks stopped behind them

'Now,' Anna said, 'tell me what your orders were.' She put her hand in her pocket.

'To obey you in all things. And to make sure the mission is brought to a satisfactory conclusion.'

So many people, Anna thought, talk just a little too much. If he had just stopped at the end of the first sentence . . . But now her suspicions were confirmed, and thus her course of action was also confirmed. 'Excellent,' she said. 'It has been a pleasure working with you. Go back and tell your people to bring the explosives up. I will get the trucks moving.'

He got out and hurried along the line of vehicles.

'Are you still with me?' she asked Rudent.

He hesitated. 'You mean to kill these men?'

'I am acting on the orders of the Führer. This is for the Reich.'

'And if I do not agree to help you, you will kill me also.'

She rested her glove on his arm. 'I would hate to have to do that, Joachim.'

'I have no weapon.'

'All I require from you is to stay alive.' She opened the door and got out. 'Drive the cargo into the shaft,' she told the first driver. 'It stretches about half a mile. Go to the end of that and park. Then return to us here.'

'Yes, Countess.' He re-started his engine and the truck rolled down the slight slope.

Anna walked along the line, giving each driver the same instructions. Until she reached the last. He had already started his engine. 'Are you armed?' she asked.

'No, Countess. I am only a driver.'

'Very good. Switch off your ignition. I wish you to stay here. Remain in your cab, and keep your head down.'

'Countess?'

'Just do as I say.'

The rearguard had arrived, Werter sitting in front beside the driver. 'What is happening?' he enquired.

'I am obeying my orders,' Anna said. 'I wish the explosive charges set,' she told the SD agents.

They looked at Werter, received a nod of confirmation, got out and unloaded the sticks of dynamite.

'How close can we be?' Anna asked.

'We need to be about two hundred metres further back, Countess.'

'Very good. Off you go. You,' she told the driver, 'back up two hundred metres. And you, Captain Rudent.'

Werter watched them. 'I do not understand,' he said. 'Why did that truck not go in with the others?'

His back was to her. Anna drew the silenced pistol from her left-hand pocket, and transferred it to her right hand. 'Because I wish it to remain here.'

He turned back to her, blinked into the gloom. 'What is that? What is happening?'

'I am anticipating the orders that were given to you, by, I assume, Reichsführer Himmler.'

'You—'

'But I am also doing something that should have been done long ago. Signorina Ratosi sends her love.'

He took a step towards her and she shot him through the head.

'Countess?' Rudent called. Two hundred yards away in the darkness neither he nor the truck driver could see what had happened.

'Stay where you are,' Anna commanded. She replaced the pistol in her left-hand pocket, rested her hand on the gun in her right-hand pocket, watched the three men looming out of the gloom, unrolling their coil of wire. 'All set?'

'Yes, Countess, but we must go further back.'

'Then go.'

Two of the men continued unrolling the wire. The third stopped beside her to peer at the mound on the ground. 'What is that?'

'Herr Werter. He seems to have had a heart attack.'

'We must get him to a doctor.'

'Later. Move back.'

'We cannot leave him here. The blast—'

'Is not going to affect him where he is,' Anna asserted with absolute conviction. 'But it will affect you if you stay here.'

The man hesitated, then walked at her side. 'The drivers—'

'Are also where they will have to stay.'

The other two men had stopped and were waiting for them. 'Is this far enough' Anna asked.

'Yes, Countess, but—'

'Blow it.'

They looked at their commander, and Anna drew her pistol. 'I said blow it.'

The commander tried to unsling his tommy gun and Anna shot him, then turned back to the other two. One of them had also reached for his weapon and she shot him too. The third man dropped to his knees beside the control box.

'Blow it!'

He drew a deep breath and pressed the plunger. The blast was greater than Anna had expected, a great gush of sound and wind that, as she had been standing with her back to the shaft, threw her forward on to her knees, gasping for breath. The man, kneeling, took the shock with less effect, and leapt at her, wrapping his arms round her body and rolling her on the ground. She lost her grip on her pistol before she could recover, and then he had her on her back, holding her shoulders to press her down. 'You killed them,' he panted. 'You killed them all.'

Anna realized that he was too heavy, and too strong, for her to throw off, and as he was pressing on her shoulders she could not swing her arms for a blow. So there was only one thing left. 'Shit!' she muttered. She had grown very fond of this coat. She got her left-hand into the pocket, while he worried her like a dog, obviously afraid to release her but equally uncertain what to do next. She was not an expert shot with her left hand, but she managed to get the pistol up and against the material and against him, lying on her as he was. She squeezed the trigger and he gave a shriek of pain and rolled off her, writhing and clutching at his shattered thigh.

Anna sat up, drew the pistol, transferred it to her right hand, and put him out of his misery by shooting him in the head. Then she scrabbled around in the darkness to find her other gun; she was covered in snow and feeling distinctly chilled.

She looked up and saw Rudent and the driver coming towards her, curiosity making them unable to obey their orders any longer. 'Countess?' Rudent asked.

Anna stood up, shaking herself like a dog to get rid of some of the snow; remarkably, her hat had not come off. The noise of the explosion was still ringing in her ears and reverberating around the hills. She had no doubt that the inhabitants of Eisenach, who would have had their windows rattled at the very least, were sufficiently conditioned to bombing raids and to minding their own business that they would not immediately react, but she fully intended to be far away from here by dawn. 'I will come with you,' she told the driver. 'In the truck. Captain, you will follow with the command car.'

'But . . .?' Both men looked from the other car to the dead bodies to the mine shaft, now completely blocked by falling stone and earth; the entire front of the hill had collapsed.

'They will have to stay here,' Anna said. The fact that Werter and his fellow agents would all carry SD identification wallets should delay an investigation still further; there were few people who would risk getting involved with that organization. 'Now we have to hurry.' She got into the cabin beside the driver, sat with a pistol in her hand. 'You understand that I will shoot you also, if I have to.'

He gulped, and engaged gear.

'Go back to the river,' Anna told him, 'and follow the road along the bank.'

This he did, and they came to the bridge over the tributary that she had marked on her map. 'There is a track just on the far side of the bridge. Turn down it.' She looked over her shoulder to make sure that Rudent was following.

They followed the bumpy track, slithering on the snow, and came to a clump of trees, again as she had marked on her map. 'Stop here,' she commanded, 'And get out.' She followed him to the ground, still covering him with her pistol. 'Now, open the tail gate and unload the contents. I wish you to stand on the bank beneath the trees, and throw them into the water.'

He obeyed, opening the first box, and gaping at the contents. 'This is gold bullion, Countess.'

'I'm glad of that,' Anna said. 'Otherwise we would have done all this for nothing.' Rudent had joined them. 'Perhaps you would give him a hand,' Anna suggested.

The two men worked with a will, but it took them two hours to throw the last ingot into the water. Anna stood on the bank and watched each one sink out of sight. There was a fallen branch nearby. She picked it up and estimated it was some eight feet long. She prodded into the water and could find no bottom. But when she pulled the branch up there was soft mud on the tip, exactly as the guide book had indicated. The river might not be all that deep, but the soft bottom into which the heavy ingots would have sunk seemed to be as secure a hiding place as she could devise.

A cock was crowing by the time the task was completed, but she reckoned it still needed an hour to daylight. 'All right,' she said. 'Let's get moving.'

Again she sat beside the driver in the truck as they regained the road. 'You mean to go back for that gold, Countess?' he asked, having considered the matter for several minutes.

'That's my idea,' Anna agreed.

'After the war,' he mused. 'I'll take you back, for a share.'

'I'm sorry. No shares.'

'But I know where it is.'

'Yes,' Anna said. 'You do.'

He gave her a startled glance.

'This is far enough,' Anna said. The road was empty, and there was nothing to indicate that the truck had ever left it. 'Stop here.'

He braked. 'Now Countess . . .'

Anna seized the handbrake and pulled it hard to make sure there wasn't an accident, and shot him through the head. He slumped across the wheel while the truck, starting to move again as his foot slipped off the foot brake, stalled and skidded before coming to a rest.

Anna pocketed the pistol, opened the door, and climbed down. Rudent had brought the command car to a slithering halt behind them. 'What happened?'

Anna got in beside him. 'Can you get round that?'

'I think so. But—'

'Just do it, and drive.'

He gulped and obeyed, but could not stop himself glancing sideways as they passed the truck, and the dead driver. 'My God!' he said. 'You have killed ten men.'

'Fourteen.' She took the two spare magazines from her pockets and reloaded.

'But . . . fourteen men! You!'

'Listen to me, Joachim, and remember what I say. For the past seven years I have worked for this ghastly regime. In that time I have been forced to kill, and lie, and cheat: I have been beaten, tortured by both water and electricity, raped, and shot. I am now making plans to leave, and I think they owe me some back pay. As for the fourteen men who have just died, ten were condemned to death, by our masters, to prevent their ever revealing where the bullion is hidden. The other four were sent to kill me, and you, the moment the task was completed, for the same reason. They were not aware of it, but they also were condemned to death the moment they returned to Berlin. I merely changed the order of things. Because it is my intention to survive.'

'And you need me to get you back to Berlin,' he said. 'Then you will kill me as well.'

'I would really not like to have to do that.'

He turned his head to look at her, then concentrated on the road again; they were entering Eisenach. 'I know where the bullion is hidden.'

'And I know that only you can know that, Joachim. Would it not be better for you and I to be friends than for you to spend the rest of you life, no matter how rich you might then be, waiting for me to step out of the shadows to settle accounts? I always do, you know.'

He considered for a while. 'And you are not afraid I may betray you to Herr Himmler?'

'You would be signing you own death warrant. Herr

Himmler does not know who I am employing as my driver. But I was instructed to kill him. Your only hope is to melt into the background and wait for me to contact you.'

'Will you do that?'

'As soon as it is safe.'

'But are you not also still intended to die to keep the location of the gold secret?'

'Of course.' Anna squeezed his hand. 'But I have friends in even higher places than the Reichsführer.'

She could only hope and pray that she was right. It was nearly midnight before they regained Berlin, and the bombers were overhead. None of the night staff in Prinz Albrechtstrasse seemed surprised to see her at that late hour, but they were able to confirm that the Reichsführer had not yet returned from his trip to the north. So she went to bed and slept soundly, and at breakfast informed Birgit that they would probably be moving out.

'Oh, Countess! We are leaving Berlin? Oh, that will make me so happy! I am so frightened all the time.'

'I think in the first instance we may just be leaving this apartment. But you never know your luck.'

She had her morning bath then walked through the pitted streets and between the still burning fires to the Ministry of Propaganda. She understood that she was taking perhaps the greatest risk of her life, but however much she loathed the man, he was about the only completely sane leader left in the regime, and she had also come to realize over the past couple of years that when he gave his word, he kept it. And he had once promised to protect her.

'Dr Goebbels is not in yet,' the secretary said.

'Then I will wait for him, in his office,' Anna told her.

The woman raised no objection. She no doubt knew all of the doctor's peccadilloes, and that Anna was one of them.

He arrived an hour later, actually wearing uniform, although entirely lacking in any medals or insignia. 'Anna!' he said. 'You are as always a ray of sunshine on a gloomy morning. You want my advice. Or is it my help?'

'Sir?' Not for the first time he had surprised her.

He sat behind his desk. 'I am sure you are perceptive enough to know that the game is up.'

Again she had to collect her thoughts; if she had known

the Nazi game was up for some time, she had never expected to hear a man like Goebbels admit it. 'The Führer . . .'

'Oh, he knows it as well as anybody. The Russians are over the Oder, the Americans are at the Elbe, the British are on to the north plain. But he means to fight to the end, here in Berlin. Did you know that he has given Eva permission to join him? He has always refused to allow her to come to Berlin before, because of the danger from the bombs. Now, he wants her with him at the end.'

Anna drew a deep breath. 'Then . . .'

'He has no more use for you?' He smiled. 'My dear Anna, he has had no more use for you for a long time. Have you not gathered that? He has no more use for sex, and you are a sexual animal. Now he wants company and comfort, in his last days, and you are not a comfortable person. Does that upset you?'

Anna met his gaze. 'No, sir.'

'Do you know, I did not think it would.'

'But you . . .?'

'I of course will remain with him. I have no future without the Führer. Magda is joining me.'

To die? 'But, your children . . .' She knew he had five.

'She is bringing them.'

Now she spoke the words aloud. 'To die?' She also knew that the oldest was not yet ten.

'Of course. They have no future without me.'

She swallowed.

'But you do not wish to die, because you have never been a Nazi, have you?'

Another deep breath. 'Yesterday I was condemned to death.'

'By whom?' He seemed genuinely concerned.

'The Reichsführer. You know that I was placed in charge of the detail to place the gold reserves beyond reach.'

Goebbels nodded. 'You were selected by the Führer personally, as both best fitted and most capable for such an assignment.'

'The SD escort was under orders to execute me the moment the assignment was completed.'

'My God! But—'

'As you can see, they did not complete *their* assignment.'

He stared at her for several seconds. 'And they . . .?'

'They are dead, sir.'

'You are unique. Which is probably a good thing. And Herr Himmler?'

'Would you like me to tell you what Herr Himmler is doing at this moment, sir?'

'Don't tell me you have disposed of him as well? I thought he was inspecting troops in the north-west. However, tell me.'

Anna related the reasons for her two trips to Stockholm, sticking strictly to her meetings with Bernadotte. Goebbels stroked his chin. 'I can see that he would regard you as a highly dangerous person to have around,' he said when she was finished. 'And as he also has no more use for you . . .'

'Will you use this information, sir?'

'I am glad to *have* this information, Anna. For use as and when I consider it appropriate. However, as I have said, you are clearly too dangerous to be allowed to remain around.'

Anna drew a sharp breath. Had she made a terrible mistake?

'That being the case,' Goebbels went on, 'I do not see that any of us have any more use for you, here in Germany. But I believe you can still be of enormous use to the Reich, to the legacy of the Third Reich. You are like an enormous, powerful bomb, just waiting to explode and cause immense destruction. To toss you into the world from the ruins of Berlin to wreak havoc is the best possible parting present we can give to mankind. Do you not agree?'

Anna found that she was holding her breath.

'And it has to be done now, before the Russians get even closer. So tell me, what do you require to get out of Germany? Where will you go?'

'Switzerland.' Anna's voice was hardly more than a whisper. She still could not believe her ears.

'Of course. I suspect you have made contacts there from your visits in the past. So?'

Anna drew one of her long breaths. 'Passports for myself, my maid and my driver.'

'Who I assume are all loyal to you and no one else.'

'I think so, sir.'

'And if they prove false, you will know what to do with them, eh? But Anna, do try to remember that outside of the Reich people are inclined to view things differently from us. I would hate you to get yourself hanged before you have done some exploding. Anything else?'

'A passport in the name of Anna Fehrbach, not the Countess von Widerstand. A carte blanche signed by you to get us through any checkpoints. And sufficient petrol coupons to take us to Switzerland.'

He nodded. 'That makes sense, although how effective the coupons will be depends on the availability of petrol itself. The documentation will be with you tomorrow morning. I recommend that you lie low until then.'

'Yes, sir. There is one thing more.'

'Oh, yes?'

'My parents, sir. I cannot go without them.'

'Ah, yes. Your parents. Very good. I will provide you with passes for them as well.'

'Thank you, sir. But I cannot do anything about them until I know where they are.'

'Of course. Himmler's big secret. They are at Dr Cleiner's Training Establishment at Görzke, outside Potsdam.'

'What?' Anna shouted.

'You trained there yourself, didn't you. When was that?'

'Seven years ago,' Anna said absently. And they have been there since July, she thought. Virtually within touching distance.

'Cleiner is still there. Although whether he is still churning out beautiful young women to serve the Reich I do not know. But I am sure he will be pleased to see you again.'

As I will be pleased to see him, for a last time, Anna thought. He would be number fifty-four, and hopefully her last, which would be appropriate, as he had started her on her blood-stained career in the first place. She stood up. 'I thank you from the bottom of my heart, Herr Doctor.' Words she had never thought she would ever use. He was the only man who had ever raped her who remained alive, and he was going to die, even if at the hands of the Russians. Or his own?

'However, another word of advice. I think it would be unwise for you to travel as your usual flamboyant self. In fact, in view of the reported conditions out there, I would say that you should not travel as a woman at all. Go to wardrobe and have yourself fitted out as a man. As an officer in the Wehrmacht, not the SS.'

'Yes, sir. I will take that advice.'

'You will need documentation. I will provide that along with your other requirements.'

'And for my maid, sir.'

'Of course. You are taking her with you.'

'I don't feel that I can abandon her, sir.'

'Very loyal of you. And your driver?'

'He is an officer in the Luftwaffe, sir. Seconded to me for last night's mission. I would like to retain him for the time being.'

'You are incorrigible. However . . . I have no doubt he has his own identity cards. Tell me what else you may need?'

'I think that is everything, sir. And now . . .' She could not stop herself glancing at the settee. She actually felt that she owed him something more than his survival, for a little while longer.

He smiled. 'No, Anna. Having held you naked in my arms when we were all on top of the world is an enduring memory to take to my grave. I would not like to spoil it with lachrymose farewells.'

'Yes, sir.' She was, actually, feeling a sudden sense of loss. She had hated this life, but it was the only life she had ever known, as an adult. And she had hated this man. But he was giving her back her life, even if not for any altruistic reasons. 'And the Führer?'

'I think seeing him again would be an even more unsuccessful venture. We are history, Anna. It is predatory, man-eating monsters like you who are the future.'

Well, thank you for those kind words, she thought. She turned to the door.

'Anna!'

She paused. Had it all been a dream?

'Will you tell anyone the location of our bullion?'

'Do you wish me to do that, Herr Doctor?'

'Yes. Tell anyone, and everyone, you can think of, when you consider the time is right. It may well be a useful cachet to ensure your survival. I am launching you into space as the Angel of Doom and Destruction. The more confusion and mayhem you can cause the better. *Auf wiedersehen*, Anna.'

'And to you, Herr Doctor.' Until we meet in hell, she thought, and closed the door.

Two Can Play

Clive Bartley threw the report on Baxter's desk. 'The Russians are at the Oder.' He sank into the chair; his recently healed leg was still tender.

'You're out of date. The Russians are *across* the Oder.'

'What? But that means . . .'

'That they have Berlin in their sights. At the moment they are north of the city. But they will soon be over in the south as well. The plan appears to be to surround and isolate the city, and then crush it and of course all the Nazis in it, out of existence.'

'What about us? Or the Americans? Can't we get there before them?'

'I think we probably could have, if we'd started thinking about it a few weeks ago. But apparently the idea was not considered. I don't know whether the decision was taken by Eisenhower himself – his hatred of the Nazis is just about paranoid – or whether the orders came from Washington, which is most likely, given Roosevelt's apparent determination to keep Stalin happy no matter what the cost, but there it is: Berlin is being left to the Russians. The Yanks have stopped at the Elbe. Of course, one has to bear in mind that taking Berlin by storm, which is the only way it seems it is going to fall, given Hitler's determination to fight it out, is going to cost one hell of a lot of lives. So it makes some sense to let those lives be Russian instead of ours.'

'Billy,' Clive said, 'at this moment I am not interested in military or political double-talk. What about Anna?'

'Has she been in touch?'

'No, she has not been in touch. How the hell can she have been in touch, if she's in Berlin? I want to know what we are going to do about her.'

Baxter began to fill his pipe, a sure sign that he anticipated a crisis. 'If Anna is in Berlin when the Russians surround the city, there is nothing we *can* do about her.'

'You mean just to write her off?'

'I am not a magician, and neither are you. Face facts, Clive. She always was living on borrowed time. All loans have to be repaid, eventually.'

Clive kept his temper. 'As you say, Billy, if she is in Berlin when it falls that's probably it. But you have to admit that if anyone is going to get out of Berlin *before* it falls that person will be Anna. What do you think she will do then?'

'If she has any sense, she'll try to get to our forces.'

'Our people are stuck in the north-west of the country. And if the Russians are across the Oder north of the city, to get to us she will have to skirt across the front of their advance.'

'She'll have to chance her arm.'

'Billy, Anna has survived for seven years, as you say, on borrowed time. She hasn't done that by chancing her arm. She has done it by taking an ice-cold look at every situation, by making instant decisions that have invariably turned out to be the right ones. To leave Berlin and attempt to make her way north-west would be the throw of a gambler. If the Russians are not yet in position south of the city, she'll make for Switzerland, where she feels sure of a welcome.'

'You mean she'll go to this character Laurent? You could be right. Well, if she does that, and makes it, Bob's you uncle. She can call us up and we can go and get her.'

'I want to be there, Billy.'

'Oh, come now. You're starting to sound like a lovesick schoolboy. Come to think of it, you *are* a lovesick schoolboy. What good can you do, hanging about in Switzerland on the off chance that she might turn up? And if she does turn up, we've just agreed that she's home and dry. You're just afraid that she'll wind up in Laurent's bed, and discover that she likes it better than yours.'

'Jealousy has nothing to do with it. I don't trust the man.'

Baxter leaned back in his chair, puffing smoke. 'Pardon my obtuseness, but didn't you, quite without authority, second him into this business in the first place?'

'I did that because Anna seemed to trust him absolutely. But since then . . . he agreed to send one of his people to warn Anna off Johannsson. His messenger never showed.'

'If she was in Sweden, he must have missed her.'

'Oh, come now, Billy, I don't believe Laurent ever sent her the message. There was always something about him that wasn't quite right. And we know he's spent the last couple of years, at least, working for Himmler. Billy, you can second me to Basle. Just for a week or two. Just to make sure that if she gets to Switzerland she also gets here.'

Baxter knocked out his pipe. 'You do realize that we are not allied to the Swiss, and that therefore we have no clout in Switzerland? If you start throwing too much weight around, you are going to find yourself being deported and listed as persona non grata. If they don't lock you up.'

Clive grinned. 'I'll keep that in mind.'

'Comrade Commissar!' Colonel Smyslov stood to attention, his eyes drifting from Tserchenko to Olga Morosova at his side. 'Is there a problem?'

'Should there be a problem, Comrade Colonel?' Tserchenko stripped off his gloves; inside the small command post the heat was intense, mainly emanating from the samovar bubbling on the fire. 'I wish to congratulate you on your rapid advance.'

'We obeyed our orders, sir. But you do understand that this is a very exposed position.'

Tserchenko nodded. 'Major Morosova and I will have some tea.'

Smyslov snapped his fingers and an orderly bustled.

'You are the furthest advanced position in the Red Army, at this moment, at least down here,' Tserchenko stated. 'You are ten miles south-west of Berlin.'

'Thank you, sir. But that also means that we are in constant touch with the enemy.'

Tserchenko raised his eyebrows. 'I hear no firing.'

'Well, it is dark. Anyway, they normally wait for us to start something. Their morale is low. And so are their ammunition reserves.'

'Hm.' Tserchenko sipped tea. 'I assume you are aware that it is Marshal Zhukov's intention to surround the city?'

'I am, sir. That will be done within the next fortnight, as soon as we have sufficient men in place. We should be able to link up with the northern arm in a week, and then . . .' He snapped his fingers.

'But is there not the chance that before the encirclement is completed, some of the top Nazi leaders may leave the city and attempt to escape to the West?'

'That is possible. But really they have nowhere to go, except to surrender to the Americans.'

'There are certain of them that it is considered essential should be taken by us.'

Smyslov raised his eyebrows, and glanced at Olga. But she, also drinking tea, did not change expression. 'I understood,' the colonel said, 'that Herr Hitler has publicly declared his intention of remaining in Berlin to the end.'

'That may be. However, my concern is the assassin the Countess von Widerstand. You know of this woman?'

Smyslov frowned. 'The woman from Warsaw?'

'And several other places. Her capture is regarded as more important that that of Hitler himself.'

'Well . . .'

'The reason you are here this far forward, Comrade Colonel, is that we have been informed by an agent in Berlin that this criminal intends to flee the city either tonight or tomorrow. I wish you to push sufficient men forward to block all usable roads from the city in the direction of Magdeburg. According to the map, there is only one good road, anyway.'

'But that is impossible,' Smyslov protested. 'I have not the men. And to send my people towards Potsdam while considerable German forces lie on our flank would be criminal. And suppose the lady goes north-west?'

'I wish that road blocked, Comrade Commissar. The commander of the force north of the city, has already been instructed to block all roads leading in the direction of Hamburg, but our information is that she will be coming this way.'

'And if she makes due west, for Wurttemberg, and the Americans?'

'She will not do that,' Tserchenko said urbanely. 'They have promised to hand her over to us should they take her, and I have an idea that she is aware of this.'

'The Americans are already close to Magdeburg,' Smyslov pointed out.

'I know that. I did not say that she will make for Magdeburg, I said that she will make in that direction, to get south of us before we encircle the city. Then she will go south-west, for

Switzerland. She must be stopped before she can do that. I have given you an order, Comrade Colonel. I expect you to carry it out. Major Morosova and I will remain with you until this operation has been completed.'

Anna placed the large parcel and the accompanying box on the table, together with the two steel helmets. Birgit and Rudent watched her in bewilderment. 'I should be getting back to my station, Countess,' Rudent said. 'I was only seconded for forty-eight hours. And that was two days ago.'

'You have been seconded again,' Anna told him. 'To act as my driver, on another important mission.' He gazed at her, wide-eyed, and she smiled at him. Was it really going to happen? She still felt she was dreaming, that she would suddenly wake up and find that none of it was real. But . . . 'I am expecting some documents,' she said.

'Oh, yes, Countess,' Birgit said. 'This envelope came for you an hour ago.'

It was a large manila. Anna sat at the table and emptied the contents, heart pounding. But it was all there. Petrol coupons, an open pass, requiring her to be given, in the name of the Reich, any assistance she might require, a letter, signed by Goebbels himself, releasing Johann and Jane Fehrbach into her custody, a passport in her real name, and a military identification wallet in the name of Major Wolfgang Schmidt. 'How frighteningly original. But you, Birgit, are to be Corporal Hans Schweiger.'

'Countess?'

'We leave as soon as it is dark,' she announced. 'But first of all, we must try on some clothes.' She undid the string and opened the parcel. 'This is for you, Birgit. I hope it fits.'

'But that is a uniform,' Birgit said. 'A man's uniform!' She was scandalized.

Anna opened the box and took out a pair of boots. 'These may be a little large, but we will stuff them with paper. Now this belt and holster, there is no need to worry about it. You will not be required actually to fire the gun.'

'I cannot wear those, Countess. I mean—'

'Our superiors feel it would be unsafe for us to risk the open road as women. So you either wear these or you stay here.'

Birgit bit her lip.

'But you may pack a valise with a change of our own

clothes so that we may resume being women as soon as it is safe to do so.'

'Am I allowed to enquire where we are going, Countess?' Rudent asked.

'I don't see why I am required at all,' Birgit grumbled. 'I would prefer to remain here.'

I am trying to save your life, you silly woman, Anna thought. But she knew she had to be careful. Rudent might have been utterly seduced when actually in bed with her, and Birgit was used to obeying her without question, but they were both fanatical Nazis. Their weakness, and her strength, was that they thought she was also. 'We are going to the SS training camp outside Görzke,' she said. 'To pick up someone who is waiting there for us, and escort her back to Berlin. Please do not ask me who this person is. We are undertaking it at the command of the Führer.'

She could almost see their brains tumbling; they were both thinking of Eva Braun.

'So you see, Birgit, that she will need a lady's maid. You will have to do for both of us. Now try the uniform.'

There was no further demur. Anna tried hers as well, tucking her hair up under the steel helmet.

'You make the prettiest major I have ever seen, Countess,' Rudent commented.

'You say the sweetest things.' There was no full length mirror but she held her hand mirror at every possible angle. 'It's not too bad a fit. Birgit, you look absolutely delicious. If I was homosexual I could have you in bed in a moment.'

'My hat is too big,' the maid protested. 'I can hardly see.'

It certainly came right over her ears. 'Well, you only need to put it on when we are in company. Now Joachim, kindly remember at all times that I am Herr Major and Birgit is Corporal Schweiger.' She was feeling almost hysterical with excitement, and looked at her watch. 'There is another hour to darkness. Prepare a meal, Birgit, and we will open that last bottle of champagne.'

There were still decisions to be made. Obviously her fur would have to be abandoned, which was a shame, although the bullet hole had ruined it in any event. But her jewellery . . . Wehrmacht majors did not wear rings or earrings. But she was not abandoning her most precious possessions. There was a cartridge pouch on her belt. In this she placed her gold bar earrings and her ruby solitaire, nestling them in the midst of the bullets. No one was going to see inside her tunic much less her shirt, so she left her crucifix and watch in place. She put her spare magazine in her tunic pocket.

They sat down to their meal, even Birgit in a good humour at the idea of getting out of Berlin, if only, as she supposed, for a few hours, and on such an important mission. They were drinking champagne when there was a knock on the door.

'Shit!' Anna said. Could Himmler have returned? Or had Goebbels changed his mind . . . or perhaps been countermanded by Hitler? Birgit pushed back her chair, but Anna waved her to sit still. 'I'll get it.'

She went to the door, drew a deep breath, opened it, and gazed at Stefan.

'Countess?' he asked incredulously, taking in her masculine uniform.

'What are you doing here?' Anna asked.

'I have come to see you.'

'You had better come in.' She closed and locked the door again. 'Why have you come to see me?'

'I was worried about you. It is so long since you came to the gym . . .' He looked past her at Rudent. 'Or have you been too busy?'

'Yes, I have been too busy. On government business. Would you like a glass of champagne?'

'That would be very nice.'

Anna signalled Birgit, who poured a fresh glass and gave it to him.

'Birgit, my maid,' Anna explained. 'Captain Rudent, my driver. This is Stefan Edert, my trainer,' she explained.

Rudent showed no inclination to shake hands. He was, in fact, looking as disgruntled as Stefan with this new development. Which gave Anna an idea; she could not escape the suspicion that he might prove difficult when her true plans became apparent. But Stefan was utterly devoted to her – or so he claimed. Certainly he wanted to possess her more than anything else in life – or so he claimed.

'So,' she said. 'Is all well at the gymnasium?'

He shrugged. 'No one comes any more.'

'So what do you do?'

'Nothing. Wait for you to come back.'

'Did you think I had deserted you?' She squeezed his hand.

'So, you have lost your job.'

'It is more correct to say that my job has lost me.' He drank some champagne, and licked his lips as he looked at the still laden table.

'Have you dined?'

'Not recently.'

'Then dine with us.' She sat beside him. 'What are you going to do?'

He shrugged. 'Wait for the end, I suppose.'

'Have you family in Berlin?'

'No. My family live in Bonn.' He gave a sad smile. 'They are safely prisoners of the Americans by now.'

'Then why do you remain here?'

'I have no means of leaving.'

'Yes, you do. You can come with us.'

'What?' Rudent demanded.

'Stefan could be very useful,' Anna said, placatingly. 'He is highly trained in both unarmed combat and with weapons.'

'You are leaving Berlin?' Stefan asked. 'Dressed as soldiers? You are abandoning the city?'

'Of course we are not. We are going on a highly secret mission for the Führer, to meet someone of the greatest import-ance and bring her to him.'

His eyes glowed. 'Fraulein Braun!'

'I'm sorry. I am not at liberty to reveal her name. Will you come with us?'

'Of course. It will be an honour.'

'Well, then, finish your meal. We leave in fifteen minutes. Are you armed?'

'No.'

'Give him your gun, Birgit. He knows more about it than you. And here is a silencer.'

'Countess?'

'Put it in your pocket,' Anna insisted. 'You never know when you may need it.'

She had no doubt that there would probably be storms ahead, but she was employing the age-old political ploy of divide and rule.

*   *   *

It was now utterly dark outside, and distinctly chilly, although it was not actually snowing. The sentries knew better than to question the Countess von Widerstand's movements, however oddly she might be dressed, and although the officer in charge of the fuel dump grumbled, once he had scanned Goebbels' orders he not only filled their tank but at Anna's request gave them four spare five-gallon drums of petrol. These they placed in the boot.

'How far is this training camp?' Rudent asked.

'About forty kilometres,' Anna said.

'Well, you know, Countess, we can go and return on one tank of petrol. And having all that in the boot . . . suppose we were to get hit?'

'It always pays to have a reserve,' Anna said. 'And it is up to you to make sure that we do not get hit. Let's move.'

She put Birgit in the front beside Rudent – it seemed more appropriate for the enlisted 'man' to ride beside the driver, while the major sat in the back with the civilian. They proceeded slowly out of the city, having to use a very circuitous route as so many of the streets were impassable.

'Do you know how much that uniform becomes you?' Stefan whispered. 'But then, anything becomes you.'

'You say the sweetest things.'

'Are we really just going to this camp for Fraulein Braun and then straight back to Berlin?'

'Those are my orders. Why, would you prefer to do something different?' She turned her head to look at him, holding her breath.

'You must obey the Führer,' he agreed. 'But when we get back . . .'

He still had only sex with her in mind. She had to hope that his desire was greater than his loyalty to the Reich. 'We'll talk about it again when we stop,' she promised.

They were at the first checkpoint. 'You need to keep your eyes open, Herr Major,' the captain said; he could not see her clearly in the gloom. 'We have received a report of a Russian patrol on this road.'

'That is impossible,' Anna said. 'The Russians are still thirty miles south of the city.'

'That was their last communiqué, certainly, and this report

is unconfirmed. There is another checkpoint ten kilometres along the road. They should be able to tell you if it is true.'

'And after that?'

'It is thirty kilometres to the Görzke checkpoint.'

'Thank you, Captain. Drive on, Captain Rudent.'

Rudent engaged gear and the car moved forward. 'What are we going to do?'

'Continue to our destination,' Anna told him. 'Stop at the ten-kilometre checkpoint, and then do not stop again for any reason until we reach Görzke.'

He made no comment, but drove on into the darkness. He had to use headlights because of the state of the road, but these were dimmed, and for the moment there did not appear to be any air activity. In fact, they seemed to be utterly isolated, the sounds of gunfire distant to the south of them, their only company the occasional village of shattered houses. There were no people; everyone who could had got out, either to the west and the Allies, or to the doubtful protection of Berlin.

They reached the ten-kilometre checkpoint. 'We heard a report of Russian activity on this road,' Anna remarked to the lieutenant.

'That is correct, Herr Major. A patrol from Görzke came under fire, and they naturally assumed it was Russians. But none of them were hit, and we have heard nothing further.'

'How long ago was this incident?'

'About three hours.'

'And nothing since? It was probably deserters.'

'On the other hand,' the lieutenant said, 'since that patrol, there has been no traffic from Görzke.'

'Well, what do you expect, on a night like this? Raise the barrier.'

'You are going on?'

'Of course. I have my orders.'

He hesitated, then saluted, and stepped back. The barrier was raised, and they followed their wipers into the darkness.

'Now remember,' Anna told Rudent. 'You stop for nothing until Görzke.'

Once again the darkness, and the isolation. The rain became heavier, but Anna reckoned it gave them added protection. And there was no sign of any Russians. She was beginning to feel quite relaxed when Birgit gasped, 'A light! I see a light!'

It was waving to and fro in the wet darkness. Rudent slowed.

'How far are we from the last checkpoint?' Anna asked.

'Eight kilometres.'

'Then drive through it. Full speed!'

Rudent hesitated, then the car gathered speed. Anna could now make out several vehicles beside the road. She drew her pistol, but as she did so, as it had become obvious that they were not going to stop, the people behind the light opened fire. Bullets smashed into the car, shattering the windscreen. Birgit uttered a shriek and slid off her seat to the floor. Rudent gave a gasp, reared back in his seat and then fell forward, slumping over the wheel.

Anna, seated immediately behind him, had instinctively ducked behind the front seats, and before she could recover the car had left the road and was rolling over down the parapet and into the water-filled ditch. I'm going to drown, she thought, as water flooded through the shattered windows. She cast a hasty glance to her right, saw that Stefan was already out of his door. The bastard, she thought. Her door was jammed into the earth, but she pushed herself up, pulling herself through the open door, gasping for breath.

There was no sign of Stefan. Whatever he had decided to do, he had done it very promptly and apparently without a thought for his companions. Birgit was still screaming. But at least she was alive. Anna knelt on the side of the car and tugged the front door open. Birgit peered up at her. 'Oh, Countess! Those people were shooting at us.'

'Are you hit?'

'I don't think so. But Captain Rudent . . . he's all bloody. I think he's dead.'

'You win some, you lose some,' Anna pointed out, while she thought, Poor Rudent. But that had been his likely fate in any event, and at least she had not had to do it herself. 'Come on, up you get. We have to get away from here.'

But even as she spoke she realized that they were too late. Figures were emerging from the wet gloom to stand around the car, which, surprisingly, although on its side, had not caught fire; but then, all the bullets had been directed at the windshield.

She held Birgit's hands and dragged her up. 'Oh, Countess,' the maid gasped as she saw the looming figures. 'What is going to happen to us?'

'Take each moment as it comes,' Anna advised.

The Russians surrounded them. 'Well, well,' one said, as Anna understood; she had become fluent in Russian during her stay in that country. 'A woman, pretending to be a man!'

Shit, Anna thought as she put up her hand and discovered that her helmet had come off; her wet hair was plastered to her head, but it had uncoiled and was obviously very long.

She slid off the car and dropped to the ground, and heard another man say, loudly, 'What was that? A woman?'

'Two women, Comrade Captain,' the first man said.

The captain advanced, and a light was held up to shine in Anna's face. She had dropped her pistol in the crash and they could see that her holster was empty. The captain peered at her, then stretched out his hand to grasp her hair and give it a slight tug. 'I think,' he said, 'that we have won the prize, Corporal.' He switched to rather bad German. 'You are the Countess von Widerstand, eh?'

'Do I look like a countess?' Anna asked, in Russian. For the moment she could do nothing more than follow the advice she had given Birgit.

'Ha! You speak Russian.'

'I would have thought that was obvious.'

He stared at her, then without warning hit her in the stomach. She gasped with pain and loss of breath, and fell forward. The captain stepped aside and she landed on her knees, using her hands to stop her face ploughing into the ground. 'In Russia,' he said, 'we beat rude women. Krassner, use the field telephone. Call Colonel Smyslov and tell him that we have captured the Countess von Widerstand. Then pack up this post; there could be an escort back there. Get her up.'

Two men grasped Anna's arms and pulled her to her feet; she was still breathless and felt physically sick from the blow to her stomach.

'I am told she has a reputation,' the colonel said. 'You had better secure her wrists. Behind her back.'

A cord was produced, and Anna's arms were pulled behind her back and secured. Then she was bundled into the back of a truck, to sit on the floor beside a shivering Birgit, whose wrists had also been bound behind her back. 'Countess!' she whispered. 'What is going to happen to us?' Although she had been in Russia with Anna, she had never troubled to learn the language.

Three men had got into the truck behind them. 'No talking!' one of these snapped, his meaning unmistakable even if the maid could not understand the words.

But even if they had been allowed to talk, Anna would have had nothing to say. As the pain subsided her brain was starting to work again, but at the moment it was going round in circles. Quite apart from the catastrophe of Rudent's death or Stefan's cowardice – had he actually got away? – there was the far more catastrophic problem of her situation. From what had been said, this road block had been set up specifically to capture her. But how could they have had any idea that she would be on this road, and tonight?

Even more importantly, how was she going to get out of it? The Russians not only knew who she was, but this time they seemed to have no doubt at all of what she was capable. They were not likely to make the mistake of giving her the slightest room to manoeuvre again.

One of the soldiers knelt in front of her. 'She is very handsome,' he observed. 'And very buxom.'

Anna stared at him, and he unbuttoned her blouse, exposing her camiknickers. Apparently he had never seen an undergarment like this before, because he started fingering it instead of what lay beneath. Then he unbuckled her belt to pull down her pants, before raising his head to gaze at her. 'You and I will have good sex, eh? There is time, and I am ready. Are you ready, German whore?'

Anna spat into his face. His head reared back, as did his hand, and Anna braced herself for another savage blow. But one of his companions caught his wrist. 'She belongs to the Commissar. If you mark her you'll be in deep shit.'

The man stared at Anna, and she returned his gaze. Then he put his hand inside her blouse and squeezed her breast, before withdrawing to sit on the far side of the truck. His companion pulled her pants back up and refastened the belt.

It was not a very long ride, no more than a few kilometres, Anna estimated, and then they reached the Russian outpost, situated in an abandoned village, and were marched into a smoke-filled room to confront Colonel Smyslov and the two NKVD agents. Anna drew a sharp breath as she recognized Olga, and realized that she could be in even deeper trouble than she had supposed.

'Well, Comrade Commissar,' Smyslov said. 'Are you satisfied?'

'I am very satisfied, Comrade Colonel. You were right, Olga. She is a most striking woman. Far more so than her sister.'

Olga stood in front of Anna, brushed wet hair from her face. 'You are a mess. Do you remember me?'

'I remember you very well,' Anna said.

'As I remember you, very well. So, do you suppose some knight in shining armour, like the man Andrews, is going to rescue you this time?'

'They are thin on the ground, nowadays,' Anna agreed. 'Am I allowed to ask what has happened to my sister?'

'She is waiting for you, in the Lubianka. You can share screams, when we get you back. Let me introduce you to Commissar Tserchenko. He has been trying to meet you for so long.'

'Tserchenko?' Anna's gaze swung to the big man.

'I am sure you remember that name as well.'

Tserchenko stepped up to her. 'You broke my sister's neck,' he said. 'With a single blow. I find that hard to believe. But I could snap your neck, now.' He wrapped his fingers round Anna's throat, and she caught her breath, while Birgit gave a little shriek.

'Ahem,' Olga remarked.

The fingers relaxed. 'Yes,' Tserchenko said. 'Comrade Beria wishes that pleasure for himself. After Marshal Stalin has finished with you. But I shall watch your last moments.'

'And I also,' Olga agreed. 'When can we leave?' she asked Smyslov.

'Not before tomorrow morning.'

'What?'

'As I thought might be the case, our probe has aroused the Germans. Our presence on the road has been reported, and my scouts tell me there is a considerable force moving behind us.'

'You mean we could be cut off?' Tserchenko's voice was suddenly anxious.

'I think we are already cut off,' Smyslov said, urbanely. 'But there is no need to be alarmed. I have radioed for assistance, and we will be relieved tomorrow. All we have to do is hold our ground until then.'

'Hold our ground? You mean, we may be attacked? I did not come here to be involved in a battle.'

'That we are this far advanced, and therefore in danger of being cut off, was on your instructions, Comrade Commissar.' Smyslov could not quite keep the contempt from his tone. 'However, the Nazis have virtually no armour left, and we can protect you until our relief arrives.'

Tserchenko looked at Olga, suddenly adrift.

'Well, we must wait until then,' she said. 'Where can we put these prisoners overnight?'

'There is a bedroom through that door. Put them in there.'

'But they must be under constant guard,' Tserchenko insisted.

'I will guard them myself,' Olga said. 'In there, Countess. And you.'

Anna went through the door, followed by Birgit. Olga came in, carrying a lantern, and closed the door. 'How nice,' she said. 'There is a bed for me to lie on. You two can sit on the floor. Or lie, if you like.'

'Do you mean to keep our wrists tied all night?'

'Of course. I know all about you.'

'I need to pee.'

'Wet your pants. You are soaking wet anyway. I am not going to fall for that one either.'

Anna leaned against the wall, and slowly slid down it until she was sitting. Birgit followed her example, and their shoulders touched. 'Countess? What is going to happen to us?'

'It doesn't look too good right this minute,' Anna said.

'If you are going to talk,' Olga remarked, 'I will gag you.'

There was a pillow on the bed, and she propped this under her head as she lay down, drawing her pistol and resting it on her stomach. She closed her eyes, but even if she went to sleep Anna couldn't see that they could accomplish anything; she would undoubtedly wake up if they tried to reach the bed, and with their hands tied there was nothing they could do even if they got there.

Almost she felt like screaming in sheer frustration. Apart

from the discomfort of sitting on a hard floor in soaking wet clothes, for the second time in a year she had been on the verge of completing her self-appointed task, and for the second time her hopes had been dashed. That had got to be more than just bad luck. It meant that now and always, she had been challenging forces too great for her, had, in the youthful confidence of the skills she had been taught, and indeed had possessed inside herself, cut a bloodstained path through all those who challenged her, with this single objective in view, an end which would have justified all the crimes she had been forced to commit. To be now faced with failure.

And not just failure. Extinction. Ahead of her lay nothing but weeks of torment, and at the end, a hangman's noose; she did not suppose the Soviets would grant her the charity of a bullet in the brain. As Olga had said, there was no Joe Andrews, no Clive Bartley, not even an Henri Laurent, to come to her rescue now.

Goebbels, she thought. She had actually trusted him, had actually been grateful to him. But only he could have betrayed her. He had boasted that he was turning her loose, so that she could wreak havoc amongst the enemies of the Reich, but not so loose that she could simply disappear. He wanted her to sew unrest between the Allies, to be put on trial, not only to cause unrest but to pull the plug on any of his colleagues who might escape the catastrophe. Himmler, certainly.

If she felt that he had overvalued her importance, he had still ended her chances of survival. But then, he was not going to survive himself, and before he died, he would murder his wife and his children. While she would live a while longer, in torment and despair.

There was—

Her head turned as she heard the noise. Birgit heard it too. 'Countess!' she whispered.

But Olga had also heard it, and sat up as the door opened. 'Who are you?' she demanded, her hand dropping to the pistol on her stomach. 'What do you want?'

There was a *phut*, and she gave a gasp as the bullet smashed into her chest. The door closed, and the man, wearing a Soviet uniform, moved forward to stand beside the bed.

'Stefan!' Anna gasped. 'Stefan!'

Stefan bent over Olga. 'She is dead.'

'But how . . .?'

He knelt beside Anna, laid down the pistol to use his knife and cut her wrists free. 'I am not as good as you, Anna. But I am better than these people. I train SD agents for combat.'

She rubbed her hands together; the returning circulation was the most delicious agony she had ever known. 'But how did you get here?'

Stefan was freeing Birgit, who was giving little whimpers of pain as she also felt the returning flow of blood into her hands. 'It was not difficult. The Ivans were so interested in you that I don't think they even knew I existed. While they were all clustered round you, I climbed on to the top of one of the trucks, and allowed them to drive me here. Now come.'

'Just a minute.' Anna went to the bed and took Olga's gun. 'A Colt automatic,' she commented. 'American Army surplus, I suppose.' She looked down at the woman. 'That should have been done four years ago.'

'We must hurry. The truck is outside.'

'The guards?'

'We can make it.'

For the first time she realized that his tunic was stained with blood. When she followed him into the outer room, she saw the two guards, both dead, shot at close range. One of them had had his tunic and cap removed. Birgit gasped, and Anna squeezed her arm. 'If you scream I'll hit you.'

Stefan was standing by the front door, looking out. 'The perimeter is guarded,' he said. 'But if you are willing to risk it, Countess, we can burst our way through. They are not expecting anything from behind them.'

'I am willing to risk it.'

'Countess . . .'

'If you stay here, Birgit, you are going to be killed. After being tortured.' She checked the pistol she had taken from Olga; it was fully loaded. 'We are with you, Stefan,' she said.

At the end of seven years of torment, she thought, this adorable man was her saviour. Because he adored her. But that, she reminded herself, was her greatest asset.

Stefan opened the front door, checked the street outside. It was deserted, the village somnolent. The truck, decorated with a red star, was parked by the roadside. 'Clear,' he said.

'You in the back, Birgit,' Anna said. 'Lie down and stay down, no matter what. Go.'

They darted across the road and scrambled into the truck. The keys were in the ignition, as Stefan had undoubtedly ascertained earlier. He started the engine and they drove up the street.

'Halt there!' someone shouted.

Stefan gunned the engine and the truck surged forward. A shot was fired, followed by several others, and Birgit screamed as bullets tore through the canvas walls. But a few moments later they were out of the houses and bumping along the track leading out of the village.

'The road is not far,' Stefan said. 'And then it is only about eight kilometres back to that last checkpoint.'

'But we are going the other way,' Anna said.

He turned his head in consternation. 'But Countess . . .'

'We have not yet completed our mission.'

He gulped, but when they reached the road, he turned left as instructed.

An hour's driving on a deserted but cratered road brought them to the Görzke checkpoint. It was just one o'clock. Lights flashed and orders were barked, while an array of weapons was presented when the truck was identified as being Russian.

Anna opened her door and stepped down, fluffing out her hair. 'I am the Countess von Widerstand,' she announced. 'I have an urgent message for Dr Cleiner.'

The lieutenant peered at her. '*You* are the Countess von Widerstand?'

'I know I look a mess,' Anna agreed. 'Take me to the doctor and he will identify me.'

'Do you know the time?'

'Does time matter, in warfare? Look, I have come directly from the Führer. Obey me, or suffer for it.'

He gulped, but did not lack courage. 'I must look inside the truck. It could be filled with high explosive, or Russian soldiers.'

'Then look, but be quick.'

He parted the canvas rear shield, and peered at a terrified Birgit.

'My maid,' Anna explained.

'My apologies, Countess. Open the barrier,' he commanded. 'I will provide you with an escort.'

'I know the way,' Anna said.

A few minutes later Stefan was driving through those so well remembered gates, into the multiple buildings surrounding the huge parade ground, the squares of sandbags that concealed the firing ranges . . . it was in one of those that she had killed her first victim, at Cleiner's command. Well, she thought, things have changed. And not only in her situation; she could tell that the camp, which had housed whole detachments of recruits when she had last been here, was just about deserted.

'That is the house,' she said, and Stefan brought the truck to a halt. 'Give me your pistol.'

'Countess?'

'You can have the Colt.' As the Russians had been so happy to capture her they had not searched her, the spare magazine for the Luger was still in her pocket, as her jewellery was still in her cartridge pouch.

'But you mean to shoot somebody?'

'If I have to,' Anna said equably. 'You two stay here. I shouldn't be long.'

She got down. There was a sentry on the door, and he now advanced, having identified the truck as Russian. 'Who goes there?' And then identified the insignia on Anna's collar. 'Herr Major? But . . .?' as he saw her hair.

'I am the Countess von Widerstand,' Anna assured him. 'I have urgent business with Dr Cleiner.'

'The doctor is asleep.'

'Then we will have to wake him up, won't we?'

He hesitated, but the authority in here voice carried the day, and a few moments later she was facing a somewhat Brunhilde-like figure in a dressing gown and pigtails. 'Who are you?' she enquired.

'I am Dr Cleiner's housekeeper,' the woman announced. 'Who are *you*? And what do you want at this hour?'

Anna had never been in the doctor's house before. 'I am the Countess von Widerstand,' she told her. 'I am from the Reichsführer. I have urgent business with Dr Cleiner.'

'You mean we are to leave this place? Oh, thank God for that.' She turned to the stairs, down which Cleiner was at that moment descending, wearing a dressing gown and slippers.

He had not changed at all from the last time Anna had seen him, five years previously, remained short and fat, with a bald head and heavy glasses, through which he was peering at her. 'Anna Fehrbach?' He was incredulous. 'You?'

'I know I am not looking at my best, Herr Doctor. But I must speak with you, urgently. I am from Berlin.'

He licked his lips. Having trained her as a schoolgirl, he knew all of her skills, just as he knew that she had graduated as an assassin. 'Yes. Well . . .'

'In private, Herr Doctor.'

He gulped, looked at the holster on her belt. 'You had better come into my office.'

He gestured at the door, but Anna said, 'After you, Herr Doctor. And you, Fraulein, go back to bed.'

The housekeeper looked at her employer and received a hasty nod. Cleiner went into the office; Anna followed and closed the door. The doctor sat behind his desk. 'I have served the Reichsführer faithfully and well for the past ten years.'

Anna stood in front of the desk. 'And I am sure he appreciates it. Do not be afraid, Herr Doctor, unless you disobey me. I am here to collect my parents.'

'Ah! Your parents.'

'You were ordered to make sure they remained in good health.' Anna allowed a touch of steel to enter her voice.

'They are in good health, yes. But they cannot be released without authority.'

Anna felt in her breast pocket and took out the folded piece of paper. 'I am afraid the ink may have run. I was very wet earlier this evening. But it is legible.'

Cleiner unfolded the paper. 'This is signed by Dr Goebbels. He has no authority here.'

'He is Reichsführer Himmler's superior.'

'I cannot release the prisoners without . . .' He blinked as he found himself looking down the barrel of Anna's pistol.

'I promised that you would be in no danger unless you attempted to disobey me.'

'You would not dare.'

'Dr Cleiner,' Anna said patiently, 'almost from the moment of our first meeting I formed the opinion that the world would be a better place without you in it. However, I am grateful to you for having taught me everything I know, almost. It may interest you to know that I have now put your lethal training into practice on fifty-three occasions. One more, especially if number fifty-four happens to be you, is not going to cause me loss of a moment's sleep.'

He gulped, and muttered, 'What do you want?'

'I have told you. I want you to pick up that telephone, call whichever barracks my mother and father are situated in, and have them sent here, immediately. Then order a command car to be made ready, with all the petrol that is available, and with two days' supply of food. And some bottles of water. Make any mistake about this, and I shall blow your brains out.'

Fifteen minutes later Anna was in her parents' arms. 'I never believed this could truly happen,' Johann said.

'It hasn't quite happened yet, so let's move. Come along, Herr Doctor.'

'Me?' Cleiner cried. 'I have done everything you wish. The car is being made ready . . .'

'And you are coming with us, for at least a little way. I will release you when we have gone thirty kilometres. Then you can walk back here.' And I am not going to kill you, she thought, after promising herself that pleasure for so long. But she was on her way to freedom, and was turning her back on her past. That was as big a dream as any.

'Thirty kilometres?' he protested. 'You expect me to walk thirty kilometres?'

'You are not that decrepit. Come along.'

'I must get dressed.'

'We have not time for that. You will come as you are.'

'In my nightclothes?'

'Modesty does not become you. It is cold, but not freezing. If you do not like this idea, I will take you sixty kilometres away, but if I do that, you may well be overtaken by the Russians before you can get back here. Out.'

Cleiner swallowed and stumbled from the house. The housekeeper had returned to bed as instructed; by the time she woke up, Anna reckoned they would be beyond pursuit, not that this establishment had anything to pursue them with.

'Countess,' Stefan said, 'you are unique. But I always knew that.' He surveyed the command car. It was very crowded, with the Fehrbachs and Birgit in the back seat, and Cleiner in the front beside Anna and himself.

'The doctor will be leaving us soon,' Anna pointed out.

'And we will be with the Americans within twenty-four hours.'

'We are not going to the Americans.'

'What? But—'

'They wish to place me on trial as a war criminal.' If they let me get that far, she thought. 'So we are going south, to Switzerland.'

'Switzerland?'

'Switzerland?' Birgit cried.

'I have friends there.'

Early on the second morning they ran out of petrol. They had had a comparatively peaceful journey, as the south of Germany had not yet become a serious war zone; the Russians were apparently concentrating on Berlin, and the Americans, although their planes constantly roamed overhead, had not yet moved down here except in patrols, which could be easily evaded. Now Stefan got out and gazed at the car in disgust. He had, in fact, been growing more and more morose as they moved south, despite the fact that Anna had honoured her promise and allowed him to share her blanket. But she could understand that with neither of them able to have more than a dip in a cold stream, and now lying on the hard ground, while it might seem terribly romantic in the abstract, was not an ideal way to have sex in reality. And he had to be exhausted as he had been doing the driving.

Now he said, 'Well, this is it. We have nowhere to go.'

Anna pointed into the morning; the mist was thinning as the sun rose. 'What do you think those are?'

He squinted. 'Mountains?'

'Those are the Alps, Stefan. Switzerland. They can't be more than forty kilometres away. We can walk it.' She looked at her mother and father. 'Can't we?'

'If there is freedom at the end of it,' Johann said.

'Well, then, the sooner we get started the better. Pack up the food, Birgit.'

'You are abandoning the Reich, Countess.'

'Well, of course I am. I thought you realized that. There is nothing for me here, any more. Nothing for any of us.'

'Because you are not German. Because you are not a Nazi. I don't believe you have ever been a Nazi.'

Anna stared at her in consternation. She had never expected a mutiny from Birgit. 'You wanted to surrender to the Americans,' she pointed out.

'I never wanted to surrender to anyone,' Birgit said. 'I came with you because you told me to. I cannot desert the Reich, desert my Führer.'

Anna regarded her for some seconds, then looked at Stefan, who was watching her. His pistol was still tucked into his belt, but he knew better than to attempt to use it, against Anna. 'Are you going to shoot us, Countess?'

Anna sighed. 'No,' she said. 'You saved my life. And I like to think that you were both my friends, once upon a time. Go back to your Führer. Or to the Americans, or wherever you wish. You can take half the remaining food.'

She watched them trudge into the morning and disappear over the last rise behind them. Then she turned to her mother and father. 'Let's take that walk.'

'Your powers of deduction are really remarkable, Mr Bartley,' Laurent said.

'You mean you agree with me that she will almost certainly come here, in preference to attempting to reach our forces in the north?'

'Whether I agree with you or not is immaterial. The point is that she is here.'

'Thank God for that. Well, take me to her and we'll be out of your hair.'

'I'm afraid it is not that simple. Anna is under arrest.'

'What?'

'She is thought to be the woman who is suspected of the murder of the two Gestapo agents here in Geneva, in July 1943.'

'Oh, for God's sake. Surely they can't make that stick? And what do you mean, thought to be? You said she has been arrested.'

'Yes. You see, she crossed the border, with two other people. She was wearing the uniform of a German major, which was suspicious. So she was detained. She is travelling under the name of Anna Fehrbach. That is also the name of the people with her, from whom I imagine she adopted the identity. As I say, her disguise made the border guard suspicious, and

when they telephoned for instructions, they were told to hold
her for investigation.'

'If they don't know she is the Countess von Widerstand,
there should be no problem securing her release. Let's go.'

'I don't think we can do that.'

'What's stopping us?'

'Well, you see, she did kill those men.'

Clive stared at him. 'I thought you had something going
for her. In fact, she told me that you were in love with her.'

'It is very easy to be in love with Anna, physically, as I am
sure you know, Mr Bartley. Unfortunately, circumstances, I
will admit beyond her control, have had a considerable effect
upon her character, her personality. It is difficult to see her
ever living a normal life.'

'So you have decided to abandon her. You should try
studying your own character, your own personality. Tell me
where I can see her to sort this out.'

Laurent did not take offence. 'If you wish, you can see
her right here in this office, in a couple of hours. She is on her
way here now, under police escort.'

'They are bringing her to you? Why?'

'Well, you see, I am the only person who can identify her.
My receptionist was able to identify, very vaguely, a tall
woman in a dark coat and hat calling at this office. But she
changed her clothes and her appearance after we had met, and
left by my private exit. I am the only person who knows that
the woman who came in, and the woman who left, are the
same, just as I am the only person, certainly in Switzerland,
who knows that she is the Countess von Widerstand.'

'You mean you went to the police? You are even more of
a bastard than I thought.'

Still Laurent would not take offence. 'I did not go to the
police, Mr Bartley. They came to me, to see if I had any information upon this mysterious woman.'

'And you identified her. As the Countess von Widerstand.'

'It is my duty to do so.'

'You—'

Laurent held up his finger, 'I think you are about to repeat
yourself. I did my duty, as a citizen. It is time to face facts,
Mr Bartley. Anna is a self-confessed mass murderess. If she
were to be arrested by the Russians she would be charged as

a war criminal. I can understand that you are upset, as she is one of your employees. But you know, she is actually better off here than anywhere else. If you were to have a private word with the prosecutor, which I can arrange, and explain the circumstances, I am sure he would not ask for the death penalty, in which case, well, fifteen years, with the possibility of parole after ten, I mean, she would only be thirty-five years old. Her whole life would still be in front of her.'

'You certainly seem to have it all thought out,' Clive conceded. 'Although perhaps you have not properly considered the effect spending a minimum of ten years behind bars would have on that personality you have analysed so competently.'

'Debts must be paid, Mr Bartley.'

'Thus speaks the conscientious banker with a reputation to protect. However, we seem to have reached a stage where you have removed not only the gloves, but every rule of civilized conduct. So you will allow me to enter the fray.'

Laurent frowned. 'What do you mean?'

'I mean that, for example, is it not a fact that since July 1943, since, indeed, the night of these "murders" that are so concerning your police, you have been laundering money for Herr Himmler, just about the most vicious of all the Nazi leaders, a man who will certainly be put on trial as a war criminal when he is captured?'

'That is confidential information.'

'Oh, really? Have you any idea how much the media adores access to confidential information? Have you any idea how strong are the waves of revulsion that are sweeping across the world as the extent of the Nazi horrors are uncovered? At the revelation of Auschwitz, a death camp created by Himmler? That revulsion is going to include anyone who has done business for them, or with them. Do you seriously think that you will attract any future clients, or indeed retain any of your present ones, should that news be released? You could well find yourself indicted for war crimes yourself.'

'You—'

'And all to no purpose. I am prepared to testify, and if necessary to prove, that I was in that bedroom when Anna shot those men, that they were Gestapo agents sent to arrest her, and that she killed them in self-defence after they had drawn their weapons. No doubt she will be deported, but she will certainly be acquitted. While you business, your reputation, and I would say your life, would be in ruins.'

Laurent stared at him as a rabbit might stare at a snake. 'There is nothing I can do,' he muttered. 'The police have her.'

'But they can prove nothing against her, without your identification. So all you have to do, is fail to recognize her as the woman with whom you have been dealing.'

'But they know who she is,' Laurent almost wailed.

'No they do not. They have arrested someone named Anna Fehrbach, who may bear a faint resemblance to the infamous Countess von Widerstand. All you have to do is say that she is not the Countess von Widerstand, and that you have never seen her before in your life. Be a man for once in your life. Then neither Anna nor I will ever trouble you again.'

Anna and Clive sat together in the back of the Lysander, her parents in front of them. 'What are you going to do with me?' she asked. 'With us?'

'Your parents will be settled in some quiet place, and we will find your father a job in journalism. As for you, young lady, the first thing we have to do is give you a new identity. The papers are being prepared, but as of now, you are Anna Fitzjohn.'

'Isn't that a little archaic? And theatrical.'

'Not at all. Your father's name is Johann, right? So, son of, or in this case, daughter of, John. Then we intend to place you in absolute security, where only Billy and I will have access to you.'

'For how long?'

'Until things settle down, and we can make arrangements. But the arrangement will be made. Believe me.'

'Oh, I believe you. And I think I could do with a good long rest, a freedom from tension. But . . . you will come to see me?'

'I will come to see you at least once in every week, until we have sorted out a permanent home for you.'

'Will that home include you?'

He squeezed her hand. 'I have that in mind.'

Epilogue

'*W*as it that simple?' I asked.

Anna made a moue. 'Nothing is ever that simple. Neither Clive nor I had any idea of what was going to happen, that far from remaining bosom buddies the Americans, after Roosevelt had died and Truman had taken over, discovered that the Russians under Stalin were only half a degree better that the Nazis.'

'That must have been good for you.'

'There were plusses and there were minuses. They still had me very much in mind, if for a different reason. You know, when I walked away from Stefan and Birgit, I genuinely wanted to turn my back on the past. But one can never do that.'

'Did you ever have cause to regret sparing their lives?'

'I'm afraid I did.'

I knew she would tell me of it, in her own good time. 'What about Joe Andrews and the OSS?'

'The OSS very rapidly became the CIA. Their reputation for skulduggery has become legendary. As was mine.'

'Don't tell me you worked for them?'

'They had something they wanted done, and they felt that I was perhaps the only person who could do it. So . . . there is a very important rule for success in life. Indeed, for survival. If you can't beat them, you simply have to join them.'

I considered. 'And Laurent? Did Clive ever tell you the truth about him? How he wanted to betray you to the police?'

Once again she looked into my eyes, and once again I felt that chill. 'Yes, he did.'

'But—'

'As he himself said, debts have to be paid.'

I drank some wine. 'But anyway, Hitler and his gang all got their comeuppance. He and Eva, Goebbels and his wife and children, Goering, at least, all committed suicide. Were *you sorry not to have been there to watch them go? To see Goebbels get his comeuppance after the way he betrayed you?'*

'If I had been there, Christopher, I would not be here now. Besides . . . they were the most horrendous people who have ever walked this earth. But I knew them all . . . so well.'

'And Himmler?'

She shrugged. 'I would have liked to finish him myself, but things do not always work out the way we would like. I do not know what transpired between him and Bernadotte, but I know that he returned to Berlin. Perhaps he wanted to complete the deal by releasing me and my parents. I have often wondered what his reaction was to finding out that I had already left.'

'But Goebbels did not denounce him to the Führer.'

'Apparently not. I don't know the truth of that, either. He eventually betrayed himself. He left Berlin just before the Russians completed their encirclement, ostensibly to rally the troops in the north-west, and once he was out, he stupidly radioed Hitler to inform him that as he, Hitler, was now trapped in the city, Himmler intended to take over as Führer. Hitler apparently went berserk and ordered his execution. But it was all too late. He was captured by the British. They didn't know who he was. He was wearing civilian clothes and had completely changed his appearance. They actually held him for three days, apparently without even searching him. Then when the penny finally dropped, and they charged him, he bit his capsule and died. I only learned all of that later. But by then –' she brooded – 'there was so much unfinished business. Katherine . . .'

'Did you ever find her?'

She made one of her moues. 'She found me.'

I waited while she drank some wine. Then I asked the question I had really been after. 'Did you ever go back for that ten tons of gold you buried in the river?'

Anna Fehrbach smiled.